HELL with the LADIES

HELL with the LADIES

Julie Kenner
Kathleen O'Reilly
Dee Davis

BERKLEY SENSATION, NEW YORK

THE BERKLEY PUBLISHING GROUP
Published by the Penguin Group
Penguin Group (USA) Inc.
375 Hudson Street, New York, New York 10014, USA
Penguin Group (Canada), 90 Eglinton Avenue East, Suite 700, Toronto, Ontario M4P 2Y3, Canada
(a division of Pearson Penguin Canada Inc.)
Penguin Books Ltd., 80 Strand, London WC2R 0RL, England
Penguin Group Ireland, 25 St. Stephen's Green, Dublin 2, Ireland (a division of Penguin Books Ltd.)
Penguin Group (Australia), 250 Camberwell Road, Camberwell, Victoria 3124, Australia
(a division of Pearson Australia Group Pty. Ltd.)
Penguin Books India Pvt. Ltd., 11 Community Centre, Panchsheel Park, New Delhi—110 017, India
Penguin Group (NZ), Cnr. Airborne and Rosedale Roads, Albany, Auckland 1310, New Zealand
(a division of Pearson New Zealand Ltd.)
Penguin Books (South Africa) (Pty.) Ltd., 24 Sturdee Avenue, Rosebank, Johannesburg 2196,
South Africa

Penguin Books Ltd., Registered Offices: 80 Strand, London WC2R 0RL, England

This book is an original publication of The Berkley Publishing Group.

This is a work of fiction. Names, characters, places, and incidents either are the product of the author's imagination or are used fictitiously, and any resemblance to actual persons, living or dead, business establishments, events, or locales is entirely coincidental. The publisher does not have any control over and does not assume any responsibility for author or third-party websites or their content.

First edition: October 2006

Library of Congress Cataloging-in-Publication Data

Kenner, Julie.
　　Hell with the ladies / Julie Kenner, Kathleen O'Reilly, Dee Davis. — 1st ed.
　　　　p. cm.
　　ISBN 0-425-21182-7
　　1. Devil—Fiction.　　I. O'Reilly, Kathleen.　　II. Davis, Dee, 1959–　　III. Title.

PS3611.E665H46　　　2006
813'.6—dc22　　　　　　　　　　　　　　　　　　　　　　　　2006020600

PRINTED IN THE UNITED STATES OF AMERICA

10　9　8　7　6　5　4　3　2　1

Authors' Note

We began critiquing together in early 1999, back when we were young (sort of), naive (not really), and unpublished (that part's true). Since we were each determined to do something about the unpublished part of the equation, we committed to brutally and honestly reviewing and commenting on each other's work (the brutality and honestly softened by the presence of coffee, tea, and chocolate). To that end, we met in the café at a local bookstore once each week from 7 p.m. until closing (and often hanging around afterward, once the staff had kicked us out onto the sidewalk).

Our standard ritual was to share a chapter of an ongoing work each week by e-mail, then take turns critiquing the pages at the weekly in-person meeting. And it wasn't long after this process began that we realized how successful the collaboration was, both on a professional and a personal level. Not only did we soon see our books bought by publishers (and then on the shelves!), but our friendship grew as well, eventually matching and overshadowing the ritual of critiquing (cue heartwarming music).

For years, we've thought it would be fun to work on a book together, but we never had the opportunity or the idea. And then, one day . . .

We were sitting at a table during a conference talking about bad-boy heroes. And who better to be the ultimate bad boy than a son of Satan? And if there were three sons? And the three of us to write a story for each . . .

Needless to say we were excited about the idea. And, thankfully, so was Berkley, to whom we give our heartfelt thanks for letting us bring Jack's, Nick's, and Marcus's stories to fruition and, in doing so, giving the three of us the chance to work together on a project, just like we've been wanting to do for years!

And to our readers, we hope you enjoy reading the stories as much as we enjoyed writing them.

Julie, Kathleen, and Dee

CONTENTS

HELL with the LADIES

Prologue

Lucifer stared into the mirror, pushing his dark hair back from his forehead. The office was decorated with a contemporary feel, light, mirrors, space. He'd arranged a complete renovation of Hell several years back, needing to get away from the dark, dank, outdated styles that he had lived with for so long. All that black and red was very troubling to the soul. "Eustace, do you think it's receding? I think it's moving farther back. Definitely farther back."

The servant, long used to the whims of the ruler of the Underworld, couldn't repress his sigh. "It's all in your head, sir. The stress is starting to get to you."

Before he had a chance to ask for it, Eustace handed him a crystal snifter of cognac, and the devil downed the drink. Baron de Lustrac, 1906, the very best his minions could provide. Pools of warmth settled the worries in his gut.

Eustace was right, he was doing too much. Each day it was becoming more difficult to get out of bed and face the challenges. A perpetual cycle, allowing him no free time whatsoever. When he was younger, maybe it had been fun, but now he was simply tired.

Handing off the glass to his manservant, he made his way to his desk and looked at the infinite piles of contracts, papers, and reports. Lucifer closed his eyes, wanting to make them all disappear. It would be easy enough. He certainly had the power. But unfortunately, magic couldn't run a conglomerate the size and scope of Hell. His responsibilities would always be there.

"What choice do I have?" he asked, settling himself in his chair, holding out his hand for the pen, which Eustace efficiently supplied. In front of him was the dossier on the Reverend Burnett. A stupid little man who continued to cross him.

"There is one," said Eustace, pausing for effect. "Retirement."

The devil laid down his pen.

Retirement.

For thousands of years, he had pulled the same old grind. Maybe the chores were too much. Eustace handed him a memo from the acquisitions office, the latest information on the Devil's Delight. Lucifer scanned the document, trying to concentrate on the missing gem, but the words were meaningless.

Retirement.

The word kept ringing in his head. He felt for lines around his hell-dark eyes, but the skin was as young and supple as it had always been. No, the tension he was feeling was all in his mind; it hadn't affected his body—yet. But still, the thought of retirement, lounging on a Caribbean beach, piña colada in hand, or an uninterrupted round of golf, no disasters to coordinate, no souls to recruit, well, it sounded like . . .

. . . Heaven.

He leaned back in his chair, for the first time truly contemplating the end of his reign. Maybe it was time. But first he had to decide which of his three sons was the worthiest. Jack, Nick, or Marcus.

"I should give Jack first crack," he said, plotting aloud.

"He is the eldest, sir," said Eustace, taking away the memo and handing him a newspaper clipping about the latest publishing blockbuster: *The Book of Souls—Investigating the Myth*. The devil pushed the article aside. "You don't think I'm too young? Maybe I should hang on for a while. A transition period."

This time Eustace opened a folder. Full of travel brochures. Tahiti. Aspen. Miami. Copenhagen in the spring.

There it was. An entire world, just waiting for him. Every day, with nothing to do but live.

Suddenly retirement didn't seem so bad. "You think I should, don't you?" he asked.

Eustace gave him a single nod.

The devil smiled for the first time in years, decades, really. *Free.* "All right. I'll do it."

"You need to speak to your sons, sir. Clue them in, as it were."

Lucifer looked down at the glossy pictures in the brochure. A bikini-clad blonde frolicked in the surf, waves splashing around her. He'd always loved the beach. Already he could hear the seductive beat of steel drums, their inviting rhythm calling to him. It was the life he craved. Days soaking up the warmth of the sun, long nights of living out his every desire. After all, he was the devil; surely he was allowed some fun.

"Find Jack," he ordered, picking up the newspaper clipping in his hand. "And pack my scuba gear. It's past time, Eustace."

He gave his servant a critical once-over. "Pack the suntan lotion, too. With that fair skin, you're going to need it."

JACK

Kathleen O'Reilly

Chapter One

Vegas. It was the epitome of all the world's vices rolled in neon and smothered in gin. Jack Vassago surveyed his birthright and smiled. The cacophony of the casino was deafening to a lesser man, but to Jack there was nothing more lyrical than the *cha-ching* of chips falling into the drop boxes.

Pleased with the brisk Tuesday night business, he walked down the crowded floor, the dealers nodding respectfully as he passed. Slots rang in the background, punctuated by the squeals of the winners and the moans of the losers. It was the moaning that he loved best, the signal that someone's fortunes had been lost—to him.

A cocktail waitress in her tight, red-satin uniform accidentally bumped him and then jumped when she realized whom she'd just run into. He took a drink from her tray and waved her on her way; indulging the hired help wasn't in the policies and procedures manual for a reason. Besides, he had a meeting to attend.

Just ahead, a large crowd had gathered around one of the craps tables, the air filled with the intermittent cheers indicative of a player on a roll. The dealer announced the winning numbers and the shouts got even louder. Jack, who ran a tight ship, and an even tighter craps table, paused to investigate. *Not good, not good at all.*

The "winner" was a businessman, or he had been thirty-six hours and twelve beers ago. The tie was loose, the sleeves pushed up, and his eyes held the drunken leer of greed. Jack considered the pile of gold chips fanned out in front of the sloshed broker and shook his head. He'd let women break the bank, but never men—bad for the casino's image. So when the player held up the dice, blowing on them for luck, Jack did what he did best and fixed the game. The dice fluttered through the air, the gawkers holding their breath. It took only a split second to focus his energy on the two cubes of ivory, one second to ensure the streak was over.

After that, Jack walked away, confident his fortunes were restored. Moans, loud and pained, followed in his wake. *Just as it should be.*

One moan rose more painful than the rest, the mournful wail of a man broken. Feeling an unaccustomed twinge of charity, he backtracked. As the dealer raked in the chips, Jack cuffed the poor sucker on the arm. "Better luck next time," he murmured, giving the destitute sap a complimentary cigar. PR wasn't his strong point, but he still needed to make the effort.

To be a successful gambler, you had to follow two basic rules when betting. One: Bank half your winnings. Two: Don't lose your head to either the juice or the game. Happily, other people's follies were the source of Jack's millions, so he didn't complain.

The green forest of blackjack tables sat quietly at the beginning of the week, nights usually limited to the hard-core gamblers. A luscious redhead playing her last twenty-five-dollar chip caught his eye. She smiled, an invitation on her glossy-red lips. After checking his watch and realizing he had thirty minutes to kill, he moved in beside her.

"Are you here to bring me luck?" she asked, leaning forward with an eye-popping view of cleavage and the ten of hearts in her hand.

"Of course," he answered, because it was expected. He focused on the cards for just a moment, and then, voila, her next card turned into an ace.

Her eyes widened appreciatively. Jack was no stranger to a woman's frank appraisal. For 906 years, he'd been hit on, seduced, flirted with, and even kidnapped—twice. After 906 years, there wasn't anything he hadn't done before. But the redhead didn't know that.

She patted the seat next to her and he sat down. "You're my lucky charm," she said in a soft, Southern drawl, her fingers tracing the hard lines of his hand. Jack merely smiled, because she was right; she just didn't know how right she was. After her next win, she gave him a long kiss, curling her tongue around his. "For luck," she said. The next hand, when her nineteen beat the dealer's bust, she took his hand from the table and pressed it between her thighs. "For luck?" he asked, raising a brow. This time she gave him a saucy look. "For me."

Jack sighed to himself and went to work. That was the difficult thing—the word "difficult" a slight exaggeration—about being the bastard son of Satan. People always wanted things from him. He inched his long fingers beneath her skirt, finding—no surprise—nothing but wet, swollen flesh. Suppressing a yawn, he began to perform. Expertly he worked her over, her hips rocking back and forth each time he stroked her. He gave her blackjack twice, an orgasm three times, and she almost blew it on the fourth hand, when she gasped, "Hit me, hit me," at nineteen.

Eventually, Jack had had enough. As old as he was, the excitement wasn't there. There was a sameness to his days, twenty-four hours giving way to twenty-four days, giving way to twenty-four years, et cetera, et cetera, et cetera. As hard as he tried, the world never changed. He gave the redhead a parting kiss, ignoring the room key that she slid across to him, and headed off to the meeting of the board.

The boardroom was empty when he arrived, the long, cherrywood table a tribute to the many souls lost within these very walls. Sometimes he came here to think, to ponder, to escape. But now he was restless, his hands itchy for something. Anything. If he'd known the other members were late, he would have stayed longer with the redhead. Not that she was *that* appetizing, but a man had certain needs to fulfill, and getting his rocks off was part of the basic four for Jack.

Hell. He drummed his fingers on the table impatiently. If he were lucky she'd be there when the meeting was adjourned. Of course, Jack was always lucky. Women tended to wait long hours, days, even decades for him. He heaved a sigh and sat down, pulling out the computer keyboard, checking the latest numbers from Tokyo. There'd been a slight downturn in crude oil, but he could fix that. He placed a buy order and clicked over to Wall Street.

By the time he'd earned himself a cool four billion, the door finally opened.

Instead of the members of the board, he got the chairman of the board, the devil himself. Jack stayed seated, a gesture of power, but did push the keyboard out of the way. His father smiled; he knew what Jack was doing, but approved.

"I'm glad you don't overlook the casino," said the devil.

Jack shrugged. "It's a big piece of the pie. Don't want to overlook that."

"No." His father settled himself in the plush leather chair at the opposite end of the table. He had the same hell-dark eyes as Jack, the same arrogant jawline, the same night-dark hair. There was a hardness about his father that Jack looked for in himself. He'd spent his entire life molding himself in the devil's image, and after nearly one full millennium, he was pretty damned close to perfection. "You've been grooming yourself to take over the empire."

Jack nodded, pleased that his father had finally acknowledged the obvious. "I've done well for you."

"Yes, you have. But you're not ready yet," the devil answered, steepling his fingers.

At that, Jack narrowed his eyes. "Excuse me?" he said, not bothering to hide the shock of being doubted at all.

Lucifer's eyes glimmered with mischief, a look that Jack recognized, had often tried to emulate, and never quite mastered. "A test," the devil replied.

Apparently his father didn't realize how badly he'd just insulted his firstborn son, but Jack had never been shy about his emotions. Especially not to Daddy Dearest. He pulled back from the table, the wood cracking under the weight of his anger. "I don't need to be tested. I'm the best brains you have. No one can touch me and you know it."

His father didn't even flinch. That was the hellish thing about his paternity. No matter what you did, Dad was always one step beyond.

"Yes, your business sense is legions above your brothers', but this is a more basic test. I need a book."

Jack rolled his eyes. "A book? You're wasting my time."

The devil leaned back in his chair, stroking the neatly trimmed goatee. "It's a special book. Currently residing in a long-forgotten corner of a bookshop in New York. I want it. Return it to me, and the empire is yours."

"Just like that?"

"Your arrogance is showing, Jack. The book must be bought, not stolen, and the seller is determined to hang onto it."

"What is this book?" he asked, already contemplating his future. This was his heritage and he wouldn't be denied.

"*The Book of Souls*. Bring me the book of souls. Prove your birthright, Jack."

It was a walk in the park. "I'll have it for you tomorrow."

The devil laughed. "It won't be so easy."

Jack shrugged. Obstacles made the chase more exciting. And he'd never met an obstacle he couldn't overcome, a deal he couldn't close, a gambler he couldn't ruin. "That's one opinion."

"Don't fail me," said his father. Then, with a booming crack of thunder, the devil disappeared in a shimmer of light and shadows.

Jack frowned, the lingering odor of sulfur irritating his nose. *Show-off.*

Books by D'Angelis was sandwiched between a Korean deli and a parking garage in the Bensonhurst section of Brooklyn. The building was tall, stick thin, the ancient, beveled-glass door painted with the words A. D'ANGELIS, PROPRIETOR.

Jack peered through the glass, but the thick layer of dust prevented him from getting a good look. Books were a foreign country to Jack, who had seen more than his share of continental travel. In nine hundred years, a man gets around, but the written word had never done anything for him.

He glanced up at the cloudy November skies, thinking that a meteorological diversion would give him the perfect excuse to loiter in a bookshop.

Instantly the clouds billowed low to the ground, turning a steely gray. Snow began to fall, huge flakes that reminded him of times long, long ago. He took two steps from under the awning, gathering a fine dusting on his lapel, then smiled grimly and bundled the wool overcoat closer. He'd been in the western part of the United States since the California Gold Rush, and never realized how much he missed a real winter snow until now.

But this wasn't the time for Norman Rockwellian fantasies; right now he needed to go in, close the deal, and secure his destiny. *Just as it should be.* On that bright note, he stepped inside.

And immediately sneezed.

The layers of dust on the window couldn't hold a candle to the heavy blankets that coated the interior. The front room was tiny, yet inordinately tall. Jack stood an even six feet, and these ceilings towered over him. Twelve or thirteen feet he figured, with books on bowed wooden shelves, books in boxes, and books that covered what possibly was a cash register. A carpet lay ineffectually on the floor, something eighteenth-century Persian, long faded to a dull brown.

The treasures of the world, buried inside a store that time forgot.

What a waste.

And people complained about the devil's handiwork? Jack shoved his hands into his pockets, avoiding touching anything if at all possible.

How the *Book of Souls* had managed to land in such a dump was beyond his wildest imagination, and his imagination could get pretty wild.

A woman emerged from behind the counter and his imagination grew four sizes wilder—along with other parts as well.

She was a prime piece of workmanship. Golden brown hair that drifted around her shoulders, hair she wore gloriously loose. Her eyes were golden brown as well, a siren's eyes hiding a wealth of secrets and sins. The body was encased in a tight brown sweater and jeans that seduced the eyes.

Jack's smile turned to a grin.

Maybe he had misjudged his father; the stupid errand wouldn't be so bad after all.

Remembering his cover, he brushed the flakes from his coat. "I hope you don't mind. The weather's getting bad." Innocent and unassuming wasn't a natural look for Jack, but he thought he pulled it off.

"Take your time," she said, her voice lower than he would have guessed. Smooth and dusky, and his body began to thrum. So what was a blizzard for if you couldn't be trapped in a godforsaken hellhole with a divine piece of pleasure?

"Very kind of you," he answered.

"Your accent. Where're you from?"

Damn. Not something he wanted to give away right at the moment. Innocent and unassuming was the name of the game. "I usually manage to cover it up, but you found me out. North Dakota," he lied easily.

At the mention of the heartland of America, her face fell. He considered taking back the lie, telling her something exotic and debaucherous, just to put the appraisal back in her eyes. She was a woman made for sin, made for long nights in cotton sheets. Silk sheets were for the pussies of the world and Jack considered himself something of a connoisseur of both sheets and pussies.

"You must love books," he said, getting back on track. He was on a mission, a quest, there was a birthright waiting to be obtained. He repeated the mantra in his mind, but his body was stuck firmly on sheets and pussies, firmly being the operative word.

"It's only a living," she answered, one hand cocked on her hip.

"Not a passion?" he said, glad to hear that she wasn't some bookish mealy worm with Coke-bottle-thick eyeglasses. Librarian fantasies were highly overrated.

"Books are boring," she said, and pushed the hair off her shoulders. It was a marvelous move, calculated and alluring, his eyes honing in on the bounty of her breasts. Just as she intended. Jack smiled. The centuries might change, but the games stayed the same.

"Do you own this place?" he asked.

Once again her face fell. The siren disappeared and she began sorting a stack of books on the glass case. "Sorta," she answered.

Jack found himself curious. "Sorta?"

"Family. Three generations. I suppose there are worse crosses to bear; books are mine."

"Family legacies can be a bitch," he agreed.

"Got that right," she muttered.

"You're a D'Angelis, I take it."

"Gabriella D'Angelis, in the flesh," she said, holding out her hand.

Jack didn't wait to take the offered skin. Touching her was the most natural thing in the world. "Jack Vassago," he said, his hand enveloping her own. Her skin wasn't smooth, her nails were short and ragged. This was a woman who labored for a living. Jack approved.

Gabriella smiled, leaving her hand right where it was, and for a moment Jack forgot his purpose. The eyes did him in, gold swimming in brown, a kaleidoscope of changing colors that he found hypnotic.

"I didn't realize there were Vassagos in North Dakota," she said. Two minutes into the conversation and she was already poking holes in his story. He pulled his hand free. Yeah, she was a looker, but he'd spent the last nine hundred years preparing to take over the empire. The last thing he wanted was to have the empire go down in flames while the emperor-in-training diddled.

Jack took one step back away from temptation, and her warm gaze chilled. He got over it. Women were replaceable, temporary bed warmers, nothing more.

"America's the land of opportunity. I go wherever I'm needed," he said, giving her the absolute truth. He'd set up some of the first gambling establishments in San Francisco. When opportunity knocked, Jack was the first one to answer.

"You've traveled all over the country?"

Jack nodded. "And then some."

"Sounds exciting. A lot more exciting than this place."

"You could leave," he suggested, not wanting to see that lush mouth curved in disappointment. He wanted to see her smile, put the glow back in her eyes. It was the sort of sad sentimentality he'd expect from his brothers; Jack usually had higher standards.

"And leave my heritage behind?" She laughed, a bitter sound. "I'd be cursed by my grandmother D'Angelis, who, along with my grandfather Marty, God rest his soul, built the store, brick by brick, volume by volume, page by page." The magnificent bosom heaved, and Jack breathed along with her, simply because he couldn't help it. "All with their bare hands and usually battling inclement weather at the same time."

"The store does have a personal touch," offered Jack, trying to be encouraging and helpful, all the while pining for the fashion styles of the French, circa 1700. Now that was an era that knew how to showcase the female breast. Women today were more interested in practicality. Damned shifting priorities.

"So why're you here?" she said, blowing dust off on particularly old tome.

Jack coughed. "Escaping from inclement weather. Besides, I felt a pull. The call of opportunity."

She gave him a long, studious look. "You don't look like a book lover."

He shrugged. "I learn fast. You must have a lot of old books."

She glanced around the room. "You *are* a fast learner, Sherlock."

Jack forced an even smile. Not a sales bone in her body, this one, and what a luxurious body . . . His eyes moved downward and skimmed slowly back up. If he had a little more time. He heaved a sigh. *Back to the quest.* "So what's the oldest book you have?"

She rolled a ladder to the corner wall and climbed up six steps, leaving Jack to admire the most magnificent rump he'd seen in at least four hundred years.

"This one," she said, pulling down a dark-green leather volume. "*The Illustrated History of Chlorophyll*, and if plants aren't your thing, we also have a signed fourth edition of *Moby Dick*."

Jack forced his gaze from her jeans. The evil empire was calling. Lust had to wait. For a little while . . . "Nothing older?" he asked hopefully. "Something ancient. Dusty?"

She climbed down and shrugged. "There's some boxes in the basement. We're in the middle of inventory."

"You don't keep track of all your merchandise?" he said, horrified at the prospect. A business could lose thousands a year in sales alone, just because someone didn't think.

"Do I look like the numbers queen?" she asked, with outstretched palm, perky breasts, and a mouth full of sass.

To Jack, who lived and died by the numbers—in the metaphorical sense only—her attitude was sacrilege. Incomprehensible. Outside, the sky darkened to dusk, and Jack realized this wasn't going to be the sure thing he imagined. Grainy dust covered everything in the shop, probably that luscious body, too. It was both fascinating and repulsive at the same time. Jack believed in hiring people to keep his places organized and neat. Now it looked like he would have to get involved.

Hell, he would have to seduce her.

His cock stood up and applauded the plan. Jack forced himself to lean against the smudged glass case, ignoring the millions of germs that were being absorbed into his skin.

"So why New York? Is this business?" she asked, her mouth

curling in a slow smile, and he felt an answering rumble inside him, almost a purr. A flash of thunder boomed, shaking the building.

So what was a little dust in the big scheme of things? "Pleasure," he answered, matching her smile with one of his own. "Always pleasure."

She leaned against the counter. "My grandmother has warned me about men like you."

"Your grandmother's a very smart woman," he answered. "I hope you don't listen to her."

"You're here for what, thirty, forty minutes until the snow stops, and then poof, you disappear, walking out of my life, like last year's taxes."

Jack winced. "Go out to dinner with me. Someplace elegant, decadent, where you can wear—a dress."

"We could go dancing?"

Jack nodded. "Cross my heart."

She sighed. "You're married, aren't you? I know you're not gay, so that only leaves married."

"You're too young to be this cynical."

"Men feed on the still-beating hearts of the Pollyannas in this city. It's why the species is becoming extinct."

"You'll have to trust me."

"How did I know you were going to say that?"

"What can I say, we're linked. Telepathically. It's definitely a sign. Fate, kismet. Now you have to come with me. Dinner, dancing, whatever."

"Whatever?" she asked, arching her brows, the eyes dancing with mischief.

Jack felt something pull at him, nothing more than a physical urge. He needed to bed her, offer to help with the inventory, get the book, and leave. In that order.

"I'll be back at seven."

"What about the snow?" she asked.

Jacked opened the door and peered outside. "Look at that, a miracle. It's stopped."

Chapter Two

There were times when a woman knew the smart thing to do was run. Run far, run fast, don't even stop unless it's to kick off your heels. When Gabriella had looked into the "promise you everything" gaze of Jack Vassago, she could hear the echoes of a hundred Sunday homilies, a thousand lectures from Nanna, and a million long, snooze-inducing lectures from Dr. Phil.

Yet somehow she managed to ignore them all, and now she had a *date*. A date with the sexiest, most exciting, most toe-curling man on the planet. Oh, lucky, lucky day! She studied the contents of her closet, not that it was hard. The D'Angelis family, or what was left of it, was neither wealthy nor owners of large storage spaces. Gabriella had exactly two dresses worthy of the occasion, and she pulled them both free from the tangled knot of hangers. She closed her bedroom door, exposing the mirrored tiles that she'd glued on the back. Martha Stewart, she wasn't.

Of course, it wasn't Martha that was staring back at her in the mirror, either.

Gabriella smiled to herself and held up the blue one, but classy wasn't quite the look she was after.

Instead, she picked up the red one, wielding it like the instrument of war that it was. Now, this was a dress designed to take a man's jets and send them right into orbit. The thought of lighting Jack Vassago's jets sent shivers into places she usually didn't shiver. The red cashmere skimmed high on her thighs, deceptive long sleeves pulled off the shoulder to highlight and showcase her two best assets. Who said brunettes didn't know how to have fun?

Gabriella's life didn't involve adventures or excitement. In fifth grade she had tripped on her way to the altar, spilling oil all over Mrs. Delafino's brand-new pink hat. The excitement had flowed downhill after that. No college for Gabriella. "The D'Angelis heritage is education enough." That from her grandmother. "Why do you need college? You have the store."

There were no older brothers and sisters. Her mother, "the heathen tramp," had run away when Gabriella was seven, and her father had never been more than a question mark on a birth certificate. No, Gabriella was stuck.

Her life sucked, and if Jack Vassago was nothing more than a fling, an affair, a one-night stand, well, what the hell? It'd be something to put in her journal. After the entry on Mrs. Delafino's hat, she needed something new. Something she could mull over for years and decades. Okay, maybe she was exaggerating, but exaggeration was what helped Gabriella stay sane.

"Gabriella? You have finished the inventory, Gabriella?"

Nanna.

Nanna was older than God, and most of the time she thought she was wiser than God, too. Mainly, Nanna was a pain in the ass. Her heart was in the right place, but her way of life was about two thousand years too old. "Coming, Nanna," she yelled up the stairs. After stuffing the red cashmere back into the closet, she checked her watch. Five o'clock. *Oprah* was over, Nanna was on the prowl, there was a granddaughter to harass, sins to expose, and dinner to cook.

Gabriella climbed the narrow staircase to the third floor where Nanna was slaving over the stove, cooking something for dinner, something loaded with carbs and cheese. The smell of an extra five pounds lingered deliciously in the air and she covered her eyes, looking away from the light. Nanna's cooking was hell on the hips, and Gabriella spent one hour every morning climbing up and down the stairs, just to maintain a status quo. She needed her body combat ready. Her face would never make it in Hollywood, her height would never be enough for Fashion Week, but her body, well, that package could win her a new life.

For about three minutes, she had considered a career in the adult entertainment industry, weighing whether Nanna would disown her (the optimal solution) or whether Nanna would spend the next fifteen years (which was the average life span of a career in porn) calling her every night, reading from the Bible. Gabriella knew exactly which route Nanna would take, so Gabriella was forced to go the old-fashioned way out of Brooklyn. She'd have to marry out.

Nanna looked up from the simmering pot (which held enough bucatini to feed two FDNY firehouses) and gave Gabriella the evil eye. "You've finished? What do you think? The books will get counted by themselves?"

"A woman must toil and labor, honing the character until the soul is ready for its final journey from earth," Gabriella recited.

Nanna shook a waterlogged wooden spoon at her. "You should not mock your Nanna. Too much like your mother, you are, *svergognata*."

"Whatever," muttered Gabriella and moved over to sniff the pot. "I'm going out tonight."

"Not before the inventory is finished."

Gabriella knew better than to argue with a woman who thought herself wiser than God. There were better ways to get what she wanted. Namely lies and deceit. "I'll go finish right now," she answered in her best Madonna (the Holy Mother, not the singer) voice. She raced down into the basement, checking her watch on the way. Less than two hours. She'd didn't have a chance in hell of finishing before Jack came to pick her up, but she could make a dent. A total heathen, she was not.

The next forty-five minutes were diligently spent writing down titles, authors, and print dates on her legal pad. At last she crept upstairs to the second floor where she showered, perfumed, shaved, and lifted arm weights in a record eighty-three minutes. With seven minutes to spare, she slunk back downstairs, leaping over the seventh step, the one that creaked ominously if you weren't careful. All that was left was to wait for the man of her dreams.

The man of her dreams. Gabriella took a deep, calming breath, because it was important not to seem too naive or too innocent. She wanted to be Mae West and Shakira all rolled into one package of sultry sophistication that would be impossible to resist. In fact, she'd conquered most of the men in the neighborhood. Of course since she'd grown up with the majority of them, it wasn't a huge challenge. But Jack Vassago was different. He was M-A-N in a way that none of the other boys could even touch.

"Jack Vassago, Jack Vassago, Jack Vassago," she said, closing her eyes, conjuring up the vision in her head, and knowing that if he stood her up, she was going to hunt him down and castrate him.

Magically, the door opened and he appeared. "Someone called?"

Gabriella jumped down from the counter, smoothing her skirt, cocking one hand on her hip, a move she'd practiced over and over again. "I like a man who's prompt."

His eyes swept down her body, and she felt hot, then cold, then hot one more time. "I like a woman who's beautiful," he said, taking her hand and bringing it *to his lips*!

Gabriella nearly passed out, a wussy move that would make Mae West hurl in the grave. "Are we ready?" she asked, shooting a fast look upstairs. Nanna would be watching *American Idol*. The coast was clear.

"Not yet," he said, moving in closer until breathing was impossible, which was really stupid because the last thing she wanted to do right now was die.

His hands spanned her tightly muscled hips (God bless stairs!), and skimmed lower, settling on her ass and pushing her toward him until she could feel his bulgy places. Oh, man, he wanted to take her right here.

Gabrielle's knees buckled, but he didn't let her fall. His head dipped low and she caught a whiff of something wow. A scent guaranteed to get you loosy, juicy, and laid. His mouth touched hers, lightly, gently, not the moray eel approach some guys used. This was Technique with a capital T.

He kissed her once, twice, his lips lingering longer each time. Gabriella didn't want to close her eyes, she wanted to watch this, keep it for all time, but her lids felt heavy and in the way. Her mind slowed until all she was sensing was him.

His tongue stole into her mouth, at first easy, and luxurious, but then the kiss turned. She felt his heart beating beneath her fingers, his mouth demanding things from her that no man had ever asked before. Deep inside her, everything was vibrating and humming, like the entire planet was spinning as fast as her head. Her hands slid into his hair, pulling him closer, wanting him closer still.

His body was hard against hers, his chest flat against her breasts, liquid pooling between her thighs. One knee slid boldly between her legs, and she sighed in relief at the welcoming touch. She lowered herself a couple of inches, because her nethers were starting to throb with something so intense, it was more like pain. She heard herself whimper, needing something more.

Almost there . . .

Almost there . . .

Just one hair more and she'd be sitting pretty. But the bastard pulled his knee away. He lifted his head and stared, his chest heaving. "Fuck."

Gabriella wanted to respond, but all she could was gaze helplessly into the dark eyes. Suddenly he was the face to every fantasy she'd ever had, the cure for ever longing she'd ever known.

"Gabriella?"

Nanna.

Oh, God.

"We have to leave. Now." She grabbed his hand and pulled him out the door. There was gonna be hell to pay later, but looking into

Jack's eyes, feeling his body (Those abs!) pressed against her, feeling the world turn on its axis . . .

He was her third rail, and tonight she was gonna touch it.

Gabriella ran into the street, skirt at eye-popping levels, raised two fingers to her lips, and whistled. Jack could do nothing but stare. Instantly cabs lined up four deep.

The limo he had reserved was two hundred feet away, but he motioned for the driver to leave. Gabriella was oblivious.

He suspected there was a lot of things she was oblivious to, mainly the tiny tremor that shook the foundation of the house.

It had been a long time since he'd lost control. Fourteenth century, right before the plague. The woman had been a weaver, and Jack's father had been furious. Furious enough to cause the death of millions of people? Jack didn't know, he didn't want to know, but he wouldn't have been surprised. He'd practiced masterful self-restraint ever since.

Until now.

His jaw tightened. For nine hundred years he had dreamed of this chance. If anything would have made the world spin faster, it should have been the reality of touching his dream, not touching Gabriella.

She motioned for him to move forward and then hopped in the first cab, exposing a long thigh, and the merest shadow of her rear.

Discreetly Jack adjusted the rock in his pants. She was going to give him a heart attack, and he hadn't even seen her naked.

Yet.

The driver glared at Jack when he ducked into the taxi. "Where to?"

"The Metropolitan Museum."

Gabriella turned. "I thought we were gonna eat?"

Jack smiled, now fully in control of the situation. "Trust me."

She lowered her chin in a look that said "not a chance in hell."

"It's a surprise," he added, because most people liked surprises, unlike himself.

"I'm going to be so pissed if you're taking me to some thousand-year-old exhibit involving people that would never make it in the real world."

"You don't like old things, do you?"

She snapped her fingers. "Life's to short to worry about the past. I like to live in the now."

Not the best thing to say to a thousand-year-old man. With age came wisdom and the responsibilities that accompanied it. Jack had learned early on how to ignore the distractions of the world. When Queen Isabella had offered him the crown to Aragon (and Ferdinand V was a mere jester at the dinner feasts), Jack had walked away because he had whole continents left to conquer.

The cab careened around a corner and Jack put an arm around Gabriella, not to cop a feel, but to keep her from heading through the windshield. He had forgotten about the vagaries of the New York cabbies. Gabriella curled closer and Jack pushed aside his past. It was a heady luxury to live in the now as she had suggested, and he thought that he could take one night off. One night out of three hundred thousand. It seemed a fair trade.

After crossing the Brooklyn Bridge, they inched through the Friday-night traffic on Park Avenue.

The dazzling marble columns of the museum would provide the perfect setting for the evening he had planned for her. Quiet, romantic, an experience that few could ever know. He could picture the way the evening would play out: he'd ply her with champagne, use his charm to lower her defenses, and when the moment was perfect, he'd tell her how badly he wanted to be alone with her, skim the dress from her shoulders, and feast on the sight of her bare flesh . . .

. . . *In her basement with the books.*

Jack scowled. Hell and damnation. He might be a devoted son, but there were limits.

"We're here," Gabriella said, her low voice flowing over him like myrrh. Tonight was about her. They passed through the main hallway where the lone night security guard nodded briefly. "Good evening, Mr. Vassago."

"They know you?" she asked, awe in her voice.

Finally he'd done something to impress her. Jack felt a bit of pride creep up through the dark depths of his soul.

"Close your eyes and come with me," he whispered in her ear.

"I can forgive you if you're married, but if you're some Ted Bundy serial killer . . ."

"I promise you'll be fine. Safe *and* fine."

"You swear?" she asked, dragging her heels.

Jack stopped. "I give you my word," he said. He didn't need to hurt her, he just needed the book. A little voice inside reminded him that he wasn't going to find the book at the Metropolitan, but Jack, who had spent his entire life listening to little voices, ignored it. They climbed the stairs to the second floor, past the European sculptures, past the armory, finally coming to a stop in front of the gallery.

"You can open your eyes now," he told her, more than a little eager to see her reaction. It was a re-creation of a fourteenth-century Italian merchant's house, the designs simple and more elegant than what the French threw together. The simplicity had always appealed to him. His life revolved around noise and neon and the high drama of billions of dollars in play. It wasn't a surprise that he needed quiet, and a place such as this was the refuge he'd always wanted.

Gabriella opened her eyes, her mouth gaping open. Then she spun like a compass, taking it all in. "We're not in New York, anymore, are we? That was a magic cab, and we flew out to some foreign country, didn't we?"

"Just a museum. Medieval art. Boring stuff."

She arched a brow. "You making fun of me?"

"I would never dare," he answered solemnly, watching as she rushed to the window, watching the snow fall outside. Jack had been born in the Ukraine, the son of a novice, who had been seduced by the sly promises of Jack's father. The winters had been long and harsh, but he loved the winter, loved the snow, loved the look of the world covered in the purity of white.

"We're going to be socked in here," she said as the white obliterated the dark.

"We have food. We have heat. What more could you want?" he answered, not telling her that the snow was part and parcel of the deal and that it would be stopped when necessary.

She turned and looked him. "You think of everything, don't you?"

Jack nodded. "Of course."

A discreet crew laid out the table, while she wandered through the room, fascinated by each piece of furniture, every piece of art on the wall. One tapestry captured her interest above all. "I wanted to believe in unicorns when I was a little girl," she murmured.

"But you didn't?"

"I didn't see them in Bensonhurst, ergo, they didn't exist."

"There's a lot that's out there that we never see," he told her, watching her face rather than the intricate stitchery. He'd learned long ago that nothing was ever as beautiful as it seemed. There was always a cost, and it was usually high.

"You're a dreamer?" she said, grabbing his hand. The spontaneous touch surprised him, and he almost drew back.

Jack laughed. "Not hardly."

"Don't lie. I'm very good at reading people. You're definitely a dreamer. Probably a Taurus."

He could only laugh again. Dreams were for the unfocused. Jack had goals, plans, a finite agenda that had no room for dreams.

Still, her words touched him. If she wanted to see him as some poet longing for the stars, so be it. It'd only make things easier. The approval in her eyes would only speed things along. He kissed her, just as an ordinary man would kiss her.

Her lips touched his, and he felt the tremors again. Instead of pulling away, like an intelligent, focused man would do, he leaned in closer, pulled her tighter, and kissed her like he could forget who he was, could forget all about the *Book of Souls*, forget all about his destiny in Hell.

She leaned against the cool stone walls, and he could feel his flesh heating up beyond the normal 120 degrees.

When he pulled away, she gave him a measured look. "I better be good at reading people. If I'm wrong about you, you're a dead man. I mean it."

It wasn't the threat that frightened him, but the truth behind it, matched by the wariness in her eyes. Guilt tugged at him, but Jack pushed it aside. His eyes skimmed over a body that promised paradise. No need for guilt. He was an adult, she was an adult.

But the guilt stayed on.

In silence they walked to the table, and magically, a tuxedo-clad waiter appeared with silver dishes.

He pulled out her chair and managed a polite smile before seating himself.

"What do you do in North Dakota?"

"Insurance," answered Jack, fascinated by the way she organized the food on her plate. Not eating, merely . . . stalling, he thought.

"Claims or underwriting?"

Jack swallowed a large piece of sole, then answered, "You know a lot about insurance."

After carefully watching his own table manners, she pierced the filet delicately with her fork. "My third fiancé was a claims adjuster for Travelers."

Jack coughed. "Third fiancé?"

She shrugged. "I like to think I inspire men to commit to me, but I think I'm just desperate to leave. It's the D'Angelis curse. Mother wanted to be an actress. She told me my father wanted to be a musician. Nanna wanted to be a doctor."

"And what do you want?"

"Excitement. To see the world," she answered, toying with the mushrooms.

Jack moved aside the mushrooms on his plate and watched as she copied the move. "And that's why you get engaged to claims adjusters?"

Her brows formed a long, thin line.

"Maybe you don't want excitement," he offered.

"And maybe you'd be wrong," she snapped. But the uncertainty was back in her eyes, and Jack was left wondering if maybe she was just looking for love.

"I've never met a woman like you before," he said, and he meant it. When a man skirted the underworlds of society, he came into contact with people who shared the same moral compass that he did. Gabriella displayed a courage that belonged to people like his mother, yet Gabriella was no novice. Not even close.

Thank God.

As the evening progressed though, he forgot about his own personal hell and began to enjoy himself. Throughout the dinner, Gabriella's dress had crept lower and lower. He was getting her drunk—on champagne, on him, he wasn't quite sure. But her eyes would find his, again and again, and soon the food was long forgotten.

By the time the clock struck ten, Jack's appetite had moved to something much more tangible. Kisses were fine for ten-year-old boys, but Jack needed more. Much more. He needed to bed her. Soon. The entire evening had been meticulously planned. A dinner at the museum, then a drive to the Waldorf, where he could seduce her properly. A long bath, a bed, a night of champagne-fueled satisfaction. But the luxuries of his life didn't match the simple honesty of the desire in her eyes.

"I'm supposed to be at the store right now. Doing inventory," she confessed.

"I'm glad you're here."

Gabriella shrugged her bare shoulders and took a sip of champagne. "The books aren't going anywhere. One night won't make a difference."

Jack's cell phone dinged, a discreet reminder that this father was calling. Without missing a beat, Jack pressed the "ignore" button. Usually he was prompt, conscientious, the reliable son. Tonight he was intent on Gabriella. The way her eyes glimmered in the low lights. The way her entire body moved when she spoke. His only intent now was to slip the dress from her smooth shoulders, past the full breasts, down the path of her thighs, and spend the rest of the night in blissful ignorance with her in his arms.

A clever scheme designed to garner the *Book of Souls*.

Of course.

"Let's walk," he said, because he needed to touch her.

He rose and pulled out her chair, his hands lingering on her shoulders, itching to explore further, but Jack was a master of control. He hooked her arm through his and led her around the museum.

They walked in quiet, the silence appallingly loud. Jack was grateful Gabriella didn't try to fill the void. They reached the Hall of the Byzantine, a place he visited every time he was in the Metropolitan. The empire had been fierce, elaborate, yet primitive compared to the complexities of the modern world. He knew he didn't belong in the modern world, but within these four walls, he could travel back to the places he loved best. Back to a world where he was not the son of Satan, but merely a man.

"Do you like art?" he asked.

"No," she answered.

"Good. Neither do I," he said, already reaching for her.

She slid close, as if they'd fit together for ages. They sank to an ornately carved bench, more Romanesque than Byzantine, and Jack leaned her back against the dark wood. Gabriella was a woman who expected nothing from him, other than his company. He wasn't an artist like his brother, Nick, but the image of her burned in his mind. The dress had moved dangerously low on her chest, but it was the look in her eyes that drew him. He leaned in, his mouth covering hers. His hands slid up to her shoulders, and then, because he couldn't help him, he drew the soft material down lower, baring her to the waist.

He lifted his head to stare, to touch. "You are perfect," he said, his hands tracing the curve of her breasts, slipping underneath to test their weight. Her skin was golden brown against the midnight gleam of the wood, and Gabriella watched him with a heavy-lidded gaze, arching her back when his thumb brushed against her dark areola. "So young," he murmured to himself.

She sat up straighter. "I'm twenty-four," she said defensively and he nearly laughed. It was the first time in his life he felt old— and tired. He took one of her nipples in his mouth in order to show her the joys of an experienced—infinitely experienced—lover. He was hungry for the taste of her, the silk of her skin, and he sucked hard, pleasuring her, but pleasuring himself as well. Her hips ground against his cock and his vision blurred. He hadn't meant to rush her, but her sensual response was killing him. He leaned his forehead against her breasts, needing to get control. After a few minutes, the world had calmed.

His hand slid between her thighs, pushing the skirt to her waist. A thin scrap of silk was the only barrier separating his touch from her flesh. An odd combination of sexuality and innocence.

One finger slipped inside her, testing the moist confines, and he was delighted with her soft gasp. Determined to pleasure her even more, he used his mouth on her neck, teasing, suckling, telling her exactly how he planned to love her. He hooked his arm under her leg, tilting her hips up, his finger sliding deeper inside her. Instantly her thighs tightened around him.

His thumb rubbed against her clit, circling and teasing, her body jerking each time he returned home. He took her mouth, his tongue matching his finger, and her whole body began to move with the rhythm he was setting.

"Somebody could come," she breathed against his lips.

"That's the idea."

"Security. Guards."

"They wouldn't dare," he answered, trailing hot kisses from her breasts and then discovering the flat planes of her stomach. He sucked against her navel and she jerked.

"Ticklish?" he asked, but she only shook her head no.

He trailed lower still. He slid the dress and panties over her hips, tossing them over an ivory vase. She leaned back against the bench, nude in black heels. Her pose was erotic in its simplicity, her breasts full and mature, her thighs parted to expose her bare nether lips; yet for all her sophisticated posturings, there was a vulnerability in her eyes, a woman who knew she was in over her head.

Jack cursed himself for rushing. "We can go back to the hotel," he said. "I promised you dancing."

She tilted her head to one side, the heavy fall of her hair coyly concealing one breast. She studied him carefully. "I wanted to dance."

He started to stand, but she held out a hand and pulled him back down.

"We're alone?" she asked, her voice a whisper, but still echoing inside the great room. Jack drew an X over his heart, and a slow smiled bloomed on her face. "This is good."

He laughed. "This is more than good. This is perfection."

Then he pushed her thighs apart and proceeded to show her the advantages of sleeping with the devil.

Her world was exploding, piece by piece.

Gabriella opened her eyes, staring at the treasures of the Byzantine Empire framing the dark head buried between her thighs. Never in her wildest dreams. Never in her wildest fantasies. She tried to focus, to keep everything boxed tightly in her mind, but all her senses concentrated on the rhythmic suckling that would bring her closer and closer to orgasm. Helpless to fight against it, the waves would start to build inside her, but instead of letting her ride the big one, he'd pull his tongue back with one long, slow stroke that made her muscles tighten and clench.

Oh, God.

The third time that happened, she whapped him on the shoulders with her first and he laughed—*laughed*.

"Do you think this is funny?"

He grinned, a devilish smile playing on his lips. For a second she forgot her words because there was such a look on his face; he looked young, happy, and carefree, and it was only then that she realized how old he had seemed before. A bubble caught inside her chest. "Go on. Do your worst. Torture me," she commanded, and he brought her to an earth-shattering orgasm three times, the third of which shook the floor underneath her feet.

The air was cold on her bare flesh, but she felt so hot everywhere he touched. Like fire. Again and again she came, trying desperately to find some toehold on reality.

She pulled him up until he lay on top of her, and her fingers worked feverishly to get rid of his jacket and shirt.

The tie was more difficult, some exotic knot she'd never seen before. Finally, she decided to just let it hang loose on his neck. It thrilled her to see him with his hair ruffled, pants half off, definitely unkempt.

It made him look . . . human. Alive. She'd tried to be the sophisticated vamp that she thought he would want, but his cosmopolitan attitude intimidated her, and seeing him like this made her feel like they were equals. Like she had a chance. She kissed him, using her tongue to taste inside his mouth, nipping at his lip, and then he groaned, and took over, kissing her until her toes curled.

Then his pants were gone, the tie removed, and he stood before her, the most magnificent man she'd ever had the pleasure of seeing unclothed. "I think my heart just stopped," she said, not completely a joke. "Are all the men in North Dakota like this?"

Underneath the tailored suits, she never realized the size of his shoulders, the brawny arms, the hard planes of his abs. A swathe of dark hair covered his chest, arrowing down to his . . .

Ohmygod . . .

Man, oh, man, oh, man. *This* was a man. A perfect sculpture that belonged in the museum, but currently on display for her private viewing pleasure.

Ohmygod . . .

Her mouth grew dry.

His eyes burned into hers and she knew there'd be no turning back. She'd never wanted a man like this, never needed a man like this, but every inch of her knew he was trouble. Jack moved, his big body covering her own, and for a second he froze, the tip of him poised, waiting, teasing between her lips.

Trouble or not, she really didn't have a choice. She moaned at the touch and her hips rose up to meet him.

He slammed inside her and the world turned black. *The pain.* She hadn't expected the pain. She was no virgin, and her body had been nicely juiced up, ready for liftoff. Jack noticed the tension in her face. "Did I hurt you?" he asked, even while he was sliding out of her, and then she clued in on the source of the problem.

Apparently, size did matter.

Her hands grabbed his hand and held on tightly. "Don't go any-where, bub. Just give me a minute," she said, curling her hips until it felt just right. "There," she said triumphantly.

"You're sure?"

"Absofuckinglutely."

He kissed her again and began to move, his cock slowly sliding in and out. His eyes never left her face, treating her like some yuppie princess from the Upper East Side. Her body began to adjust, oh, yeah, even welcome his size, and soon she understood the benefits, her muscles clenching in sweet relief with each powerful thrust. It was exquisite, this give and take, his thick cock moving deeper and deeper inside her, her body flying higher and higher. With each powerful stroke, her breasts rubbed painfully against the crisp hair on his chest, her sensitive nipples aching for just a tiny touch.

"Oh. God," she cried, feeling the orgasm approaching.

"This is killing you," he said, his chest glistening with sweat.

"No!" she yelled, her hips moving faster to keep up with him. She locked onto him, as he drove faster and faster. She didn't think she could take anymore, but each time, he was there again, and her heart was pounding, her blood racing, her entire brain lasered on the pulsating beat between her legs.

With each thrust she thought she died, only to be brought back to life once again. The cycled continued over and over, and she felt the wear on her body.

There was a rumble in the building. An earthquake. A bomb. Dear heaven, maybe it was all inside her, she didn't know.

Unable to keep the pressure bottled up, she cried out, and Jack's body quivered in response. Then he collapsed on top of her, his skin feverishly hot.

She struggled to regain her breath, needing to find a pulse once more. Eventually sanity returned. Every muscle within her ached; she was exhausted, she was drained, but damn, she felt sated. His heavy body was slick with sweat, and the heat . . .

"Are you okay?" she asked, because he felt so amazingly hot.

Groggily he raised his head and nodded. Once. "Am I too heavy?"

Was he kidding? She thought she could happily lay like this forever. And she told him just that.

He pressed a sleepy kiss on her lips. "I'm glad. I can't move."

It was a disquietly intimate moment, the inelegant afterglow with two bodies fully joined. Gabriella had never met a man who seemed perfectly content to remain inside her.

They had an odd connection, she and this man so far removed from her tiny universe in Brooklyn.

Another thousand years, and Jack still wouldn't want to move. Moving meant leaving her body, going back to a musty old store, and digging through boxes of books. No, this was where he wanted to be. Unfortunately, sacked out on a six-hundred-year-old bench was hellishly uncomfortable. With a long-suffering sigh, he sat upright.

"Come to the hotel with me," he said, because he wasn't ready for the evening to end.

"What time is it?" she asked, sitting up and leaning back on her hands, not uncomfortable at all. His cock took notice, started to harden.

No, no, no.

The next time would involve a bed where he could love her properly.

Which reminded him . . . he checked the time. "Fifteen after one."

"You have got to be shitting me!" she yelled, jumping up and pulling her dress on.

"I shit you not," he replied. "To the hotel?" he asked hopefully.

"I have to get home. Nanna will kill me." She smoothed the dress over breasts, hips, and thighs. A feeling of inordinate sadness swept over him as he watched golden flesh disappear beneath a mountain of cashmere. "I have to finish inventory."

"At two o'clock in the morning?" Jack asked, the vision of cotton sheets and bare flesh getting flushed down the toilet.

"A little Red Bull, and I'll be good as new."

His cock twitched painfully, knowing it was beaten. Besides, hers was the better plan. He'd drive her home, gallantly volunteer to help her with the books, buy the damned *Book of Souls*, and then disappear into the night, ready to take over his rightful place as heir to the devil incarnate. Jack knew his place in the world, actually the Underworld to be more precise. He practiced and trained and worked his butt off to be what his father wanted him to be. Nine hundred years was too long to waste.

Her hips swung dangerously as she downed the stairs two at a time, and he groaned with frustration. Would one more night have been too much to ask? Tonight he had felt something he hadn't in a long time. *Alive.* It had started as a tingle when she made him laugh, then spread to his chest when she shot him a slow smile, and after they'd made love . . .

Jack stuffed his hands in his pockets.

He didn't want to feel alive. A man didn't rule over the denizens of Hell by feeling anything but dead.

Chapter Three

After the cab carted them back to Brooklyn, Gabriella grabbed her keys. Oh, God, this was going to be a nightmare on Elm Street. Literally. Nanna got all freaky and possessive-like when Gabriella stayed out too late. She had learned to preplan alibis for her nights out, but this time . . .

She glanced over at Jack, who seemed impervious to the whole thing. Okay, so it'd been worth it. And what was the worst Nanna would do? Kick her out on the street like she threatened to do about eighteen million times before? Probably.

Gabriella snuck another look at the cause of all her problems and then sighed. He was *so* worth it. How many times did she get a chance to eat at a sublet Metropolitan Museum of Art—not that she really cared about all the pictures and joujou crap, but still . . . Talk about your grand gestures.

She leaned back against the seat, trying to relax.

"You're nervous?"

Gabriella flashed him a confident smile. "Oh, no. It's just so late."

"I'll see you to your door."

And wasn't that sweet? Gabriella flashed another smile because the last thing she needed was to show up on the stoop of the store with a *man*. Sordid assumptions were one thing, but if Nanna got one look at Jack, well, even Gabriella wasn't a good enough liar to cover up that one.

When they got to her street, he went around and opened the cab door. "So chivalrous," she murmured, getting out into the cold, still completely enthralled. Good God, was there anything this man couldn't do?

The lights out front were dimmed, which meant Nanna hadn't stayed up.

Excellent. Maybe it was her lucky day after all.

The snow crunched underneath her heels, a glowing white instead of the usual mucky gray-black, and she realized she should see the new snow at 1 a.m. more often. The wind whipped around her, and she pulled her coat closer.

Jack fell in behind, his hand on her back. His touch was always so warm, his hand burning into her flesh, even through the layers of her wool-blend coat.

She fumbled for her keys and unlocked the door, then turned around because she was dying to kiss him again, and also because she knew she couldn't let him into the store. Flirting with danger was one thing; flirting with Nanna-incited death was another one entirely.

He put an arm across the door, effectively blocking her way— not that she was really hankering to get inside; right now, she really just wanted to melt inside that body of his again. "Let me come inside. I'll help you," he whispered and then gave her a soft kiss.

A warm breeze caressed her cheeks. Heaven.

Like the potato chips, she wasn't ready to stop at only one. Tempting the fates, she pulled him inside. What would a little kissing hurt?

And immediately the lights flashed on.

There, on the foot of the stairs, was Nanna, dressed up in a black nightgown, her gray hair hanging down her back in one long braid. Nanna pointed a finger at Jack.

"You!"

Jack, who'd obviously never tangled with Nanna, took a step forward, trying to play a hero. "Is there a problem here?"

Uh, hello! Gabriella stepped in front of Jack. "No problem. Nanna can be dramatic." She backed into him, trying to push him out toward the door. Finally, she turned her back on her grandmother (never a good thing) and decided to be more forceful. "I'll see you tomorrow," she whispered.

"He has the mark of the devil," began her grandmother.

Oh, God, not the mark of the devil again. Gabriella felt her cheeks flush bright red, and not in a charming way, either. "She says that to all the men I date," Gabriella whispered to Jack, just in case he thought that crazy blood might be hereditary.

"You will not get the book," Nanna continued, her eyes never wavering from Jack, and this time, even Gabriella was getting slightly freaked.

Jack froze. "What book?"

"The *Book of Souls.* The D'Angelis family will never surrender the book."

Gabriella covered her face with her hands. This *Book of Souls* crap was all new and fresh from the pages of the latest *New York Times* thriller.

Thankfully, Jack didn't look either appalled or ready to run. The smile he flashed at Nanna was George Clooney–smooth, maybe better. "I'm just an ordinary guy who likes bookstores. The *Book of Souls* sounds great, but I was thinking of buying something a little more exotic. *The Illustrated History of Chlorophyll*, for instance," he said, giving Gabriella a discreet wink.

What a trooper. Gabriella pushed her grandmother up the stairs, but Nanna wasn't finished yet. She glared at Jack, although no pointing, which was definite progress. "A choice confronts you. The book can give you great power, all that you've ever dreamed. Or . . . you, and only you, can destroy it, losing everything you seek. The blood in your veins will not be denied. Go. Leave now." Nanna grabbed Gabriella's arm in a clawlike vise grip. "We will talk."

Gabriella glanced over her shoulder at Jack, who looked more amused than alarmed. She held up her pinky and thumb to her mouth and mouthed, "Call me."

He nodded once and then walked out into the night.

Nanna was furious, more furious than Gabriella had ever seen. She started out in Italian, hands flying. Gabriella listened, her hands crossed across her chest, and eventually Nanna lapsed back into the language Gabriella understood best.

"He is one with the devil. Leave him alone. Tell him to go far away."

"Nanna, he's sexy, he's rich, he's single, he's fun. If you think

I'm going to let him out of my sights, you're crazy. Men like that don't grow on trees."

"You don't understand. He only wants the book."

There it was. The book again. Gabriella hadn't read the thriller, but she understood the plot. An ancient book, believed to be a myth, was unearthed, and mayhem ensued. Blah, blah, blah.

"It's a myth, Nanna. Right up there with the Holy Grail, the silver bullet, and the perfect wax job. It doesn't exist."

"You're so young, you think that you know everything. You know nothing, Gabriella. The book exists. The man bears the mark. He comes seeking it for—"

"I know, I know, evil purposes."

Nanna nodded.

"What sort of evil purposes, Nanna?"

"It contains the souls of the holiest of holies. Saints through thousands of years."

"In a book? Come on."

Nanna crossed herself. "There was a time, hundreds of years ago, when the Church had a great flood that destroyed the catacombs, the tombs were disturbed, and bad men came. They took the bones of the saints, performed rituals to return the souls, and the souls returned. A great battle ensued for hundreds of years, dark forces at work, but finally one priest managed to capture the souls and return them to a tiny book. A very dangerous book that could only be destroyed by a descendant of the dark forces that had raised the dead. Your man, so sexy and fun, is one of those descendants. He comes seeking the book."

"And I suppose we have it."

Nanna dodged her eyes, which Gabriella took as a "no."

"Well, if we don't have the book, then we're in no danger, right?"

Nanna stared at her with golden brown eyes, measuring her granddaughter. Gabriella knew she'd never live up to the D'Angelis standard, so it was easier not to try. Finally her grandmother pulled her sweater close and turned away, muttering something old, dark, and ancient that Gabriella couldn't understand.

Jack had planned to return to his hotel. A hot shower sounded like just the thing, and although he was the son of the devil, he tried to get his requisite seven hours. But instead of a shower and sleep, he found himself watching the bookstore instead.

So the book was there after all. Power, hot and blood-red, pulsed in his veins. How could Father have even doubted him? The old woman was right about the book: It was the key to all Jack had ever wanted.

Finally, there would be no more worlds to conquer. Almost sad, really. He stood alone in the dark cold street, empty except for the creatures of the night. Creatures like him. This glimmer of loneliness was new, mainly because Jack didn't believe in getting too close. People lived, people died, but not Jack. Jack endured, and prospered, and soon he would take over the empire. Now he just had to convince Gabriella to sell it to him, then the book would be his.

Just as it should be.

The lights in the basement flickered on, drawing his attention. Gabriella, dressed in a long T-shirt and sweats, was dragging a folding chair across the room. Then she climbed up on the seat, pulling a box from the shelves, only to have it fall to the ground. The glass window did nothing to mute the clearly audible sound of disaster.

With growing horror, Jack watched the scene, telling himself that he needed to wait it out, not to look too obsessed with the book. If he showed his cards too soon . . .

Another box fell and he sighed. She'd probably destroy the damned book herself before he even got a look at it. Deciding that intervention had its purpose, he slid down into the dark window well and tapped on the glass.

Startled, Gabriella looked up. When she recognized him, she smiled and pointed to the front door, where she greeted him with a sloppy kiss on the cheek. "What are you doing here?"

"I thought I should see if you survived, and if maybe I could help," he offered, trying to ignore the line of dust cutting through her white T-shirt. It would've been nice to just zap into something more casual. Unfortunately, he had never been a big believer in business casual. The caste system was there for a reason, and proper dress reinforced the creed. She smiled again, and thoughts of dust and grim disappeared. "As long as you know I really have to work this time."

"I wouldn't leave you here, alone, slaving away. What kind of man does that?"

"Most of 'em," she answered. "Come on, then. You don't know what you're getting into."

Sadly, he did. Burying himself inside her body was one thing, but getting elbow-deep in years of dust mites and cobwebs, trying to restore order to an inventory system not practiced since the Mongols overran East Turkestan . . .

The things he did for Hell.

The basement was in worse shape than the store upstairs; ten freestanding shelves, supported by absolutely nothing, were loaded with boxes, and crates, and books. Even the floor was covered with books. The single lightbulb illuminated the silvery webs of spiders that were nearly as old as he was.

There was no time to waste—the faster he got out of this hellhole, the better.

Jack picked up a box from the top shelf and promptly sneezed. *Shit*. And just think, the night was young.

Together they worked through two shelves of books, which went much faster after a laptop magically "appeared" in Jack's briefcase, which had magically appeared as well. When his watch chimed three, he realized Gabriella had spent far too long logging a third edition of *Silas Marner*. He looked around the room, and finally found her fast asleep, a can of Red Bull lilting dangerously in one hand. Her head was pillowed against a stepstool, her neck crooked at an awkward angle.

For long moments Jack watched her sleep, confounded by the contented smile on her lips. He didn't understand what she found comforting in her sleep, especially surrounded by . . . he glanced around . . . *this*.

Still, contrary to rumors propagated by Marie Antoinette, he wasn't completely heartless. He conjured up two blankets and four pillows, then gently settled her in for the night. Which left just him, one computer, ten thousand books, seventeen spiders, and a thousand pounds of dust.

Hell.

Jack

Gabriella awoke to the sun in her eyes. Immediately she burrowed deeper into the blankets, grateful for the soft warmth. That wasn't right. She sat up, rubbing her face with her palms, trying to crank her brain back to life.

As was her usual morning ritual, she quirked open one eye, peering around, and finding no reason to believe the giant alligator in her dream was anything more than a dream, she safely opened the other one.

It was the storeroom . . . yet not the storeroom. There was order, there was cleanliness. Oh, my God, she was still stuck in her dream. She slapped her arm, and yes, it hurt. This was no dream. And then she saw him.

Jack.

He had turned the place upside down, but in a good way. The books were ordered, even alphabetized, and the dust had disappeared.

He was hunkered over a shelf against the wall, computer in hand, wearing wire-frame reading glasses.

He wore *glasses*. She felt her heart go *thumpa-thumpa* and sighed, a little louder than she'd planned. Jack looked up. "Awake?"

She smoothed her hair, climbing to her feet. "Where are the elves?"

He lifted a volume to the top shelf in one smooth move that flexed muscles that she had touched. "You don't believe I did this by myself?"

"Do I look like a sucker?"

His dark eyes skimmed over her, and she felt that curious heat once again. This man was downright dangerous. "Not at all."

51

She crossed the room, determined to play hardball this time. "I think it's time you started telling the truth." That got his attention. He pocketed the glasses, but the gesture didn't mask the shutter that came over his eyes. "You're no ordinary insurance dweeb, so don't even try and pull that one with me."

She waited for his reaction, but he was a cool customer. *Why was she not surprised?*

"I'm sorry, but I don't usually tell people who I am."

"Who are you, then?" she asked, because she knew that anybody that could close the Met had clout, spelled with a serious dollar sign.

Finally he nodded. "Vassago is short for Vassonovich. It's an old family. We made a lot of money during Prohibition."

It was starting to make sense. "Like the Kennedys?"

He nodded. "Sorta."

"And the insurance?"

"My family deals in life insurance. It's one of the companies under the family umbrella."

Gabriella looked into his eyes, not trusting him a bit. "Google reveals all. If you're lying . . ."

"Look it up," he said calmly. "Want my social security number?"

He sounded legit, acted legit, and he made love . . . well, okay, like no guy she'd ever slept with, and certainly not anybody she'd read about in *Cosmo*.

Case closed. For now.

"You finished the inventory?"

"Red Bull," he said. "Amazing stuff."

"It never worked *that* good for me." Gabriella glanced around at the spotless cement floor. "So did you discover any dead bodies down here? I always thought Nanna was part Gambino."

"Nothing but books. Some really old ones, too." He was all business today, with none of the urgency he had shown her last night. It was as if there were two of him. One she wanted, and one she didn't understand.

"We should take 'em upstairs. The store could use the fresh blood."

"You'll be happy to note that no *Book of Souls* was down here. I think your grandmother's just getting old."

Slowly she lifted her chin. Something in his tone was just a little too casual. One thing she'd learned very quickly about Jack—nothing was casual. "You interested in buying it?"

He closed the lid on the computer and slid it into his briefcase. "Look, I don't want to embarrass you or anything, but if your family has something that's worth a lot of money, well"—he shrugged—"I could broker it for you. Maybe pull your family out of a jam. The book is worth a fortune."

"I thought you weren't interested in books."

Jack reached out and stroked her hair, and she had to keep herself from turning into mush and tilting her cheek toward his palm. "You're smart, Gabriella D'Angelis. You know what's keeping me here, and it's not some book."

Their eyes met and Gabriella wanted so badly to believe him.

"Find the book for me," he said, his voice making her skin hum. "Don't you want out?" It was a rhetorical question, because Gabriella wanted out more than she wanted to breathe. She was tired of four walls, inadequate heating, and a mattress that caved in the center. "You have no idea," she answered.

"You'll find it for me?"

Gabriella nodded. She'd find it for him, but she wouldn't be Miss Speedy about it. Something inside her—most people called it a brain—told her that as soon as she got him the book, Jack Vassonovich would disappear. And she wanted to hold onto him for as long as she could.

Chapter Four

By the following Wednesday, Gabriella knew that Jack Vassago had a very large brain, but she wasn't so sure about the size of his heart. Oh, he was certainly generous enough; generosity wasn't the problem.

Every night, Jack would take her out on the town (although she usually snuck out the back to avoid any accidental run-ins with Nanna). On Sunday, he'd gotten orchestra seats to a sold-out show on Broadway. When Gabriella had leapt to her feet at the end, clapping until her palms hurt, Jack had rose much more quietly, clapping four times before calmly sitting back down.

She didn't let it bother her, but on Monday they went to a movie premiere in the Hamptons, a real tearjerker that made her mascara run. When the mother died of cancer in the end, Jack had simply frowned, like he didn't understand.

Tuesday, she vetoed all the movies and plays, and let him take her shopping, first at Barneys, then at Agent Provocateur. She wore her new dress and silk unmentionables that very night.

After shopping until she had nearly dropped, they retired to his hotel, a not-so-shabby suite at the Waldorf—a far, far cry from Bensonhurst.

For Gabriella, it was the excitement she'd always craved. Especially the nights. Once in their room he ordered champagne and caviar, strawberries and cream. The food of the gods, or at the very least, the obscenely rich. With the noise of Manhattan far, far below, she slipped out of her dress (Dior!) and posed in the doorway, the silk strap of her bustier strategically slipped down on her arm.

The bottom silk triangle was nothing more than an accessory on a string, because there wasn't much of her left covered.

He lay on the bed, shirt off, pillows piled behind his head like some Middle Eastern sheik. When he saw her, his eyes flashed with fire. She felt the heat burst through her, budding her nipples and dampening her thighs.

Somewhere along the line, she'd left the minors and was playing in the big leagues now.

"Very nice," he told her.

"Which parts are your favorite?" she asked—not exactly scintillating dialog, but she'd never had the cash to sign up for the *Penthouse* seduction classes, so she was just gonna have to wing it. Of course, when he looked at her like the fourth course at dinner, it wasn't that difficult.

"I have to pick?" He folded his hands behind his head, looking more than comfortable, although the *Venti*-sized swelling in his pants convinced her that he was feeling the heat, too.

She slipped down the other strap and gravity kicked in, her

breasts peeking over the lace edge. "Only one," she said with a sultry smile.

"Turn around," he ordered, and obediently she whirled, one hand braced on the wall. Again with the "very nice," only this time his voice was deeper, a little shakier. "Show me the front," he said.

"Top? Or bottom?" she asked, not sure what he was asking.

He shifted uncomfortably, the bulge growing larger. "Start with the top."

Gabriella paused, deciding which was better: coy or trampy. Eventually, she decided coy was the best route, so she began to untie the tiny bows that kept the front together. There were a lot of them, but Jack didn't seem to be in a hurry. Slowly she worked down the front until there was just two left, and she opted to keep them closed, mainly because she was cold.

Trying for sophisticated casual-*cum*-lap dancer, she shimmied and the front gaped, exposing her bare-naked ladies for his approval.

He didn't move.

Opting for daring, she touched a finger to her tongue and then rubbed her nipples.

His zipper burst.

"I believe we have a winner," she said, moving two steps closer to the bed, his heat now so intense, she could feel her skin burn.

"Wait. I don't make any conclusions without examining all the facts."

Gabriella swallowed. She'd pretty much covered her entire repertoire of moves learned from *Cosmo*, but then she spied the chair. She'd seen *Basic Instinct*. Twice. First she dragged the antique froufrou piece across the marble floor, planting it squarely in front of the bed. Then she settled her bottom primly (or as primly as possible when wearing a bustier) into the seat.

All she had to do was . . .

All she had to do was . . .

Oh, God, her nerves were shot.

Sensing her hesitation (it didn't take ESP), he looked at her with a question in his eyes. "You're sure?"

The tone was surprised, pleased, and it slid down her spine. She considered him, considered the modesty she'd already lost, and decided that some times risks were made to be taken.

The air heated, and she swore that her blood was going to explode, but before that happened she was going to see this through. She placed both feet on the mattress, but he was faster. He grabbed her by the ankles and pulled her onto the soft cotton sheets. Gabriella had always felt like she had a very modern attitude about sex, but Jack was so far ahead of her in matters of the carnal world, which was saying a lot.

He slid the last two ties free, his hot hands skimming her breasts. "Your body wasn't made for these," he said, drawing his tongue across one nipple and then the other. She arched her back, savoring his touch and realizing that these nights would never be forgotten.

Smoothly he drew both hands up over her head, holding her quivering and helpless . . . and desperately aroused.

Then she felt his lips against her neck, teasing, nibbling, nipping. "Why do you trust me?" he whispered in her ear, his cock thick and hard between her thighs.

She shifted, her legs parting to accommodate him. "I don't," she managed, tilting her neck as his tongue slid in her ear.

The pleasure fest stopped, and Jack raised his head, meeting her eyes. "Then why are you here?"

"This is sex, nothing more," she answered, forcing a smile, but she quickly looked away, in case he read something in her look that she wasn't ready for him to see. Sophisticated, carefree—that would be her middle name.

He freed her arms and rose up on one elbow, his dark eyes curious. "Why not?"

"Why not what?" she asked, playing stupid.

"Why don't you trust me? Do you think there's somebody else?"

She shook her head. "You're not in a relationship, you're too . . ."

"What?"

This time she shrugged, not finding the rights words.

"Go ahead, say it."

Gabriella licked her lips and sighed. "You're too closed off. Like nobody else exists," she managed.

"How do you think I should act?"

"I don't know. Sometimes I feel like nobody matters to you."

The curiosity in his gaze changed to something darker, more dangerous, and he sat upright on the bed. "You think I'm not thinking of you? I've given you everything." The truth was, he hadn't given her anything important.

"There's things, and then there's nonthings. You got the things down solid. It's the nonthings you suck at." She really hadn't meant for it to come out that way, but okay, the words were out there, and she wasn't going to take them back.

He didn't move; he was cold, frozen, like her words had bounced off his chest. She had wanted to hurt him, to get an emotion out of him. Anything. She was feeling so much, and he never seemed to feel at all.

His mouth drew together in one hard line, and she realized that she had succeeded.

"So it's just the things that are keeping you here?" he asked in a deceptively silky voice. "I thought that's all you would need."

Gabriella moved off the bed; her stomach hurt, and she felt cold. When she was little, there were a lot of things that she wanted to be when she grew up. Whore was not one of them.

Quickly she pulled her blue jeans and blouse out of the Barneys bag and started to dress. "What the hell is wrong with you?" he asked, which was the stupidest question in the universe.

"I don't have the problem," she said, determined not to cry. She was not going to cry. Not in front of Jack.

"Yes, you do. You should be happy."

She flashed him a cold smile. "Yeah. I look happy, don't I?"

"I don't understand. After everything I've bought . . . ," he said, getting up and padding over on bare feet. He was such a magnificent piece of man. For the first time, Gabriella realized that a hot body and loads of cash did not make a perfect man.

"Everything, nothing. What's the difference?"

"What more could you possibly want? A penthouse? Diamonds?"

A loud war cry erupted from her mouth, and she threw the shopping bag at him. So smart, so dumb. "It's crap, Jack. This is bubble gum, nothing more. I kept thinking there was something else to you; I was wrong. Go down on Tenth Street, 'cause that's where the real pros hang out."

She was halfway to the door when he grabbed her arm. "You can't leave me." There was a plea in his voice. Something she'd never expected to hear.

It was too little, too late. Gabriella D'Angelis had never been stupid. Well, maybe just this once.

"Welcome to the real world, Jack. Welcome to New York." Then she slammed the door and left.

Jack sat alone for a long time, waiting for Gabriella to show up. Eventually he realized she wasn't coming back.

Damn.

He stalked to the bar and poured a shot of whiskey into the glass. The liquid burned going down, but did nothing to ease the cold inside him. Three shots later he realized the whiskey wasn't going to work.

Television was no better. He turned it on, then turned it off when the noise did nothing to fix the silence.

What the fuck was wrong with her? He'd offered her a lot—a helluva lot more than most women got from Jack. He hadn't looked at another woman. He'd ignored his businesses. Hell, he'd been with her *constantly*. Five solid days where he'd never once sought solitude. In all of his nine hundred years, he'd never spent so much time with a woman. So why didn't she realize what he'd done for her?

Jack paced around the room, working himself into a white-hot rage. There was nothing in the world but things. Nothing. And she, of the family with nothing at all, should know that more than anyone.

She had nothing. Nothing except the book.

God damn it.

A loud bang cracked behind him, but Jack knew exactly what had happened.

Dad was here.

Oh, the joy.

"She dumped you?" said the devil, seated comfortably on the couch, like he owned the place.

"Fuck you."

"Touchy. Your heart's not supposed to hurt."

The glass on the table exploded. Mainly because Jack needed to hit something, he wanted to hurt something, to make up for the hurt inside him.

"You did manage to get the book, didn't you?" asked the devil, picking up a travel magazine and casually thumbing through it.

It wasn't often that Jack hated his father. Now was one of those times.

Chapter Five

Gabriella spent Monday morning playing "I told you so" with herself. Having her sorry lot in life illuminated with 100-watt clarity did nothing for her self-esteem, but she did manage to sell four first editions, seven third editions, and one autographed copy of Bill Clinton's memoir. Maybe she should've climbed on the reality express earlier.

After *Oprah* was over, Nanna trundled downstairs, a confrontation Gabriella had tried to avoid. It was one thing to play "I told you so" with yourself, an entirely different (and rotten) kettle of fish to hear it from your eighty-year-old grandmother.

"You're working today."

Gabriella finished dusting the glass plates on the counter and threw the rag in the trash.

"Yes, Hell has frozen, Nanna."

Her grandmother picked a book off the shelf and pretended to read. Gabriella wasn't fooled. She waited for the lecture, pretending to reorganize the history section. And wasn't even to the French Revolution when it came.

"He was no good."

"Will it lower your blood pressure if I tell you you're right?"

"You're better off without him."

It was margarita salt to the wounds, but Gabriella let her grandmother continue. The painful truth needed to set inside her like cement, because deep down, Gabriella was no different from any other lily-livered, weak-kneed female who'd ever called a man at 4 a.m. just to hear his voice. Some of the weaker sex would proposition the cad, some (before caller ID hit it big) would hang up, but all clung to the same hope: that their man would be the exception to the rule.

"Are you listening to me?" her grandmother yelled, interrupting Gabriella's funk.

"Of course I am."

"He's an evil man and will do bad things with the book."

Nanna spoke with such absolute certainty. "What's up with this book?" Gabriella asked, for the first time entertaining the possibility that her grandmother wasn't a crazy person. Her grandmother eyed her, taking stock to see if Gabriella was trustworthy. Eventually she must've realized that Gabriella was the end of the D'Angelis line and she really didn't have a choice.

Nanna bent down behind the cash register, back behind the black cast-iron safe, and came up with a small book: *101 Uses for a Dead Cat*.

Gabriella sighed and went to put the book back.

"Take off the dust jacket," her grandmother said, a pleased smile cutting through already lined cheeks.

64

Underneath the jacket was a black leather volume, looking more like a Day-Timer than an ancient book. Inscribed on the cover in tiny gold letters was the title, *The Book of Souls*.

It seemed such a tiny thing, and Gabriella could only wonder if it was the real deal. She moved to open the cover, but Nanna slapped it shut, then took the book away and hid it back behind the safe.

"Now you know the secrets of the D'Angelis family."

"I didn't think it existed," Gabriella whispered.

"There are many things, Gabriella, many things you do not know. The world is not such a simple place."

Then it dawned on Gabriella that the secrets of the D'Angelis family would be worth a fortune. "Can we sell it?"

Nanna gave her an indulgent smile. "Only to the right buyer."

"The right buyer not being Jack?" she snapped, because of course they couldn't give the rich, handsome, sometimes charming Prince Charming what he wanted.

Things like Gabriella; things like the book.

Her sigh was not a complete surprise, and Nanna, not the indulgent grandmotherly type found in movies and fairy tales, waved it off. "You will survive this."

Maybe she'd survive it, but it would be nice if she could survive it with someone else—like Jack, or maybe a kinder, gentler Jack, one with sensitivity and feelings. Feelings were important.

After her grandmother went back upstairs, Gabriella's thoughts returned to the book. Having her own Pandora moment, she rooted around behind the safe and was just about to open the cover when the bell over the door jangled.

She didn't have to see through the counter to know—

It was Jack.

She stuck the book in her wool sweater pocket, locking her hands there, too, mainly to avoid touching him. "Well, well, well," she said, because she didn't have anything better to say.

He nodded politely. "Jack Vassonovich, CEA Vassonovich Enterprises."

Did it always have to be a mystery with him? "Chief Executive Auditor?" she asked, not really liking this game.

"Asshole," he answered.

Oh. An apology. That was a better game. He made no move to touch her, which was both a relief and a torment. "You're here for the book?"

He shook his head, his mood dark. "It took me a long time to acquire people skills. Longer than most. Humanity is not a concept that runs in my family."

She locked her arms across her chest. "All my problems are due to my parents? Sell it to Geraldo," she snapped.

"No. All my problems are due to me. I want to start over. I'm sorry." If he thought she'd be a pushover, he thought wrong. She had pride; she had principles.

"Hands and knees are usually the best position for groveling," she said, halfway serious.

Outside, a crash of thunder shook the entire block. Jack ignored it and climbed down on his knees. His eyes held hers, dark, fathomless pools that she could never understand. This was no game to him; maybe he'd learned something after all. She waved a hand. "Oh, get up. Two jerks don't make a right and besides your pants weren't cut out for our not-so-spiffy floors."

A pained expression crossed his face, as he climbed to his feet. "I know."

Gabriella, pride now firmly in tact, and principles, not so much, took a deep breath. This time she was going to get it right. "First we establish a code of conduct. No shopping. No expensive dinners. No red-carpet razzmatazz."

"Why?" he asked, with all the dense insightfulness of those who've never know the embarrassment of having a credit card declined.

"You tempt me, Mr. Vassonovich. You tempt me to be a person I don't like. When it comes to money, it's too easy for me to sell my soul, and I like my soul, thank you very much. It's my way or no way," she finished. Her principles came roaring back and patted her on the shoulder.

"What if I can't do it your way?"

Now that was a toughie. It was possible they were too different. It was possible he required some bimbo Barbie who believed that money was as necessary to life as silicone. However, Gabriella chose to ignore it.

"Piddle. You're selling yourself short."

He stayed quiet and considered it. When the silence ran on two beats too long, he finally spoke. "All right. So what is allowed?"

"Where were you born?"

"Kiev."

"Favorite food?"

"Caviar."

Gabriella rubbed at her temples. There must be *something* he did that wasn't superluxe.

"Second favorite?" she asked, hopefully.

"Pierogi."

Much better. She could work with that. "Brighton Beach it is."

"I beg your pardon?"

"The best pierogi in Brooklyn. You'll have to educate me on the finer appointments of dumpling tasting."

"I can do that," he answered seriously, way too seriously.

She shook her head. One small step at a time.

It wasn't nearly superluxe; it wasn't deluxe; in fact, there was no luxe whatsoever. The Ukrainian was a towering hall with bad murals on the wall and a "singer" (Gabriella used the word loosely) wailing on the long, wooden stage.

"This is what your childhood was like?" she asked, nervous about what she was getting into. Some cultural differences could not be overcome. That singing, for instance.

Jack's mouth twisted into a half smile. "The music was better."

Gabriella heaved a sigh of relief. "What are the pictures?"

"It's the river Kalka. A long time ago, a brutal battle was fought on the banks of that river. Ukrainians lost, the country went downhill after that. Bad times."

"And they make a mural of that?"

"It's a Ukrainian thing. Anytime a lot of people die, pain, suffering, torture, they don't forget."

"You really know your history, don't you?"

He flushed. "I dabble. But no more than anyone. I bet you know the history of the American Revolution."

"Not a bit. We Americans are very blasé about our own past."

"History protects us from repeating mistakes."

"I've heard that before," she answered. *And usually ignored it,* she thought to herself.

He took a drink and watched her over the edge of the glass. "You never doubt yourself, do you."

"Not on days that end in 'y.'"

He began to smile, his body looser, freer somehow, even with the bad music. Her Jack was back, and a warm glow lit her up from the inside. As hard as she tried, she couldn't break down what separated him from everyone else, but something inside him called to her. There was something lost about him, a man without a country. She wanted to be there for him, because for all his tangible aspects, he didn't seem to understand that people needed people most of all. She knew that it was her mission, destiny, kismet, whatever, to be here. With him. For him.

She wanted to know more. He'd been so evasive about who he was, and it drove her nuts. It could have been the vodka, it could have been the singing, but mostly it was an incurable addiction to meddle in other people's lives.

"Tell me about your family," she asked.

His gaze flickered to the pictures on the wall, drawn to the monastery at the top of the hill. "My mother was a very mild woman. Quiet, but still strong. She raised me by herself at a time when society wasn't open to the idea of a single mom."

"What about your father? I thought this was a family business?"

"As soon as I was old enough, he came and claimed me."

"He took you away from your mom? How crappy is that?"

"She died," he answered, his voice flat and emotionless.

Gabriella was appalled. No kid should be without their mother. She knew about it personally, and it sucked. But at least she had Nanna, which, okay, she bitched about her grandmother a lot, but Nanna was better than nothing. "That must've been very hard for you."

"He exposed me to a lot of opportunities I wouldn't have had otherwise."

She folded her arms on the table, watching his face. The eyes seemed so tired for someone his age. "You dad must've done right because you turned out okay."

"We are who we're meant to be."

Gabriella studied the singer on the stage, her short skirt, her too-tight sweater. "We're different people from our parents. If Nanna is right, I'm destined to be a slut."

He covered her hand with his own, the movement awkward for him. "You're not a slut. Trust me when I say that I know sluts, and you, Gabriella D'Angelis, are not one."

Part of her wanted to believe him, part of her still needed reassurance. "Spoken like a man who's getting a lot of snatch."

"I don't think ours is the norm for you," he said with a confident smile. A little *too* confident.

She moved her hand away. "It could be. You don't know."

"Don't even try to lie. There's something different about us and you know it."

"You really think that?" Deep inside her, she needed to believe that everything was going to be okay.

He nodded.

"Why?" she prodded.

His scowl was not encouraging. "God, I hate that word. Can't we just stop at 'yes' and move on?"

"No," she answered with a benevolent smile.

Thankfully, the man was smart enough to know when he was licked. "Fine. Look, I don't know why it's different. I mean, there's some important things going on in my life right now, and that could be it, and I wish it was that, because it'd be a lot easier for me, but I'm a realist and I like to call a spade a spade, even when it's part of a full house, but you . . ." He stopped and stared at her, shaking his head. "You make me feel," he finished, and then promptly drained his shot of vodka.

"Feel? Feel what?"

His frown deepened. "Just feel. You know, emotions."

It was like milking an answer from the IRS, only worse. "What sort of emotions?"

"All kinds."

"Good ones?"

"And bad ones."

"Bad ones?"

"Not too many bad ones," he added, his brows knitted together into one long, fierce line. Gabriella felt her heart sink.

"So why don't you look happy? You should be happy? People with feelings and good emotions are happy people."

"No, sometimes it just makes you depressed."

"Have you considered counseling, or medication? Our neighbor, Mrs. Dunlap, was a regular Biddy McBitch until she started on Paxil. Pharmaceuticals can do wonders in this day and age. You should try it."

"I don't think drugs are going to help."

She pointed her spoon at him. "That's just what Mrs. Dunlap used to say."

"I'll look into it," he answered.

Gabriella toyed with her vegetables, but put down her fork because there was one more question she wanted to ask.

"What 'important things' are going on?"

"It's a takeover."

"Oh, man, that is so cool! Or is this a bad thing?"

"It's a good thing."

"So everybody wins?"

"Yeah, everybody wins," he answered quietly.

"It must be very exciting, all the wheeling and dealing," she gushed, envying him for the life he led.

"On most days, but sometimes you forget . . ."

"Forget what?"

"You forget what life is like, you forget what bad music sounds like, you forget the taste of bad food."

Again with the riddles. "I don't understand."

"It's like . . ."

"What?"

Jack searched for words, but finally merely shrugged his shoulders. "I don't know. Forget it."

God, he was such a *man.* "No, I'm not going to forget it. Explain. Use your words. Communicate."

"You're not going to drop this, are you?"

"Are you kidding? Drop a chance to hear the man I love hash through his feelings? What kind of woman do you think I am?" she said, pouring him another shot of vodka.

He looked like he needed it.

He ignored the glass. "What did you say?"

Gabriella sighed. "I said, 'What kind of woman do you think I am?'"

This time he downed the shot and then promptly poured another. "Never mind."

Gabriella wasn't about to let him off the hook. Not know. Now when she was so close . . . "No, not 'never mind.' Let's go back to this life stuff."

"You really want to know?"

"Are you always this slow? Of course."

He started to laugh, twisting the shot glass in his hands. "Have you ever pulled yourself out of a situation? Watched your life through a camera lens?"

"Once." It'd been a date with Dwight Grunberg. His definition of "no" and hers weren't the same. It'd been a painful lesson, but she had survived.

"It's easier if you don't participate," he said, one lock of hair falling on his forehead. The lost boy was back.

She took his hand, needing to touch him, needing to break through the titanium exterior. "You got to get in the game, Jack. You gotta get your hands dirty, or else, poof, your life is over, you're dead in the ground, and you've got nothing but regrets."

"You mean like working in a bookstore that you hate?" he answered.

"Well, yeah, but you know, I'm no role model. I'm only twenty-four. You're older than twenty-four. I mean, you're like, what, early thirties?"

He smiled, his thumb absently rubbing against her palm. "Something like that. So what are you going to do with your life?"

Gabriella hadn't intended to talk about herself. Her life was a yawner, but he inspired her to do more. "I'm going to take a chance. I'm going to take a risk."

"On what?"

She knew, but she wasn't willing to voice it aloud. It was a feeling, an inspiration, a thought, and she needed to let her instincts simmer.

"That's for me to know and you to find out. Of course, that's assuming that you stick around, which isn't a high-probability occurrence, and usually I don't play Mega Millions, because the odds are stratospherically high, but sometimes you have to buy a ticket, you know? Sometimes you just feel it here," she said, fist to heart.

Jack didn't answer, but the music grew louder, the bass so amped up the whole room seemed to vibrate. Or else New York was having an earthquake. Gabriella smiled to herself.

As if.

She gave him the book when he took her home. He hadn't bought her anything, unless you counted the really bad pierogi, and she refused to take any money. It was as easy as he had bragged to his father so many days ago. It felt like ten lifetimes ago.

Now here he was, the *Book of Souls* in his hand and Gabriella looking at him with all the trust of a tiny puppy.

"I can't just take this from you," he said, because according to the devil, she had to sell it to him. They should spend time haggling over the price. Hours, days, maybe weeks. She'd drive a hard bargain—

"I want you to resell it for me," she answered.

Jack fumbled for words, wishing she wasn't making this so easy. "I need to give you something. A deposit."

"Then give me a dollar," she said.

Outside the wind picked up, freezing rain starting to pelt against the thin windows.

"You should get more than a dollar," he protested.

"Make it two."

"That's not how you operate a business."

"It's not just a business, it's my heritage, and if I want to run it into the ground, I will."

He took a deep breath. At least one of them could have a cavalier attitude about their responsibilities.

"Why are you doing this?" he asked, but he knew. She trusted him. She believed he was one of the good guys. Her dream man coming to rescue her from the banalities of a Brooklyn existence.

She loved him.

Gabriella favored Jack with a thoughtful look before answering. "Sometimes I have to get in the game. Sometimes I have to get my hands dirty, too."

At the mention of dirt, he promptly sneezed.

"What if you're wrong? What if I give you two dollars, take the book, and you never hear from me again?" Even as he said the words aloud, something began roaring up inside him, like a drowning man racing for air. When a man was immortal, there was nothing to fear—until now.

Her eyes, never serious, were very serious. Their golden brown was flat, without the familiar glow. "I have to take the risk," she answered slowly. "I have to know how it's going to turn out. If you walk away, Nanna was right. You're a bad man and not worth my time or my heart. But if I'm right . . ."

She stopped and shook her head.

"What?" he asked, wanting to hear her say it. Just once, wanting to hear someone say the words.

"You're a good and decent man, Jack Vassonovich. I don't know where you've been in the past, or what you've done, but I know you. I've known you all my life. I've loved you all my life. I just haven't met you until now."

The book burned in his hands, the heat in the room stifling hot. "You don't really know me," he argued. "You just want to see me that way. You don't know who I am. If you knew you wouldn't be saying this. You wouldn't . . . you couldn't really love me."

"Don't tell me how I feel. It's my heart, and I'll do with it whatever I want."

"You're throwing it away," he told her. "I won't be back." The sleet was coming down in torrents, the noise drowning out all else.

Gabriella blinked back the tears in her eyes. "Then I'll be wrong, but I have to believe, Jack. I have to keep believing. Someday, I'll be right."

A warm feeling stirred inside him, a candle flame flickering in the breeze, and for a second, the icy storm outside abated.

It was the opportunity of a lifetime, a chance to return the book to her, tell her that he loved her, explain his complicated bloodlines, and they would all live happily ever after.

He even opened his mouth to tell her, but the words refused to come. For nine hundred years he had clawed and worked and fought and lied to obtain the keys to Hell. When it came right down to it, that was who he was. She could believe whatever she wanted, but if she thought he could ever change . . .

Jack couldn't look at her anymore.

He turned around and walked out the door, the icy sleet cutting into his skin.

What she thought didn't matter.

Gabriella was wrong.

Chapter Six

Two days later, Gabriella woke up in bed and came to two bone-chilling conclusions.

The entire state of New York was suffering the worst ice storm on record, cold enough to freeze off even the most plastic of breasts. The other conclusion was not so easy to wrap her mind around.

The man she'd fallen in love with didn't exist. She burrowed deeper in the covers, but it didn't help. Nanna came up and pounded on the door. "Get up, you lazy bear." Gabriella pulled the pillow over her ears. "I won't." Right now she needed to wallow in bed and cry and cut herself off from the rest of the world. Only for a few days . . . maybe four thousand. And then she'd be better.

"We have customers downstairs."

"And suddenly you've forgotten this is your bookstore?"

"I'm an old woman, Gabriella."

"Not too old to nag at me."

"Of course not."

Realizing that peace would never come, Gabriella grumbled out of bed, showered, threw on her worst jeans, and pulled her hair back in a brutal, yet face-slimming, ponytail. By the time she was halfway down the stairs, she felt a little better. Not so much like throwing herself in the Hudson. And tomorrow, things would be a little better than today, because, well, how could they be worse?

"*Where is the* Book of Souls?" Nanna screamed at Gabriella, just as she hit the last step.

The entire contents of the shelves behind the safe had been emptied. Boxes of tissues, dust rags, crumpled and used, book bags, tissue paper. Everything but the book.

Gabriella pulled at her ponytail. "Imagine that."

"You sold it to him."

"Of course I didn't."

"You did."

"I didn't."

"You did."

"Maybe I did."

There weren't many places left for Jack to hide, but there was one place his father would never find him. The Cloisters was about as close to church as Jack could get, and he needed time alone. He needed to think.

The outside terrace was bitingly cold, the waters of the Hudson dark and fathomless. He leaned against the stone rail, letting the wind wash over him. The book lay flat on the wall next to him, waiting for a bolt of lightning to come down and destroy it, or perhaps a strong gust of wind would wash it away. Then Jack wouldn't have to make a choice. After a few minutes, he realized that a bolt of lightning wasn't forthcoming, and that if he wanted a gust of wind, he would have to create it himself.

People strolled by, but nobody noticed the book. They were too busy with their own lives to realize that the key to so many souls was right in front of them. His fingers traced the worn leather cover, traced the gilt lettering. The book wasn't as old as he was, and it contained a goodness that he never had. It seemed wrong for him to touch it, so he removed his fingers. No point in ruining something pure.

Still, if he was going to take it to his father, he'd have to touch it. He'd have to pick it up, put it in his pocket, and fly back to the casino. Mission accomplished. The keys to Hell would be his.

There were so many reasons to take the book to his father. More than nine hundred years worth of reasons. For so long, he had walked down one long and arduous path in order to fulfill his destiny. *Destiny*. Somehow he'd grown to hate that word, not realizing it until now.

An elderly couple stood next to him, arm in arm. The elderly man looked tired and near death, but his eyes were alive. Even in the cold, the blue eyes were dancing with love. The woman was frail—a good wind would be enough to blow her away—but she held on tightly to his arm, and slowly they shuffled forward, one small step at a time.

It was puzzling to him how mortals endured life, when death was always hanging over their shoulder. Shouldn't they be afraid? Hell, Jack was immortal and right now he was terrified.

Terrified because not only was the book his destiny, but it was Gabriella's as well. She didn't deserve to live out her meager allocation of days in the dusty bookshop in Brooklyn. She deserved something better.

As if to mock him, a strong burst of wind came from the north, ruffling the pages, but the book stayed stubbornly there. The book was her ticket out. And he was sitting here, contemplating destroying it.

And that's what he was doing, wasn't it? Walking away from his heritage, the firstborn son of Satan, walking away from his destiny, his goals, his dreams. Sadly, he couldn't walk away from everything. He couldn't walk away from his past, nor could he walk away from his blood. Those pieces were inside him and they always would be. Even if he destroyed the book, it was one tiny debit in a sea of red ink.

How could he tell Gabriella that her destiny was to never find the fame and fortune she wanted? How could Jack walk away from his entire life?

A heartless man could; an unfeeling man could. A man whose head ruled his heart would laugh. But Jack was none of those things anymore.

The thought made him smile, and he wished Gabriella was here to see it. Actually, considering he was about to set fire to all her dreams, maybe her absence was for the best.

Before he could talk himself out of it, Jack took the book and hefted it out to river. The book fluttered in the air, nearly still for a moment, and he focused his energy on the pages. A flame flickered, then caught, flaring to life. As the pages burned, the ash turned to dust, and in the blink of an eye, his destiny had been destroyed.

Jack

At the D'Angelis bookstore, the bell over the door jangled as it opened, letting in not only the customer but a brutal blast of cold air as well.

"*Vergine Santa!*" whispered Nanna, crossing herself.

Gabriella looked up from the inventory list and took a step back, and then one more because one didn't seem to be enough.

"Good morning, ladies," the man said, dark eyes gleaming above the neatly trimmed goatee. The whole room seemed to freeze in his presence. Formidable didn't even begin to describe him and Gabriella, not a religious type by nature, felt a sudden urge to cross herself, too.

"I'm looking for a book," the man said, causing Nanna to spew out a torrent of Italian, which loosely translated to "the devil is here."

Gabriella sighed, because it was a statistical impossibility that every man who stepped foot in the store was some form of Lucifer. "You've come to the right place. Did you have something particular in mind?" she asked casually, but keeping a safe distance nevertheless.

"*The Book of Souls*. I believe you have it," he said, pulling off black leather gloves. Gabriella's smile froze in place. At some point in time, even the most disbelieving of cynics must start to think that something hinky is definitely going on. "It's already been sold. Maybe you'd like an autographed fourth edition of *Moby Dick*?"

The dark eyes narrowed, spearing her in place. "That's impossible."

Gabriella worked to remain calm. "Technically it's not. There are at least five documented editions of *Moby Dick*, not counting—"

81

"Gabriella, hush," commanded Nanna, and for once, Gabriella obeyed.

"I sent my son to retrieve the book," the man said.

"You're Jack's father?" asked Gabriella as the reason for Jack's personality idiosyncrasies became crystal clear.

The older man nodded. "He already bought the book?" A pleased smile crossed his face.

"Two days ago," Gabriella replied.

"Then where is Jack?"

"And isn't that the mega-million-dollar question. If you see him, tell him not to show his face around here, or I'll be kicking some Ukrainian ass or possibly some other, more vulnerable body part."

"He didn't give you the book, did he?" said Nanna, not quite so fearful anymore.

The man's eyes flashed like lightning. "That is not your concern."

Gabriella looked at Nanna, because all at once she realized that Nanna was much more mentally competent than she had assumed. "He's really the . . . ?" her voice trailed off, and the Ruler of the Undead nodded proudly.

Gabriella gulped. "And Jack is your . . ." she started, but fumbled for the correct genealogical descriptor.

"Son," the devil finished, even though she already knew.

Her heart shattered, crumpling into a million pieces. The devil began to smirk, and she hated him then. Hated him, hated his son. Oh, God. *His son.*

"I bet all that crap about Kiev was bullshit," said Gabriella, choosing to ignore the very real, very ookie fact that she had had carnal relations with the son of Satan. It just seemed better that way.

"He told you that?" asked his father, surprise in his voice. "No matter. Yes, it's the truth."

Gabriella's opinion of Jack notched up a point. She looked at her grandmother, who seemed amazingly pleased considering the devil was looming very large and lifelike in the store . . .

. . . Looking for the *Book of Souls.*

"He destroyed the book, didn't he?" she said to Nanna.

Nanna shrugged enigmatically, but the smile on her face didn't go away.

For a moment, Gabriella let that piece of information simmer. She gave Jack a silent cheer for standing up to his father, although it was a metaphorical "standing up" since he hadn't confronted his father, merely ran away, dodging the whole issue.

Hell, in his shoes, she would've done exactly the same thing, or at least she hoped that she had the strength to deny the monster standing in front of her.

"Bad day in Black Rock?" she taunted, mainly for Jack's sake, since he wasn't here.

"Silence," the devil bellowed, the room vibrating from his voice. "I will find him; I will find the book," he said and turned to leave.

"Happy hunting, Columbo," whispered Gabriella as he opened the door.

The devil whirled around and instantly she knew she'd gone too far.

A trio of rats scrambled into the store, sending both Nanna and Gabriella scrambling as well.

The dark eyes, more mischievous than his son's, twinkled in the light. "I don't know what you've done to my son, or how you've corrupted him, but it really doesn't matter. In a few hours' time, you'll be dead."

Her heart pumped faster than a dead person's would. This so wasn't fair. She wasn't supposed to die. She needed to get married. Maybe have a family. Possibly a dog. Nanna pulled her close, and Gabriella chose not to fight it. For once, Nanna's tight confines weren't a bad thing. Over her granddaughter's head, Nanna met the eyes of the devil. "The rats?" she asked evenly.

"The plague," he answered with a smile. "The old methods of destruction have always been the best."

Then the devil strode out the door, the bell jangling happily behind him.

Chapter Seven

Jack found his father exiting Gabriella's bookstore. For some reason, it was easier to confront Lucifer than to tell the truth to Gabriella.

"You have the book?" asked the devil.

Jack glanced between the store and his father. "Why're you here?"

"Looking for my son. Looking for my book."

Jack took in air, long breaths of air. It was time. "I destroyed it," he answered. Three words. Three little words.

Lucifer's eyes flashed, turning hot, then cold. But Jack had seen his father's anger before, and he'd always survived. "You're either a liar or a fool," the devil said.

"A fool I may be, but I'm no longer your fool," he said, feeling the weight of nine hundred years lift from his shoulders. Gabriella was right. Sometimes you had to take a risk. Sometimes you had to get in the game, and for Jack, life was a bigger risk than gambling could ever be.

Lucifer stared, trying to see into the darkness that was Jack's soul.

"You're lying."

"No."

"She's not worth it."

Jack, remembering what happened to the last woman he loved, opted to lie. "A night of pleasure, a warm bed, nothing more."

"Excellent. It won't bother you if she's dead in a bit."

The earth began to shake, slow at first, but then growing in intensity. "You're lying," he whispered, as the sky began to dim.

The devil waved a careless hand. "The plague. Very sad."

Jack's heart stopped. "What did you do?"

"Ring around the rosies," sang his father in a jaunty voice, as if he hadn't just condemned Gabriella to death. A bolt of lightning flashed low to the ground, hitting a billboard on the other side of the street.

To *death*.

Pain cut through him, shocking pain like he'd never known before. He was immortal, he was immune, but this . . . this was pain like he'd never experienced. He howled, a long cry of despair. When he had destroyed the book, he had blithely assumed that his life could carry on. With Gabriella.

His anger unfurled, lightning streaking through the sky, the wind whipping up with hurricane intensity. Signs bounced like toys, the screams of frightened pedestrians filled the air. His father dodged a mailbox, his eyes amused. For the devil, this was nothing more than an elaborate game.

"Jack, I didn't think you had it in you. Does my heart proud. It's not too late, you know. I don't believe you'd disobey me. Just give me the book."

The wind whipped at him, but he had heard the words . . .

It's not too late . . .

He needed to focus. Regain calm. He needed a plan. His heart-slowed, his breath. He had to stay calm. The winds died down.

"I told you the truth. It's gone. I'll do what you want. Be what you want. But you have to make her well."

"You're in no position to negotiate, Jack," said his father, and Jack wanted to cry in frustration. All his life, he'd worked to achieve power, and now, when he needed it most, he had none.

"It's your blood running in my veins. I'm your firstborn. No one else can do a better job. Give her life."

The devil checked his watch. "So sorry."

Jack grabbed his father by the throat and pushed him up against the dusty glass windows, rain streaking down on both of them. He needed to beat at something; his father would do nicely.

Lucifer never blinked. "It's hard to kill a man who can't die."

"What do you want?" Jack asked, his hands falling helplessly to his side, begging now.

"You had your chance. You took a gamble. You lost."

They were words. Familiar words. Words he'd heard a thousand times before. Jack backed off, dusted his jacket. He would not let this happen. Not to Gabriella. She had to live, because he didn't think he could handle an eternal life without her in it. "A turn of the cards."

His father's mouth twisted. "Why?"

"For nine hundred years I have worked for you. I have tripled your profits, tripled your souls, done more for you than anyone else. I have conquered nations, brought glory to your name. I am your son. *You owe me.*"

The devil considered it for a moment, stroking his beard. "If I win?"

Jack could think of nothing he had to give. His life had been about his father. He looked around at the madness around him, the people nervously staring at the sky, waiting for the next dangerous turn of the clouds. "The whole city burns," he answered.

His father looked happy at the prospect. "And if you win? The girl lives?"

"You heal her."

The devil glanced toward the store. "And her grandmother, too," Jack added.

"One card?"

Jack pulled a deck from his pocket, and watched as his father drew the jack of spades. The devil's mouth quirked upward.

Now it was Jack's turn. He took a deep breath and did what he did best and fixed the game. It took only a split second to focus his energy, his heart on the piece of paper in his hand. He turned over his card.

The king of hearts.

His father smiled. "You should never cheat the devil."

Jack knew then that he had lost. The last bit of hope inside him curled up and died. The numbness returned. "What can I say? I learned from the best."

His father shook his head. "You'd give it all up?"

Jack didn't even hesitate to reply. "I love her."

The dark eyes, so like his own, looked at him, finding him wanting. His father had always found him wanting, but now it didn't hurt so much. "Who's going to run Hell?"

"You have two more sons."

"She won't take you back. She knows who you are."

"Then make her live, just to spite me," Jack answered.

His father looked beyond him to the doorway of the D'Angelis bookstore, and then he considered his son. He gave Jack a curt nod, but it was enough. "You'd better start running," he said.

Jack turned to see Gabriella walking toward him, the fire of Hell burning in her eyes.

"Why couldn't you have found someone more"—his father's mouth turned up in distaste—"amendable?"

Jack merely laughed. A great booming sound, louder than thunder.

Gabriella came up to him and punched him in the nose. Jack clasped a hand over his face, surprised to realize his hand contained blood. He looked at his father. "Why am I bleeding?"

"You lie with the humans, you rise up with fleas."

"I'm no longer immortal?"

The devil winced. "No. I really had higher hopes for you, Jack. Take care of yourself; you're going to need all the help you can get." And with a laugh he walked away, leaving Jack with a mess of explanations and absolutely no plan at all.

"I didn't give him the book," he said, highlighting what he considered the most honorable of his actions.

"You walked out on me," she said, bouncing on her heels.

"That's why you're angry?" he said, amazed that out of all his sins, his heritage being primary, that the one that seemed to be the cause of his possibly broken nose was his leaving her.

"Damn straight," she said, and then began to walk away, her back stiff, but her hips . . . ah, her hips were singing another song. A warm breeze flew through Brooklyn. It was going to be a day people would remember for a long time.

A smile flirted with the corners of his mouth. Life was never going to be boring.

Possibly much shorter, but never boring.

KATHLEEN O'REILLY

"I love you," he said, whispering it at first. The words sounding strange on his tongue.

"I love you," he said again, louder. This time she stopped, her back still ramrod straight. The hips no longer singing.

"What about kids? If I have a baby, is his grandfather going to come someday and claim him for his own?" she said, still not facing him.

Jack looked over his shoulder, searching the horizon for any hint of his father. "No. I tainted the bloodline. He's looking for someone more . . . amendable."

One shoulder moved. And finally she turned around, crossing her arms across her chest. The distance between them was formidable, but a plan was formulating in Jack's mind. He had new goals. New aspirations.

"Are there any oddities I need to know about you? Horns? A tail? A head that spins three hundred and sixty degrees? The last thing I want is for you to embarrass me at parties."

"I'm perfectly normal."

"But what about that weather thing. The earthquakes."

Jack worked to make the earth shake, but . . . nothing. "Powerless," he said with an ordinary shrug.

She took a step forward. "Really? I'm going to miss that. Are you still rich?"

Jack laughed. "Nope. Is that a problem?"

"The money would have been nice."

"I'll get a job."

She took a step closer. "You really meant that?"

"Meant what?" he asked, but he knew.

"You really love me?"

He drew a cross over his heart. "Swear."

"Forever?" she asked.

Forever was a loaded word to Jack. He'd never really considered the prospect of anything other than eternity. Time had always been a limitless commodity. For the first time he realized how the rest of the world did it. He realized the beauty of living in the now.

"Forever," he said and gathered her into his arms.

Just as it should be.

"Any other secrets I should know?" she asked, sliding there like she belonged.

"None."

"You know, Nanna is going to have a—" But she never finished. Jack was kissing her as if tomorrow was never going to come.

The world shook just a bit, but they were too busy. Or maybe it was just the devil laughing.

NICK

Julie Kenner

Chapter One

The evening sun outside the window cast an orange glow over the inside of Nick's SoHo loft, setting the bed on fire even more than the three women already there, their bodies slick and willing atop the satin sheets. Nick stood naked at the foot of the bed, paintbrush in hand, the canvas in front of him a perfect reflection of the hedonistic revelry of the women who now cooed and called to him, urging him to abandon his work as the day abandoned its light.

Not an unpleasant proposition, all things considered, and he felt himself harden in response to the women's call. Soon he would take his pleasure. But first, he wanted to take a bit more from these women. Just a tiny morsel to flesh out their portrait, to make the work come alive.

Almost reverentially, he dipped his brush into the paint, then dabbed at the canvas, the brilliant hues of the sun's glow now shimmering on their oil-paint skin. In front of him, the women cuddled and giggled, tasting and suckling and urging him to join them. But

Nick was lost in his art, lost in the light. He'd always loved this time of day, an expression of his artist's heart, he supposed. Or, perhaps the fiery glow simply reminded him of home.

He stroked the canvas, urging his brush to make the women more than they were in life and, yes, he *almost* succeeded. The portrait would be another Nicholas Velnias masterpiece, there was no doubt about that. But still he searched for the perfect subject. A woman so beautiful that she could awe even his jaded heart.

"Nicky . . ." The woman's pouting voice came from behind him, and Nick realized that he'd lost himself to his work once again. Now only two women were in front of him on the bed. The third—Nancy? Clancy?—stood behind him, her lips grazing his ear, her breath hot on his skin. "Nicky, baby, we miss you."

And then her arms wrapped around him and her hands stroked his chest, easing down lower. Nick closed his eyes, prepared to lose himself once again to the touch of these women.

"Oh, Nick. It's so big! Girls, you have to come look!"

Nick's eyes flew open, and he couldn't help the amused quirk of his mouth. He knew with perfect clarity what she was looking at, and he felt a twinge of pride. "You're pleased?"

"Pleased? I'm . . . I'm astounded." She took her hands off his abdomen as she moved closer to the canvas, meeting her friends as they all stood in awed wonder, staring at the larger-than-life image that filled the huge canvas. "We're so big. I had no idea the picture would be so huge. And our faces . . . It's almost as if the painting is alive . . ." She reached out, almost brushed the canvas with her fingertip, but he pushed her hand away. "How did you do that?"

He laughed, then kissed her fingertips. "That's my little secret," he said. He moved around the canvas, not wanting to look at the women's images anymore. Not wanting them to ask questions. He'd thrown his entire being into painting their portrait, and the effort had exhausted him. But his devilish little secret was that he'd thrown a bit of them into the mix, too. Not so much that they'd miss it, but he'd captured a bit of their soul.

Stolen it, really.

Could he have become such a revered artist without that little trick? He didn't know, and as the women tugged him into the bed and pulled him down between the sheets with them, he told himself he didn't care. The trick served his purpose, keeping him in the spotlight. Couldn't he have whatever woman he wanted whenever he wanted? Hadn't his face graced *People* and *Time* and all those other magazines that claimed to reveal the richest, sexiest, most eligible men the world over?

He was one of those men, and he knew it. For that matter, he loved it.

He'd always craved the spotlight. In his younger days, he'd reveled in his heritage, using his familial connections to wrangle introductions to the most stellar artists of the day. He'd sat as the subject for such brilliant artists as da Vinci, Botticelli, and even Michelangelo. Today, a walk through the Louvre was like strolling through his own private portrait gallery, and a marble image of his own perfection stood in Florence under the false name of "David." In truth, Nick was glad for the fictitious name. Michelangelo had taken certain artistic liberties, and one of Nick's best assets had been decidedly reduced in his stone image.

The glory of the spotlight faded quickly for the subject, however, while the artist's name lived on. That was a lesson Nick had learned soon enough, and in more modern times he'd been drawn to the flame of fame in the guise of an artist. Once again, he was the darling of the tabloids, caught up in the glare of photographers' lights. Now, though, he was the artist and not the subject.

Now, it was *his* name that was known.

The truly remarkable thing about his newfound career was that he'd discovered a legitimate talent. Or, at least, he thought he had. So far, he'd not revealed a portrait to the public without first enhancing it with a bit of the subject's soul. "A fiery rendition that seems to crackle with life," one reviewer had said. And how very right they were . . .

Still, there were days when he wanted to ply his craft utilizing nothing more than his own skill. Perhaps one day. If he ever found a worthy subject . . .

A tug on his hand pulled him back to himself, and he smiled at the brunette, hoping he didn't appear as uninterested as he felt. The women had obviously expected the bed to be more than simply the backdrop for a portrait sitting. And why not? That was his reputation after all. The bad-boy painter, dubbed by the press as the sexiest man alive.

Far be it from him to disappoint his fans.

As the brunette tugged, he went willingly, then slid under the sheets with the women. Above him, the blonde dipped a strawberry in chocolate, then passed it to the brunette's open, moist mouth. She took it, then bent to share it with him, a sweet, chocolate kiss.

He indulged her, taking her mouth in his, succumbing to the pressure of her tongue in his mouth, slipping his finger down to caress the wet heat between her thighs. As he did, the redhead slid down under the sheet, her mouth leaving a hot trail of kisses on his stomach and lower abs, the trail becoming all the more heated the lower she moved.

The blonde pulled away, teasing him with her teeth on his lower lip. He made a rough growling noise in the back of his throat, but really, it was all for show. Already he was bored. Already his mind had wandered to the blank canvas prepped and stretched by the north window, a canvas waiting for the perfect subject, but which had yet to see a drop of paint.

"Tell me, Nicky," one of the women whispered, "do you like that?"

He muttered a convincing "yes," then let his mind turn back to the fantasy of the woman he wanted to paint. Hair so gold it seemed to reflect the light, and blue eyes so pale that they looked right at him even from the still depths of the canvas. She was out there, somewhere.

Someday he'd find her.

Someday he'd paint her.

Until then, though, he had to take his pleasure where he could, and he forced his mind back to the three women. The redhead beneath the sheet was doing some delicious things down there, and Nick had to admit he had no complaints. The brunette was trailing chocolate-covered strawberries over his chest, then licking up the confection with decidedly feline laps of her tongue. And the blonde . . . oh, yes, the blonde was right there, her body writhing against his finger that still stroked her wet clit.

With a seductive grin, she eased off of him, then bent down and took his mouth in hers, kissing him deep and hard, then pulling away, a cat-got-the-canary grin on her face. Nick could only assume *he* was the canary and that the woman believed she had him.

Little did she know.

She leaned forward again, twining herself on one side of his body just as the brunette pressed against him on the other. They both eased up his side, their tongues playing with the sensitive skin around his ear. Soon they moved on to other pastures, one woman—he had no idea which—claiming his mouth, and the other sucking on his fingertips.

He let his head fall deeper in the pillow and gave in to the pleasure of three women whose sole purpose was his ultimate satisfaction. The women themselves may not be the perfection Nick sought, but he wasn't a stupid man. And only a very stupid man would turn down three very horny, very naked women.

He focused on forgetting about his canvas and concentrating only on the pleasure of the moment, and just when he'd finally managed to clear his head of all things but the hot and willing women in bed with him, a thunderous boom shook the loft, setting the bed to shake and rattling the crystal chandelier that Nick had kept after one of his more adventurous conquests in the eighteenth century.

Beside him, the blonde and the brunette froze, looking at him with concerned eyes. Even the redhead stilled beneath the sheet, a particularly unfortunate byproduct of the noise.

Of course, while the women feared explosions, Nick was simply bored. He knew what caused the noise—his father. Lucifer. The devil himself. Announcing for anyone who cared to listen that he was about to make his presence known.

And, of course, giving his son the opportunity not to be caught with his pants down.

Nick didn't bother to get dressed. Or to get up for that matter. Modesty wasn't in his nature. And his father had certainly seen it all before.

Beside him, the women shifted nervously. But that was nothing compared to the way their eyes widened in fright as the whirlwind of fire appeared in the middle of Nick's loft, tongues of flame licking the walls and canvases as the column spun faster and faster, finally exploding in a burst of blue flame, leaving the stench of sulfur in its wake and one very irritated-looking Prince of Darkness.

"Quite the entrance, Father," Nick said, raising an eyebrow as he leaned up on one elbow. "What brings you to my neck of the woods?"

The women, he noticed, were completely frozen. His father's handiwork, no doubt. He lifted the brunette's arm, pushed her aside, and managed to sit all the way up.

"Only two in your bed," his father said, his dark eyes flashing with something that might have been amusement, but probably wasn't. "You disappoint me, son."

Nick met his father's eyes, then lifted the sheet and gazed pointedly at the woman now frozen down there. "Three, actually."

Lucifer's eyes narrowed, and his mouth quirked at the corners. Good, Nick had managed to amuse his father. Usually that role was left to his younger brother, Marcus. "Peel yourself out from under the ladies' attentions and join me. We need to talk."

Nick considered arguing, but he didn't. As a rule, he rarely argued with his father. His position in the family tree was precarious. He wasn't the oldest, so he didn't stand to inherit from their father. Nor was he the youngest, the son who could get away with anything. No, Nick was in the middle, and he had to tread more carefully.

He slipped the sheet back and climbed out of bed, pulling on a red silk robe as he did so. His father had moved to the window, and now Nick joined him.

His father stood there, gazing out at the Manhattan night. Nick looked at him with an artist's eye, once again itching to paint his father, a request that had been denied on repeated occasions. Once the most beautiful angel in all of Heaven, Lucifer's looks had only sharpened and increased in the passing millennia. Nick had inherited the dark hair and complexion, but the shimmering gray eyes came from his mother, whoever she might have been.

In stark contrast, Lucifer's eyes were dark and unreadable, the kind of eyes that could be painted a thousand times and yet never completely captured. Eyes that reflected a million stories, and very few of them with happy endings.

Today, in fact, the eyes reflected a raging storm.

"You're troubled," Nick said. "What's wrong?"

"Jack," Lucifer said, referring to Nick's eldest brother.

Nick couldn't help the little trill of pleasure, and he hoped it didn't show. "Jack? What's wrong with Jack?"

This time, when his father turned, his eyes were no longer stormy. Instead, they were flat. And somehow, that was even more disturbing. "He failed me. One simple task I handed him. One task, the reward for which would be to inherit my kingdom."

"He failed?" Nick tried to keep the glee from his voice as he felt himself get shoved one rung up the familial ladder.

"Dismally," Lucifer confirmed. He made a motion with his hand as if shooing away flies. "But that is of the past. I'm concerned only with the present and the future. *Your* future."

"Yes?" He spoke the word calmly. Inside, however, he was cheering.

"A quest, my son. One simple quest and, if you prevail, you will rule over my entire domain."

"And if I fail?"

His father stayed silent, and Nick nodded. For this, at least, no one needed to draw him a picture. Not that it mattered. *Jack* might fail, but Nick had always been more competent than his older brother. His father had just been too blinded by his firstborn's charms to see the truth.

"So what's the quest?"

"Simply a soul," Lucifer said. "Just like you dabble in every day. Only in this case, I need the entire soul." He handed Nick a flat envelope. "Her name is Delilah Burnett."

Nick slid his finger under the flap, reached in to pull out the picture, then almost dropped the entire package when he saw the photograph inside. *Her.*

He drew in a breath, managed to recover his voice, and asked, "Why her?"

"I've nothing against her, actually. It's her father. Pesky do-gooder. A reverend. Rather famous, too. He's known for his aggressive campaigns to turn lost souls away from sin." He leaned in close and put his hands on Nick's shoulders. "It's bad for business, Nicholas. And the man deserves to be punished."

"And the girl—"

"Paint her. Paint her portrait and take her soul. What could be simpler?"

Nick couldn't think of an answer, because nothing *could* be simpler. This woman's face was the one he'd been searching for his entire life. To paint her would be the culmination of his career. And to fill that image with the fullness of her complete soul . . . well, with a force like that shining out from the pigment, the painting would surely end up being the greatest masterpiece of the ages.

"You're intrigued," his father said, amusement lacing his voice.

"You knew I would be."

"Good. I expect results, Nicholas. Jack failed me. I expect more from you."

"I won't fail."

"Of course you won't," his father said. "The price would be too high." And then he was gone with a wave of his cape and a flurry of sparks, leaving Nick standing there holding Delilah's picture, with three very confused women squirming on the bed behind him. Whatever appeal they might have once held for him, now it had completely dissolved.

He grabbed his clothing and headed for the door.

"Nicky?"

"Stay until the champagne runs out, ladies," he said. "Just be sure to lock up and be careful when you leave. There're all sorts of devils prowling this part of town."

Chapter Two

The plain white envelope taunted her, peeking as it did out of the top of her tote bag, which was now nestled under the desk near her feet. Lila powered up the computer and plugged her headset into the phone, all the while telling herself that it was just another piece of mail, nothing special at all.

That, of course, was a lie. The return address—*The Tannin Agency*—made it all too clear that her entire destiny had been typed, signed, and stuffed into that slim white envelope. And she was such a spineless wimp she couldn't even gather the courage to slide her finger under the flap, open the envelope, and pull the contents out.

It had arrived in last night's mail, and she'd almost ripped it open right in front of the mailboxes. But then she'd stopped, because if it was bad news, what was she going to do then? The Tannin Agency was her last hope. Every other modeling agency in the city had already slammed the door in her face, albeit more politely than that. But to Lila, the familiar mantra of "you're a beautiful woman who's sure to find representation elsewhere" might as well be "go away, kid, you bother me." After all, the end result was surely the same.

Just get it over with. She turned and eyed it again. Still there. Still taunting. Damn.

And then, before she could talk herself out of it, she leaned over, the cord on the headset stretching tight as she snatched the envelope out of her bag. Breathing deep, as if she'd just done something quite wicked and gotten away with it, she sat up straight and held it in front of her, staring at her name—Delilah Jean Burnett—the black letters a stark contrast to the blinding white of the paper itself.

A little devil perched on her shoulder urged her to *do it, do it, do it.* She recognized the voice. It was the same little devil that had encouraged her to leave Alabama for New York to try her hand at modeling despite her father's staunch objections. A minister's daughter, he'd said, doesn't prance around half naked, wearing clothes designed to tempt and tease a man.

"It's advertising," she'd said. "And if the men can't control themselves, then that's just too bad for them." Those were the strongest words she'd ever spoken to her daddy. But he was being unreasonable. After all, it wasn't as if she was planning to model *nude.* That really would be wicked, and Lila could just picture her mother spinning in her grave, trying to shield herself from the horror of having a harlot for a daughter.

And if Lila every once in a while had secret fantasies about taking off her clothes and posing nude for the camera, well, those were just fantasies, right? It wasn't as if she'd actually *do* something that wild. And the fantasies didn't even include magazines or billboards or anything like that. God forbid she was plastered all over the planet in her altogether! Not even in her imagination would she go *that* far.

But to undress for a single photographer? Maybe even a boyfriend? She shivered slightly at the thought, the undeniable pleasure sizzling over her skin like water on a hot skillet.

Bad, Lila. You're a very naughty girl.

She lifted her chin a little, because maybe she was. And maybe that kind of thinking proved she wasn't the perfect little princess her daddy always made her out to be. New York was right for her, and she was right for it. At least so far. She may not have made her mark yet, but the Big City still hadn't eaten her alive. Not yet, anyway.

She traced her finger along the edge of the envelope, thinking about that. The Tannin Agency had been her last hope. If the letter inside said no, then maybe New York really had just smacked her behind, but good.

Quickly, before she could talk herself out of it, she edged a fingernail under the flap. *One, two, three.*

Nothing.

Okay, no problem. Just try again.

One, two, three.

But her finger wouldn't move.

Damn it all!

Frustrated, she tossed the envelope aside, glaring hard at it, and she felt unreasonably relieved when the first call of the day came in, the businesslike buzz of the phone urging her to sit up straight and keep her mind on her job, not her mail. "Kelley-Hart," she said, punching the button to answer the first call. "Public Relations and Publicity."

And so the day began. Like most Tuesdays, the morning was flooded with calls and appointments. Everyone who'd skipped Monday for a long weekend or had spent the day holed up in planning meetings was suddenly coming back to grips with reality and wearing out their index finger dialing through their Rolodex.

Between fielding calls and greeting the steady stream of clients, Lila spent a blissful morning not thinking about the damned envelope. In fact, it wasn't until Stacey, the college intern, showed up to relieve her for lunch that Lila thought another thing about it.

What she thought, in fact, was that she was a wimp. She was just about to shove the envelope back into her tote, when Stacey opened her mouth. "What's that?" she asked, grabbing for it.

Lila snatched it away, resisting the urge to smack Stacey's fingers. "Do you mind?"

"Come on!" Stacey said. "I saw the return. It's from the Tannin Agency. Are you a model? God, if you're not, you should be."

"What?" Carrie said, swishing up in a flurry of designer labels. "You're telling me you haven't seen our girl already? She's got the biggest billboard in Times Square! That's where you hang out, right?" she added, peering down her nose at Stacey as Lila tried very hard not to feel sorry for the girl. Once Carrie decided she liked you, she was as diligent a friend as a guardian angel. But until then, she could be a little scary.

Stacey frowned, genuinely befuddled, as Carrie laughed and grabbed Lila's sleeve. "Come on! Lunch!" She tapped the face of her watch. "Tick, tick."

They were out the doors and onto the elevator before Lila realized that she'd left her sack lunch in the break room refrigerator. "My lun—"

"My treat," Carrie said firmly. "And when you're a big, famous model, you can pay me back." She looked Lila up and down. "Not that you'll ever be big . . ."

Lila crossed her arms over her chest self-consciously. "I never said I wanted to be one of the Victoria's Secret girls."

Carrie patted her on the shoulder, grinning wickedly. "And you never will be."

Lila almost laughed, then remembered that her entire fate was still tucked into her tote bag. "Honestly, I'm not sure I'll ever model for anything."

The elevator doors opened and Carrie stepped out, but not before shooting Lila a withering glance. "Since when did Little Miss Sunshine turn pessimistic?"

"Since that letter ended up in my mailbox," Lila said. She paused at the newsstand near the entrance to their building. "Hold up a second."

While Carrie waited, foot tapping since the lunch hour was ticking away, Lila bought a copy of *Vogue* and a Milky Way. She gave Harlen, the kiosk's owner, a twenty, took her change, and turned back to Carrie.

"I think I may faint dead right now. Lila Burnett, eating a candy bar?"

"I can eat as many as I want since my chances of being a model are all shot to hell. But, no, it's not for me. Stacey loves them, and she always works through lunch." From what Lila could tell, "intern" was a shortened version of "indentured." As in servitude. As in Stacey worked her tail off and only had college credit to show for it.

Carrie rolled her eyes, her mouth curving into an ironic smile.

"What?" Lila asked, fumbling to shove her change back in her wallet. "Oh, wait!" She turned and headed back to the kiosk, Carrie following behind, her heels clicking a fast tempo on the polished floors.

"Lila!" Carrie called. "If we don't hurry, we won't have time to eat!"

"Just one second," Lila shouted back over her shoulder. She hurried back to Harlen, then handed him a dollar. "You miscounted the change," she said.

The elderly man's face split into a wide grin. "You're a good girl, Lila. A real good girl."

When Carrie didn't say a thing about the letter over lunch, Lila thought she was off the hook. But that illusion shattered as they stepped off the elevator and paused in front of the double glass doors that led into the Kelley-Hart reception area.

"So?" Carrie demanded, staring pointedly at Lila's tote.

Lila stopped, hugging the tote to her chest, and feeling as gangly and awkward as a startled doe. "So?" she repeated.

"Come on. Stacey I can understand, but aren't you going to clue me in?" She turned so that her back was to the door and Stacey couldn't see what they were talking about. "I'm dying to know what's in the letter."

"Me, too," Lila admitted. "But at the same time, I'm not."

Carrie lifted one brow, but otherwise didn't say a word.

"I just mean, what if it's bad?"

"It won't be bad."

"Yes, it will," Lila said. "They don't send good news in a letter."

"Well, if you already know it's bad, then what's the big deal? Open it, toss it, and be done with it. You'll find a modeling gig sooner or later. Tannin isn't your last shot until the end of time."

As to that, Lila wasn't so sure. As to opening the envelope . . .

She rocked a little on the balls of her feet. "They don't *normally* send good news in a letter. So it's probably a reject. But so long as I don't open it, I can pretend it's a request to come in for a photo test. Or maybe a tax form, so they'll have it on file when they send me on my first job."

"You're delusional," Carrie said. "I love you, but you're delusional."

"I like to think of myself as charmingly naive." She sucked in air, then nodded. "But you're right. I'm being ridiculous. I might as well get it over with." She settled herself on the small settee in the elevator lobby. And then, with Carrie sitting beside her, she reached into her tote and pulled out the envelope. She met her friend's eyes, then slid her finger under the flap. Using her thumb and forefinger like pincers, she tugged out the letter, unfolded it, and began reading.

She didn't have to read far. "We regret to inform you" followed the salutation, and Lila didn't even bother finishing the letter. Just handed it off to Carrie with an "I told you so."

Her friend took more time, her eyes moving back and forth over the page, her brow furrowing a little bit more with each line of text. "I'm sorry, Lila. But you'll find an agent eventually."

Lila lifted one shoulder in an exhausted shrug. Would she? Right at the moment, she didn't much believe that.

"And they seem to really like you," Carrie said, still playing the supportive friend. "They just don't have a use for you in their stable right now."

"Just as well," Lila said, with a faint smile. "I don't want to be a horse, anyway." What she wanted to do was yell and scream and curse. But Delilah Burnett had been raised better than that. Somehow, this was all part of God's plan. At least, that's what her daddy would say. And, honestly, maybe that was true. The dream had brought her to New York, hadn't it? Maybe that was enough?

The elevator dinged, and Lila turned toward the doors, grateful for the respite from the thoughts smashing around in her head. The doors slid open and she heard Carrie release a slow breath.

Half a second later, Lila knew why. The man stepping off the elevator looked like some sort of demigod. Beautiful in the way that angels are beautiful, but utterly masculine, too. With near-black hair, tousled in a devil-may-care manner that seemed sexy rather than sloppy. A chiseled chin, like something carved by Michelangelo. A hint of a beard, as if he shaved religiously every day, but still couldn't control the wildness within.

He wore a tailored gray suit and walked with purpose toward the Kelley-Hart entrance, never once turning back toward the girls huddled on the small settee, staring at him like paparazzi in the shadow of Brad Pitt.

He pulled open the door and stepped through, then stopped in front of Stacey's desk, probably sending the poor intern into shock.

"Wow," Carrie whispered.

"No kidding," Lila agreed.

They leaned forward, craning their necks to better see into the reception area. He was still there, his back to them. Lila could just make out a bit of Stacey's blond hair, but mostly she was blocked by the man's broad shoulders.

Or, rather, she was at first. Then Stacey tilted to the side, her head bobbing out as if playing peekaboo. Her eyes met Lila's, and a huge grin spread across her face. Lila froze, trapped and feeling ridiculous. How pathetic was that? Caught staring at the cute guy?

And then, to make it worse, Stacey started making come-here gestures with her hand. Lila looked left and right, wondering if she could escape. "What is she doing?" she whispered to Carrie.

"I don't know, but if she keeps it up, I'm telling Mr. Hart he has to submit an F for her internship program."

Stacey obviously had no clue about her pending academic demise, because now she said something to the man, at the same time pointing directly at Lila.

The man turned, nodded a thank-you at Stacey, then looked at Lila and smiled. Lila almost melted on the spot from the heat of that smile. And when he pushed through the door—walking toward her without ever taking his eyes off her—well, Lila was certain she'd somehow morphed into the most exotic and vulnerable woman in the world.

"Delilah Burnett?"

"I, yes, I mean, yes. That's me."

His smile broadened. "I know, actually. I recognize you."

"You recognize me?" She squinted at him. "Have we met?"

Beside her, Carrie cocked a finger toward the office. "I'll just be heading on in. Don't mind me."

Neither Lila nor the man did, though somewhere in the back of her mind Lila was aware that she'd been left alone with this man. This perfect, awesome man.

"We haven't met," he said. "But I've been hoping we would."

He held out his hand then, and she took it, her whole body tingling merely from the gentle way his thumb grazed the side of her hand. Lord help her, the man was walking sin. And what the devil did he want with her?

"Wait," she said, cocking her head. There was something familiar about him. Like something she'd seen in a dream. Or, more probably, in the *Post*. "Aren't you—"

"I'm Nicholas Velnias," he said. "And it's a pleasure to finally meet the woman I'm determined to paint."

Chapter Three

"*You* want to paint me?" The words squeaked out, and Lila cleared her throat, her face flaming. She felt awkward and stupid, but how else would someone feel in the presence of Nicholas Velnias? *The* Nicholas Velnias.

"Yes." His smile was soft, indulgent, and she relaxed, but only a little.

"Oh." She pondered the answer. Straight, simple, to the point. "Why?"

"Because you're beautiful." His brow lifted very so slightly as he spoke, and his mouth curved into a hint of a smile. A small dimple flashed in his cheek, disappearing so quickly that Lila had to wonder if she'd imagined it.

"I . . . but . . . oh . . ." She cleared her throat. "I mean, thanks."

"You're welcome," he said, with undisguised amusement. He pointed toward the elevator. "Can we go somewhere and talk?"

"Um." She glanced through the glass doors of Kelley-Hart, where Stacey was making whooping motions with her arm and mouthing, "You go, girl." Lila looked away, mortified. "I really need to get back to work. They're pretty strict about my hours."

"I see." A hint of disappointment flashed in his eyes. "After work, then? There's a bar on the corner. Finnegan's. Meet me there?"

She wanted to. The thought of being painted by someone as famous as Nicholas Velnias made her all giddy inside—as did the thought of having a drink with him. But today simply wasn't possible. "I've got plans," she said.

"Break them."

She straightened, a bit taken aback. And, at the same time, not surprised at all by his suggestion. "I'm not sure I should do that." She *could*, of course. She volunteered at the literacy center twice a week, and she wasn't technically scheduled to go in until Wednesday. But she'd bought some books from a library sale over the weekend and she'd made plans to drop them off.

"We can meet another day, of course," he said. "But I'm anxious to start now. I want to paint you, Delilah. And I promise, I'll be persistent. Meet me tonight, and you'll be rid of me that much sooner." He spread his hands, his smile so self-deprecating that she had to laugh.

"It's not that I want to be rid of you—"

"Good."

"It's just . . ." She shrugged. Not entirely sure what it was. But something about this felt weird. And she couldn't quite bring herself to agree. "I'm really not sure I should—"

"Delilah," he said, taking her hand. "Please."

"How do you even know about me?"

"Does it really matter? I'm offering you exactly what you want. To be a model. And I assure you I have the means to ensure that this job is only the first of many."

"But how—"

He pressed a finger to her lips, sending warm honey flowing through her to pool right between her thighs. It was everything she could do not to moan.

"Just nod. Don't say a word. Just nod, and let me know that you'll meet me."

Mute, she nodded.

He smiled, then stepped away, breaking the contact. "Six o'clock," he said, as the elevator doors slid open.

She frowned, unable to remember him hitting the call button. He stepped on and as she watched, the doors closed, blocking him from view. She lifted her fingers to her lips, pressing there as he had done and wondering if a kiss could ever feel as magical as the touch of his fingers.

"Another one for you?"

Nick looked up, startled, into the bartender's droopy face. He lifted his glass, saw the tiny splash of scotch and the remnant of an ice cube, then downed them both in one gulp. He held out the glass for the bartender, who efficiently replaced it with a fresh drink.

"Waiting for someone?"

"Mmm."

"Been waiting a while," the bartender said, glancing up at the clock, which clicked firmly onto six-fifteen even as they watched. "Maybe she's not coming."

Nick flashed the man a sharp look, saw him cower back, then heard him start mumbling apologies.

"Not that I meant any offense," he said, grabbing a nearby rag and wiping down the bar.

"None taken," Nick said, though his tone surely suggested otherwise. The man was a jackass, an annoyance, yes, but hardly worth trifling with. And although he *could* shift the man's appearance so that he more closely resembled his true nature, giving the man a donkey tail would sap Nick's strength. And for centuries, he'd reserved his power exclusively for his paintings. Why tamper with success now? Especially for something as trivial as teaching a fool to mind his own business?

Still, the fool had a point. The girl *was* late. Could she be standing him up?

The idea was almost incomprehensible. His heritage didn't make him immune to disappointment, of course, but throughout all of his eight hundred years, never once had disappointment originated with a woman. Women, he'd learned long ago, tended to behave exactly the way he wanted them to. On his canvas and in his bed.

Of course, he had to admit that in the past, *he'd* always selected the women. Carefully choosing females who would satisfy him both artistically and physically.

This time, his father had selected the woman. And despite the fact that she was too shy, too quiet, too altogether *innocent*, Nick found himself becoming more and more irritated by her lateness.

He told himself that his irritation stemmed not from the girl herself, but from the purpose she would serve. The hint of fascination he'd felt during their encounter by the elevator meant nothing. The only—*only*—interest he had in the girl stemmed from what she could bring him. The satisfaction of painting the perfect portrait. And the even greater satisfaction of proving his worth to his father. Not to mention lording his victory over Jack and Marcus once he took his father's place on the throne of Hell.

He allowed himself a small smile as he took another sip of scotch. Almost casually, he glanced again toward the clock. Six-twenty-five.

Damn.

He slammed the tumbler down, the drink sloshing out and pooling on the polished oak. He started to stand and then, suddenly, there she was. Standing in the open doorway, the early-evening light casting her in silhouette and giving her an ethereal, almost angelic glow. She turned her head, searching, and when her eyes found him, she smiled. Not just in recognition, but with hope.

His gut twisted unpleasantly, but he forced the sensation aside. He wasn't doing wrong by this woman. Just the opposite. The file his father had given him revealed the secrets of her heart; he knew she longed to be immortalized. He could give that to her. Hell, he wanted to give it to her.

So what if the price was high? Thousands upon thousands before her had paid with their soul for significantly less than to be painted and revered as a masterpiece for millennia to come. And what did he care of the girl's fate, anyway?

Nick watched as Delilah crossed the room toward him, so

trusting and eager. He stifled a smile. The girl wanted what he could give. There was no way Nick could fail at this task. No way at all.

But if that were true, then why did he feel so damn vulnerable?

Lila gave Nick a little wave, then hitched her purse strap more securely over her shoulder before navigating through the darkened bar toward him. She almost hadn't come. The whole thing seemed too, well, bizarre. Her so desperately wanting to be a model, and him showing up and offering her that very thing on a platter. Lila had never thought of herself as a stupid girl, and she didn't intend to start behaving like one. She had questions for Mr. Velnias. And if she didn't like the answers, she was out of there, job or no job.

"You have the look of a determined woman," he said as she approached.

She felt her cheeks warm, and she nodded. "Well, yes, actually, I am."

"Determined to talk yourself out of this, I think."

"No, no," she said quickly, now afraid she'd managed to offend him. She took the stool next to him at the bar, her purse clutched in her lap.

"Glad to hear it. Since you're here, you must have cancelled your plans. I wouldn't want to end up disappointed."

"I didn't cancel," she said. "I just postponed."

The corner of his mouth twitched with amusement. "So why *are* you here, Delilah?"

Her name on his lips seemed coated with honey, and she shivered as the soft, sweet sound settled over her. She studied her hands, not quite able to meet his eyes. "I guess I just want more information."

"That's easy enough." He paused, and she looked up to find him smiling at her, his gaze hot against her skin. "And if you want a drink, I can arrange that as well. A martini?"

She shook her head. "Hard liquor wipes me out. Just a glass of Chardonnay, please."

While he ordered, she rested her chin on her fist and regarded him. She'd walked through the door determined to take control. And with no effort at all, he'd wrested all control away from her. And the worst of it was, she didn't really mind at all.

"Your determination has changed to befuddlement," he said, his voice laced with amusement.

"I'm sorry." She pulled her hands back down in her lap, once again awkward.

"Don't be sorry. Just tell me what's on your mind."

She licked her lips. "Maybe I'm just not quite able to believe my good fortune. I mean, this is the kind of thing a girl like me daydreams about. You know, rejected by all the modeling agencies, then in walks the handsome stranger to—" She stopped midsentence, mortified. "I can't believe I said that."

"What? That I'm handsome?" The dimples made a quick appearance again. "I promise you're not the first woman who's told me that."

"That, I believe. But, no. I meant the rejection part. Not exactly doing a good job of selling myself, am I?"

He took her hand, his firm and slightly calloused. This was a man who worked with his hands, wielding a brush, stretching canvas. How sweet would the rough pad of his thumb feel stroking her lips? Her nipple? Her . . . *there*?

Alarmed, she jerked her hand free, her whole body burning from a mixture of desire and embarrassment.

"Something wrong?" he said, and though his tone was innocent, his expression suggested that he knew exactly what she'd been thinking. And that he very much liked her thoughts.

She closed her eyes and counted to five. "I'm fine, thanks." Another deep breath. "I just meant that I shouldn't have told you I was a reject."

"And I just meant," he said, brushing his thumb down her arm, "that I don't give a damn what anyone else thinks. You're perfect, Delilah. You're perfect for me."

Lila sighed, then took a sip of her wine. The truth was, she did feel perfect. She didn't know what it was about Nicholas Velnias, but he made her feel both special and daring. It was a heady combination, and she tried not to lose herself in it. "But how did you find me?"

"You know who I am, right?"

"Of course," she said, sitting up straighter. "You're . . . well, you're Nicholas Velnias. You're huge. You're amazing. You're—"

"Getting a swelled head," he said with a smile, and right then she liked him even more.

"But it's true."

"Maybe," he said. "All I meant was that I'm in a position to have access to the headshots that modeling agencies receive. I saw yours and, well, here we are."

"Here we are," she agreed. Wherever that might be.

"But now I need to know what your intentions are." He picked up her hand before she could respond, then pressed it against his chest. "Are you going to lead me on? Tease me? Play hard to get? Or are you going to be mine?"

"Yours," she repeated, looking at their intertwined fingers. "That sounds intense."

"And it will be," he said, disentangling their hands and leaning back in his seat. "I expect full access to a model. I don't pretend to keep banking hours, and I don't intend to make the muse wait simply because my model is across town or at work or going shopping with friends. You'll move into my guest quarters. And you'll keep my schedule."

She shook her head, startled as much by his words as by his sudden shift to a businesslike tone. "That's not possible. I mean, Mr. Velnias, my job—"

"Can be performed by a nineteen-year-old college student. You'll quit, and I will more than compensate you for your time." He named off a figure that not only had her gasping, but was also almost double her annual salary at Kelley-Hart. "And call me Nick."

"But . . . but . . . you can't really mean you'll pay me that much! How long will the job take? I can't just up and move in with you for a year!"

He chuckled. "Am I really that unappealing?"

"Oh, no! Not at all. I just meant that—"

"I'm teasing you," he said, brushing his fingertip over her lips and sending sparks shooting through her body. "I don't expect I'll need you in the studio more than a week or so. Once I've captured your essence on the canvas, I don't need you in the room while I work. You can move out then. If you want to."

"Oh." She didn't know what else to say.

"The compensation is fair," he continued. "And if the work is licensed for any sort of advertising purpose, then you'll receive a royalty on top of it."

He looked at her, his gaze so hard and penetrating that it

seemed as if he was looking at her soul. "I want this, Delilah. I want you. Tell me that you agree. Tell me that I can paint you. That I can capture your soul on canvas for all the world to see. Don't deny yourself this opportunity. Say yes, Delilah. Say yes, and all your dreams will come true."

Chapter Four

Nick kept his eyes on her face as he waited for her response. It would be yes, of course. No woman had denied him. Still, though, his body tensed with anticipation, and when her sweet lips parted, he leaned closer to hear her response.

Her first words were a whisper, and so startling that he was certain that even with the exceptional hearing that heredity had provided him, he must have misheard. "What?" he asked. "I couldn't quite—"

"Will you sketch me?" She spoke almost too loud this time, her chin lifting as she voiced the query. It was exactly what he'd thought she'd said, and it was no less bewildering so many decibels louder.

"First, yes. A few rough sketches to test poses, compositions. But that will take only a little time, and soon your image will come alive in oil on canvas."

She shook her head. "No, you misunderstand." She took a sip of her wine, then lifted her eyes to meet his. Her cheeks were bright red, but from the wine or from embarrassment, he didn't know. "Will you sketch me *now*?"

"Here? Right now?" He looked around the bar, with its polished oak and equally polished people. Nothing in the room seemed real, and certainly nothing in here was worthy of his brush. Nothing, that is, except her.

"Yes."

"Why?"

The question seemed simple enough, but she took her time answering. "I want to know how it feels. If it's worth it."

"If what's worth it?"

"Chasing dreams, I guess. Especially when this isn't about ambition."

He found himself leaning closer, looking at her with interest. He told himself there was no danger in that; the better he knew her, after all, the easier it was to grab hold of her soul. But while he wouldn't quite let himself admit it, the truth was far more complicated. And, in a way, far more treacherous. He wanted to know what made this woman tick. Not so that he could fulfill his father's wishes, but simply because, for the first time in his life, he wanted to know more about a woman than how she'd look in the early-morning light.

"Isn't everything about ambition?" he asked. His ambition was twofold. Become an even greater artist. And prove his worth to his father.

"Maybe," she said, her eyes lighting with her smile. "But if that's the case, then it's a question of choice. Am I choosing to pursue the right ambition? Because, honestly, I'd almost talked my-self out of it."

"Out of modeling?" He couldn't help the shock that crept into his voice. "And deprive the world of your beauty?"

"You're sweet," she said. "But I didn't come her because I wanted to give the world a present," she said. "I was a little more selfish than that."

"Really?" Without thinking, he took her hand, tracing his fin-ger up and down between hers. He saw her breath hitch, realized the effect he was having on her, and smiled. He didn't, however, stop. He knew his effect on women. He also knew how to put it to good use. "I know all about selfish tendencies," he said. "Right now, for example, I want to touch you. And I intend to pursue that goal most selfishly until you tell me not to."

Another shaky breath, and then she said, "I'm not saying anything."

"Good." Her hand was warm in his, almost burning. "Now it's your turn," he said. "I told you how I am selfish. Tell me now about you. How did you end up in New York?"

"I guess you could say I escaped to here."

"A common tale," he said.

"Blond girl comes to the city to be a model," she said with a wry gin. "I never said my story was original. But it is mine."

"So you left home to find fame and fortune?"

Her brow creased. "I don't have anything against either, but I really came because I couldn't stand the thought of living my life without options in Alabama. I wanted more than working in the office at my daddy's church, answering phones, and calling people to make good on their pledges. And even if I could convince

Daddy I didn't want to do that, well what then? Work at the Piggly Wiggly? My grades weren't good enough for a scholarship, and Daddy said he wouldn't pay for anything but the county junior college."

"Sounds like a bastard," he said, and felt a secret pleasure at that. At least the man his father wanted to punish deserved it.

"He loves me. He just has a different view of the world, you know? Thinks working in the church and getting married and having babies is all a girl should want. But I wanted more." She drew in a deep breath. "So I decided to be the stereotypical small-town girl and rebel against my daddy."

"You came here."

"Sure did. I banked on the one thing I knew I had. The one thing that might be worth something."

"Your looks."

"Everyone had always told me I was pretty. And I've always secretly agreed with them." Her cheeks flushed.

"They—and you—were right. You definitely have the looks." He was equally impressed by her decision to rebel against her father. For that matter, maybe he was even a little jealous of the decision. That, however, wasn't something he intended to think about.

She shrugged. "My daddy would say pride's the biggest sin of all, and I guess he'd be right, since New York pretty much turned its back on me."

"It won't anymore," he said. "Not if I paint you." He took her hand. "And you are beautiful. It's not pride, Delilah. It's honesty and self-awareness."

"Maybe. But it doesn't matter anyway, you know? Because my

looks are what got me here. And now that I'm here, I'm staying. I may not be a model, but I'm going to stay. I can study and take night classes and maybe even get into NYU." Her chin lifted, just a little. "I can do it, you know."

"I believe you." He did, too. "And you could do it a lot faster with a model's salary." He took her hand. "I sense a 'but,' though."

"You're either perceptive or I'm transparent. But, yeah. There's a 'but.' Because even if I go to school and become a teacher or an accountant or something, I'm still going to crave this, you know? Because I really did want it. And for more than a way to escape, and for more than just a little rebellion against my dad."

"You wanted your fifteen minutes."

"No, it's not the fame. It's really not. It's the experience. The whole shebang. Something I can pull out and look at and think, yes. Once upon a time Delilah did something a little crazy. And she had a great time doing it."

She tugged her hand away from his, and the heat from her touch dissipated, leaving him cold and hollow.

"That sounds really silly, doesn't it?"

"Not at all," Nick said. He understood the need to fulfill a wild urge. To go a little crazy and let passion rule over intellect. "Was that what you had planned tonight? To go a little crazy?"

"Hardly." She grinned, clearly amused by the thought. "Maybe that's my problem. Even when I want to go wild, I don't quite know how."

Nick shook his head, not understanding.

"I volunteer at an arts center," she said. "They have painting, writing, pottery, all sorts of classes. But they also teach basic literacy. I volunteer to work with the students a couple of times a week. I'd planned on dropping off some books at the center tonight, but then you came along . . ." She trailed off with a shrug.

"So you did choose a little wildness tonight," he said. "You chose me."

Her eyes widened, and she nodded, just a little. "Yeah. I guess I did."

"But I still don't understand the sketch," he said. "Why do you want me to sketch you? And why now?"

"This may sound silly, but I'd pretty much convinced myself today that I'd lost the chance, you know? To have that experience of being a model. I figured I gave it my best shot, but got nowhere. So maybe it was time to face facts. Start applying for schools. Quit thinking about modeling. And figure that trying to be a model was experience enough."

"But you don't believe that."

She shook her head. "No, I don't. So I thought that if you sketched me, I'd know. And if the feeling is anything like what I've imagined, then I'll keep at it. At least for a little longer."

He watched her, for the first time wondering if he *could* take her soul. The women he'd painted before had been beautiful but careless with their soul, with their essence. Women who would willingly trade their bodies to get what they wanted. Women, in other words, who would have given him exactly what he'd taken merely for the promise of a brief moment of fame.

The stealing of a soul was a complex process, and he'd never much analyzed it; he simply *did*. But the one thing he knew was that it always started with the loosening of inhibitions. And with those previous women, that step had essentially already been accomplished. It had been nothing to steal a hint of their soul and, he knew, the women had hardly missed it at all.

With Delilah, though, the task would not be so easy. Certainly he wouldn't even bother trying with a mere table sketch. But perhaps the sketch would be useful if it would serve to entice her.

And entice her he needed to do. Whereas his previous models' ambition stemmed from vanity, Delilah's stemmed from a sense of self. Internal rather than external. A trickier proposition, to be sure. And for the first time, he doubted his ability to satisfy his father's quest.

No. He could do this. He *had* to do this. The woman might be more of a challenge, but certainly the task was not impossible. All that was needed was more finesse. More creativity. And a little bit of time.

Certainly, it would be necessary to get close to the woman. Close enough to earn her trust. Close enough to unravel some restraints. And, more important, close enough to steal.

Lila fidgeted on her stool, unnerved by how much she'd revealed to this man. He probably thought she was an idiot, the way she'd blathered on and on. There was something about him, though. Something that drew her in and, apparently, affected her as potently as a few strong drinks.

Lord knew, he loosened her tongue. Not to mention that his mere proximity left her feeling warm and decadent. Itchy, even, but in a wholly sensual way. Like she might die if he didn't scratch the itch . . . and she might melt if he did.

"So will you?" she asked, shaking off the languor in her bones. "Will you sketch me now?"

He leaned back, his silver-gray eyes examining her with an almost feral intensity as he looked her up, then down. She tried to sit still, but couldn't quite manage. The heat of his gaze was so intense it might have been a caress, and her nipples peaked under his scrutiny, raising hard nubs under the soft Lycra of her top. Instinctively, she started to cross her arms over her chest, but fought the urge, keeping them at her sides, and feeling more exposed—and more turned on—than she ever had in her life.

His inspection finished, he met her eyes, the corner of his mouth curving up into a silent smile. He turned away, saying nothing, then took a quick, silent sip of his scotch. He reached for two cocktail napkins, pulled them close, then patted his mouth with one.

Honestly, she wanted to scream. "Well?" she demanded, forcing her voice to remain calm and steady.

"Of course I'll sketch you," he said. He met her eyes, and a muscle twitched in his jaw. "In fact, at the moment I can think of only one thing I'd like to do more."

"Oh." She knew she shouldn't ask, but she couldn't help herself. "What's that?"

One beat, then another. Her heart pounded in her chest, the rhythm so intense she was certain everyone in the bar could hear it.

And then, just when she was certain he wasn't going to answer, he traced the curve of her cheekbone with his thumb, then leaned close. She closed her eyes as his lips brushed her hair, and his voice was a whisper against her ear, sending shivers trilling down her spine. "The only thing I want more than to sketch you," he murmured, "is to paint you."

Lila exhaled, her eyes still closed, her body burning from the remnants of his breath caressing her skin. That hadn't been the response she'd expected. But somehow his words were all the more erotic, holding a promise of things more decadent and revealing than mere sex.

. "Shall I?" he asked.

And then, opening her eyes to look at him, she nodded.

He grinned and reached into the inside pocket of his jacket to produce a stick of charcoal.

She lifted an eyebrow and he shrugged. "Accountants carry calculators," he said. "It's not that surprising."

"Do you have a pad in there, too?"

He drew the napkin closer. "No need. Now sit quietly," he directed. "And watch me."

He cupped her face, tilting her head just slightly, then urged her hand up until she found herself resting her chin on her fist, watching him from this posed position. And watching the image of herself come to life on the tiny cocktail napkin.

He started with a sweep of the charcoal. One line that seemed to have no connection to her at all. No connection, that is, except for the smoldering way that he looked at her. A smoky gaze that seemed reflected in the smudged charcoal image emerging on the paper.

The curve of her jaw. Then the line of her neck. A flick of his wrist and the tendrils of her hair seemed to materialize from so many lines on the paper. And then, most miraculously of all, he caught the expression in her eyes. And, seeing that, she knew that he could never doubt that she'd agree to be painted. Because her expression was rapturous. And she knew the truth of what he'd sketched. Because with every piercing look—with every sure stroke of the charcoal—Lila had realized that she couldn't walk away without letting him paint her. His scrutiny made her feel both alive and unique. And even if she never did another bit of modeling, the portrait he'd create would fulfill her fantasies. More, Nicholas Velnias would be giving her the chance at immortality. And, really, what girl could say no to that?

Chapter Five

Nick leaned against the door frame and peered into the only fully enclosed room in his entire loft. In front of him, Delilah frowned at her duffel bag, then withdrew a crumpled dress and tried to shake out a few wrinkles. As far as he could tell, she didn't realize he was there, and for a few moments longer, he wanted to simply watch her.

They'd left the bar for her apartment, where they'd gathered a few of her things before coming back to his place. He'd led her through the loft, trying to see it with her eyes. The wide-open space, filled with the scent of turpentine and oils, of fresh canvas and sawdust. Canvases and bits of wood for frames leaned haphazardly against the walls. Tubes of paint, mason jars with soaking paint brushes, and dozens of pages ripped from magazines littered the floor and covered the five utilitarian worktables that ringed the room and constituted the only furniture in the loft other than a luxurious bed, a small dining table, two spindly chairs, and an armoire for Nick's clothes. Nick had never before focused on the spartan quarters, but now he had to wonder what she must think of him. Devoted to his art, he presumed, and that was the truth. Once he'd found the loft—once he'd installed rows of windows to let in the light—all he'd cared about was painting. Food and sleep were afterthoughts. Even sex, though the rush that came from watching an image come forth on a canvas was often more than enough to make him hard. Fortunately, his previous models had always been understanding and flattered, if not downright demanding.

He'd built the guest room about a year ago after he'd been frustrated one too many times by the inability to get in touch with his current model when he woke up at 3 a.m. with the urge to paint.

Now he watched Delilah, and while his fingers itched to paint her in the moonlight, he also wanted simply to touch her. The urge was, in fact, so overpowering that he almost took a step forward. He reined in the urge. Time enough for that after he'd begun the task of capturing her image on the canvas.

She looked up at him, a question in her eyes. "You're staring."

"Yes. I am," he said. "Studying the way you move, the flow of your body. The way your clothing hugs your curves as you go back and forth from the bed to the closet."

"Oh." She pulled a T-shirt out, scowled at the wrinkles, but didn't bother shaking it. She put it in a bureau drawer, then started to fold up the now-empty duffel. She stayed focused on the job, her face turned away from him. Even so, he could see the way her lips curved in pleasure, as if the thought of him watching her gave her a secret little trill of delight.

Interesting.

"But you're not going to be painting me moving," she said.

"You caught me," he said. "The truth is I just like watching you."

"Yeah?" Another shy look. "I guess that's a good thing since you'll be looking at me for a while."

"A very good thing," he said.

"So, um, am I kicking you out of your bedroom? Because I can just sleep on a couch or something." A little crease formed over her nose. "Not that I saw a couch . . ."

"Decorating hasn't been a huge priority."

"Men," she said, grinning.

"I stand accused. And no, you're not kicking me out of my bedroom. I sleep out there." As he spoke, she'd come toward him, and now he led her into the room even as he pointed toward the massive bed, complete with black silk sheets and a blood-red comforter.

"Right," she said, then let out a nervous cough as she stared at the bed. "So, um, where do you want me?"

A loaded question. "Where would you be most comfortable?" he asked. He was playing a game, pretending to be the polite, considerate host, when in reality he wanted nothing more than to pull her to him, ply her body with his hands and mouth, and then leave her sated in the bed, her soft, glowing body ready to be immortalized in pigment and oil.

"Oh. I . . . I don't know. I mean, I—"

He held up a hand, amused by her befuddled expression. "Honestly, it's not a fair question. The truth is that I could paint you anywhere and create a work of stunning beauty. The real question is what composition is worthy of the creation of a masterpiece."

Her eyes flashed with gratitude, and he found himself charmed by her innocence. How quaint. And how interesting.

"I guess that's your department," she said. "I'll just do what you say."

He fought to keep his expression bland, afraid that if he commented on the more lascivious possibilities that her words suggested she'd blush so brightly she'd ignite the turpentine. Those lascivious possibilities, however, intrigued him more than he'd anticipated.

She'd had that effect on him. He supposed he'd always known that she would. Should he ever find the woman he'd for so long imagined capturing on the canvas, how could he not want to possess her fully, both body and soul? How could he not be drawn to her? Want to consume her? Want to lose himself in her?

And yet, despite everything he'd known before he'd met her, Delilah Burnett was still a surprise. He'd expected the physical craving. What he hadn't anticipated was the . . . what? Curiosity, perhaps. Or anticipation. Maybe even joy. An unfamiliar and not entirely unwelcome emotion that coursed through him.

He hadn't truly required her to move into the loft. There was a convenience to having his models near, of course. But he could have made do. Still, having her nearby made practical sense. After all, he had his father's work to do, and the sooner he satisfied that, the sooner he'd obtain his prize.

Nick didn't fear much in this world. But the course of desire that heated his veins when he looked at her had him trembling.

"Nick?"

"Follow me," he said, his voice gruffer than he would have liked. He took her to the bed, waited while she crawled on. Then he stepped back until he was right beside that one canvas he'd had for so long. The canvas that had been waiting for her.

Nick

As he sketched a few preliminary lines with a pencil, she knelt on the bed, her hands awkwardly placed on her knees. "Should I just sit here?"

He shook his head, his mind now only on the canvas and the image of the woman he was trying to coax from the lead. "Something different. Lay down," he said. "On your side, and look at me. Good. Good."

He stroked the canvas again, the faint gray line hinting at the outline of the portrait to come. Just a single gray line marring the clean, crisp canvas. But that was enough. It wasn't right. In his mind, Nick could see how every stroke would fill the canvas, like a chess player planning the game through to the end. And at the end of his game, there was no masterpiece. Not yet, anyway.

"No," he said, stalking away from the canvas. He tossed more pillows onto the bed, then took her by the elbow, tugging her back gently among them. She wore a white button-down shirt, a single button at the collar unfastened. His fingers moved to the next button, this one modestly tight. As he started to undo the button, she slapped him away, her fingers closing over her chest.

"If you'd like a wardrobe alteration, just tell me."

"Sorry," he said, coming back to himself. "I get caught up."

"But you aren't happy with it," she said. "Not yet."

"No," he agreed. "Not yet."

"Is it me?"

Such an innocence filled her voice that he was compelled to kneel on the bed beside her. He stroked her face, wishing he could somehow make her understand the perfection that he saw in her. But there really weren't words. The best he could do was render her beauty on canvas and hope that the portrait proved her worth.

"It's not you," he said simply.

She smiled, then leaned forward and kissed his cheek. "Thank you."

"For what?"

"For everything. For giving me this opportunity. And, I guess, for wanting me here. For wanting to paint me."

Nick nodded, but found himself not quite able to meet her eyes. Foolish emotion. He *did* want to paint her. And she wanted what he could give her. True, she probably didn't want to lose what he intended to take, but this wasn't about what the girl wanted. It was about proving himself to his father. And to do that, Nick had to see this through. Best to forget about the larger issue and simply focus on creating his masterpiece.

"Like this," he said, his fingers moving down to cup the still-fastened button. "The purity of a plain white shirt coupled with the invitation of several open buttons."

He started to work the buttons free, but her hands closed over his. He held his breath, hoping she wouldn't fight him on this. He needed her open and vulnerable. He needed inside this woman because he couldn't take what he couldn't see.

His fears, though, were unfounded. She closed her fingers over his, and the heat of her touch shot through him with a feeling of coming home. Her lips parted, and he had to force himself to wait for her words when all he wanted to do was lean in and capture her in a kiss. "I'll do it," she said, then undid the next two buttons.

The crisp white cotton parted, revealing the swell of her breasts, trapped in a pale pink bra that fastened with a simple clasp in front.

Nick couldn't help himself. He reached out and traced his finger down between her breasts, noting with interest the way her nipples hardened against the lace. He stroked his thumb over her nipple, his breath catching in his throat, mesmerized by the way she closed her eyes and tilted her head back.

Her movements were slow and subtle, but she tilted her breasts up in a silent invitation. Greedily, he cupped her breasts, feeling them swell against the inside of his hands. Glorious Hades! How he wanted this woman. A woman like none he'd ever had before, with a purity that seemed to reach out, begging for him to take and make his own.

"Delilah," he whispered.

That, though, was a mistake. Her eyes flicked open, and she reached for the lapels of her shirt, tugging it modestly closed even as she slid to the far side of the bed. "Sorry," she whispered. "I'm sorry."

"I'm not," he said, hoping for a smile but receiving nothing in return.

She stopped by the window, then reached her hand up to stroke her fingers along the glass. Outside, the setting sun burned orange in the sky, painting her body with an ethereal glow and setting her hair on fire.

Her shirt, though more modest now, was still unbuttoned, revealing only a hint of her bra.

Magic seemed to wash over her, as if the firmaments had both consumed and released her, leaving her trapped between Heaven and Hell, earth and the sky.

This, Nick realized, was the image he'd been waiting for.

She started to turn toward him, but he held out a hand and cried, "No! Don't move."

She froze, one eyebrow lifting. "Nick?"

"Say nothing," he said. "Just stay stay there. Stay, and let me capture this moment."

Lila stood completely still, her palm pressed against the window, the cool of the glass a counterpoint to the heat that filled her body. So intense, actually, that it was a wonder steam didn't rise from beneath her fingers.

She smiled at the thought, pleased to have something silly enter her head after all the decadent images that had filled and distracted her.

He'd touched her!

Even now, it was all she could do not to trace her fingers down her throat and cup her own breasts, remembering the feel of his hands against her. So heady, so wonderful, so very erotic.

And so very terrifying.

She'd felt the quickening in her thighs, the liquid heat in her panties, and she'd bolted, startling him and embarrassing her. But what choice did she have? She'd come here to be a model, not to fall victim to Nicholas Velnias's famous charm. No matter how real that charm might be.

The man had a reputation, after all. And she didn't want to be one of his many publicized conquests. Didn't want to be one of a line of women. More, she didn't want to turn into the very woman her father had predicted she'd become if she moved from home to the decadent hell of New York City. A wild woman, unconcerned about whose bed she ended up in, more interested in pleasure than love or morality or simple kindness.

No, Lila didn't want to be that woman.

But she did want to sleep with him. Like it or not—foolish or not—the desire coursed through her, filling her. And, ultimately, driving her.

Her eyes welled, and she fought back tears as she thought of her father's harsh words when she'd told him that she was doing it—that she was going to New York. He'd been cruel, accusatory.

But he'd also been wrong. Because she *wasn't* that woman. She had her head on straight and she wasn't going to sleep around.

But did that mean she couldn't be just a little wicked with a man she was desperately attracted to? Because right now, she wanted to be. Oh, how she wanted to be.

Nick was fully focused on her, and the sensation of being at the very center of his attention turned her on, filling her body with heat. Something about him—about this place—seemed to open her senses. The pungent scent of oil and turpentine. The larger-than-life women who watched her from canvases propped this way and that, seeming to urge her on to . . . what?

She wasn't sure. She wanted something, but she didn't know what. She felt itchy, as if she wasn't quite herself, but at the same time was more herself than she'd ever been before.

The gentle scratch of Nick's charcoal against the canvas seemed to be an incantation, something pulling her toward him. Something beckoning. Something seeking a promise from her.

She wanted to turn from the window and promise him anything he asked, just so long as he'd let her keep that feeling.

She stayed there, watching his reflection in the window as he sketched, occasionally trading the pencil for a brush with just a dab or two of color on it. His face was intense, his jaw firm. And as he stroked the canvas, she could almost imagine he was stroking her.

Her skin felt on fire, and if he did touch her right then, she had a feeling she would come so hard her body would melt right into the floor.

So help her, she *did* want him. And by the time he put the brush down and walked to her side, it was all she could do not to rip open her shirt and thrust her body against his.

"That's all for now," he said, his hand pressing lightly against her back. "We're losing the light. More tomorrow."

"So we're only going to do this when the sun's going down?"

His rich laughter caressed her. "No. You can pose here in the evenings. The rest of the time I'll work on feature studies. And, who knows, I may do a few smaller canvases as well. But that," he said, turning toward the large canvas by which he'd been standing, "that is the portrait that will change both of our lives."

She couldn't help but grin. "Confident, aren't you?"

"Very." He traced his fingertip on the back of her neck, pushing her hair aside as he did so. "You were wonderful, by the way. I know it must be boring to stand there with nothing to do but look out the window."

"I had a lot to think about," she said. She turned, letting his finger trace her shoulder as she did. Then she took a deep breath for courage and met his eyes, gratified to see the silver-gray storm brewing there. A storm that seemed to rival the tempest now spinning through her body.

"Secret thoughts?" he asked. "Or will you tell me?"

"I might tell," she said, teasing. "If you'll show me." She cast a quick glance toward the canvas.

"Show you mine, you'll show me yours?" he retorted with a grin.

"Something like that."

"Then by all means." He took her hand, leading her across the studio to the canvas. "It doesn't look like much yet."

How wrong he was, she thought when she laid eyes on the canvas. "On the contrary," she whispered. "It's beautiful."

He looked more closely at the canvas. "Do you think so?"

"Oh yes," she said, unable to take her eyes away from the orange and purple of the setting sun. Just a hint. A color study, really, but enough to give the painting a warmth. The rough outline of her hand, so delicate against the glass.

For part of the time she'd stood there, she'd imagined his body beneath her fingers, and now, looking at the image and the tenderness with which he'd painted her hand, she couldn't help but wonder if he somehow knew that.

Her face, though, was the true masterpiece, even at this early stage, a mix of pencil and paint. Colors not yet alive or accurate. Lines unfinished. But none of that mattered. Her essence was there, spilling from the canvas, crying out to be completed and yet somehow whole even as it was.

"Wow," she said. "You make me look . . . I don't know. Lit from within, I guess."

"That's how you look to me," he said, making the words sound like the truth and not a come-on.

"That's how you make me feel." She licked her lips nervously. He was watching her, and she could feel the heat of desire radiating off of him, filling her.

Earlier, she'd pulled away from him, a frightened little girl. But she wasn't frightened anymore. And she wasn't a little girl. She was a woman. Wasn't that made crystal clear by the portrait? The image on that canvas wouldn't shrink from her desire. She'd embrace it. And that's just what Lila wanted to do.

She moved closer. And then—before she could talk herself out of it—she took his hand in hers and put it on her breast.

"Are you sure?" he asked, but he had to already know the answer, because her body was answering for her. Her nipple was peaking, her feet moving closer to press against him.

"I'm sure," she said. "I want to go a little wild. Just once. Just with you."

He didn't require any more convincing. Instead, his mouth closed hungrily on hers, and she felt the low moan escape her and her knees go weak. His arm slid around her waist, holding her up. And then he picked her up, cradling her as he took her the short distance to the bed.

He made quick work of the rest of the buttons, pulling her shirt open and then unfastening her bra. Her breasts popped free, and his thumb found the nipple of one while his mouth closed over the other, sucking and licking and sending a hot wire of heat shooting through her body to tingle between her thighs.

She writhed against him, wanting to lose herself to sensation, but needing to say just one more thing first. Slowly, almost regretfully, she urged his head up, making him look at her.

"Please," he said. "Don't tell me to stop."

"No," she whispered. "But I need to hear something, even if it's a lie. I need you tell me that I'm different. That I'm not like all the women before. The ones the magazines say are always in and out of your bed."

Her words seemed to amuse him, and she fought not to blush. The request was idiotic, of course, but she still wanted the lie. She *wasn't* different, and she knew it. But this night was about her.

About taking this experience all the way. About being wild and letting go. She could be Delilah Burnett again tomorrow. Tonight, she
was going to be the woman on the canvas.

"Nick?" she prodded.

"You're nothing like the other women I've had," he said, so
earnestly that she almost believed him. "You're special, Delilah.
Let me show you just how special you are."

Chapter Six

Lila was not a virgin, a fact that would surely have shocked her father had the Reverend Burnett had a clue. But she might as well have been, because certainly she'd never felt before the way Nick made her feel now.

His hands stroked her body, which sounded simple enough. But there was nothing simple about the trill of electrical sparks that seemed to skip from his fingertips into her blood, firing her desire and loosening her inhibitions.

His kisses, too, were beyond anything she'd ever experienced. Deep and hot and all consuming, she thought she could get lost in his kisses, and she writhed against him, desperate for that deep heat to fill her and frustrated that he hadn't simply ripped her clothes off and thrust himself into her.

"Patience," he whispered, his voice laced with a small chuckle. "All in good time."

"How can you do that? How can you know what I'm thinking?"

The corners of his eyes crinkled in a grin, and he urged the shirt off her body, leaving her clad only in her bra, and that hanging open, the cups lost somewhere under her arms. "Your body," he said, pressing a kiss on her neck, and then moving down to kiss between her breasts. "It tells me."

"Yeah? Well, good." At least her body was still managing coherent thought. Her mind wasn't doing nearly as well, dipping low as it was into the swirling abyss of pleasure.

True to his word, Nick understood what she craved even though she could never have voiced her needs, not in a million years. He trailed kisses down her belly, pausing to pay special attention to her navel, his tongue flicking in and out in a manner that hinted of similar attention to come just a bit farther to the south.

And oh, how she wanted that attention. Her back arched, and she bucked up in silent demand. Her body was on fire and right then, only Nick could quench it. Damn it all, though, the heathen was doing nothing more than tossing thimblefuls of water onto the inferno that raged in her. Dousing small bits of need, maybe, but sending up clouds of steam that sizzled and popped and seemed only to give the fire that much more room to grow.

"Nick," she moaned, her voice barely more than a whisper. "Now."

He just lifted his head and smiled. A slow, sultry smile that made perfectly clear that this was his show, and that he wasn't going to move any faster than absolutely necessary.

She only hoped she didn't die before he thought it necessary.

His body was tucked between her legs, as his mouth caressed her belly and his hands stroked her thighs. Shameless, she writhed against him, trying to get some friction between her legs to quench the red-hot need she felt there.

"Don't worry, baby," he said, slipping down lower and taking her jeans with him. "All in good time."

He tugged her jeans off and tossed them onto the floor, then moved back up her body, this time trailing kisses up the inside of her legs. He paused only briefly to lick the inside of her knee, and the sensation was so wholly erotic that Lila's entire body shook from the unbridled pleasure . . . and from the anticipation.

She held her breath, her body so tense and taut that she expected to snap in two at any moment. Nick took no mercy on her, though. He trailed soft kisses, down the sensitive skin of her inner thigh, his strong hands holding her down as her body bucked and trembled.

And then—when she swore she'd die if she didn't find release—he stroked his finger against her slick, wet heat, slipping inside her with firm, even strokes. Her body spasmed, closing around his fingers, wanting to pull him inside her and yet still wanting more.

He gave it to her. With his finger still stroking inside her, he bent low and sent a whisper of breath to cool the heat between her legs. She whimpered, then nearly bit her lip when she felt his tongue caress her clit.

That was all it took. He'd wound her so tight that that one, tiny touch drove her over the edge. He held on, sucking and nipping, as she cried out with a pleasure so intense it could be mistaken for pain. She bucked and twisted, unable to stand it, desperate to get away now and at the same time never wanting it to end. It did end, though, and when her body finally went limp, he was right there beside her, his arms strong around her waist, pulling her close until he was kissing her, the taste of her sex still on his lips.

His hand crept down between them, and he stroked her. Her

body fired in response, her limp, sleepy limbs coming alive with a passion that had been hiding only too close to the surface.

He'd taken her to wonderful, erotic places. Hell, he'd just *taken* her. And now, she thought, she wanted to return the favor. Reaching down, she stroked him, her hand not quite able to close around him as she slid up and down over the velvety shaft. "It's your turn now," she whispered.

"Yes," he said, the heat in his eyes undeniable. "It is."

Nick couldn't remember the last time he'd been this turned on. Even the countess he'd met in Venice three centuries ago hadn't sent him spiraling so out of control. His hands roamed her body, her thrilled moans and excited whimpers firing his blood. He'd been with countless women, but none with such a mixture of fire and innocence. The combination was seductive; it had sure as hell seduced him, even as he'd been seducing her.

He kissed her, wanting nothing more than to consume her, to take her body the way he would take her soul. To make her *his*.

Desperately, he nipped and suckled, losing himself to everything except the goal of pleasing her and his body's ever-growing demand for release.

The silk of her skin burned under his fingers, the heat swelling to fill and surround him, burying him in a blaze of lust and greed. He wanted to hold out, to tease and pleasure this woman even while letting his own desire build until he could stand it no more. Already, though, he realized he'd reached that point. Their foreplay had been with a paintbrush, and now he wanted to take everything she was willing to give.

"Nick." Her voice, low and strangled, rasped over him. "Oh, *yes.*"

Nick groaned a response, then slid inside her with one strong thrust. She cried out, her back arching with pleasure and her fingernails digging deep into his shoulders. She was as warm and soft as he'd imagined, and he thrust again and again.

Their bodies sang together, an infinite wash of pleasure as they moved as one. Time seemed to stand still and to expand, and he was aware only of the velvety sensation of her body around him, counterbalanced by the sharp sting of her nails in skin and her desperate moans in his ears.

The friction between their bodies sparked and sizzled, lighting a fuse that wouldn't be extinguished until the violence of an explosion ripped through him. More and more and more until he could stand it no longer. He had to lose himself inside her, or be lost forever.

He cried out, his body yanked apart, then coming back together as he sagged against her. She curled against him, her body as slick with sweat as his. Her cheek rested against his chest, and one finger lazily stroked his chest. "Wow," she whispered.

Yes, he thought. *Wow.*

And not just from the intensity of his reaction when their bodies had been high on hormones and lust, sex and need. But from the pulse in him even now. A steady thrum that drew him to her, made him want to touch her. To keep a hand on her, possessive yet gentle.

To stay. To sleep.

And—for the first time in over a century—Nick felt absolutely no urge to slip out of bed and paint.

A burst of light yanked Nick back to consciousness, and he sat up, irritated and mildly surprised that Delilah hadn't moved at all. His confusion faded almost instantaneously, however, as his fuzzy mind took stock of the situation.

Nick's father, he knew, had arrived.

Slowly, Nick slid out of from under the covers, the cool air decadent against his naked skin. "One of these days," he said as he slipped on a robe, "you really need to learn to knock."

His father actually laughed at that, his usually flat black eyes now flashing with glee. He waved a hand, indicating the image that was just starting to emerge from the canvas. "I'm pleased," he said, running a hand over his goatee. "A single day and the woman is already in your bed. But it is not your pleasure I'm interested in, Nicholas. I want the woman's soul."

"You made that perfectly clear, Father."

"Did I?" His father lifted an already-angled brow. "Good. Because your elder brother seemed incapable of following even the clearest of instructions. I trust I won't find the same disappointment with you?"

"You won't," Nick said firmly.

Lucifer traced a finger over the lines of Delilah's face, the form barely emerging from the canvas. "You've begun then? With this touch I'm caressing the soul that I covet?"

Nick hesitated, unsure of the best way to answer his father. With Lucifer, the question of temper was always at the forefront. Lying, however, was not an option. If his father ever learned the truth, the punishment would be exponentially increased. And Nick was many things, but a glutton for punishment was not one of them.

"There is no soul in that canvas," he said, still not entirely sure what demon had stilled his hand, keeping him from infusing the canvas with her soul even from the first moment the bristles had stroked the canvas.

His father stiffened, his hand still resting on the soft brushlines that would soon be transformed into Delilah's flowing hair. He turned slowly, his eyes full of an anger so hot it seemed icy. "Do not tell me that you have already started down the path to failure, son. After Jack, I don't think I could bear the disappointment. Certainly," he added coldly, "I couldn't be held responsible for my actions."

Nick took a step forward, determined not to show fear in front of his father. Most of the time, that was easy. The tales about his father's temper were true enough, but Nick had known the man long enough to have learned to stand his ground. Sharing the same blood didn't hurt, either. But that didn't mean Nick was immune. And he certainly never wanted to see his father's wrath aimed directly at him.

"I'm merely toying with her, sir," he said, casting a quick glance at the woman frozen in the bed. "Taking a bit of my own pleasure before completing the task. But it *will* be completed. Sir."

"Your own pleasure?" his father repeated. He moved swiftly to the bed, lifted the sheet, then peered under it at Delilah's naked form. "Ah, yes. So I see." A lascivious grin spread across his face. "Perhaps before this is over, I'll take a nibble for myself."

Nick stayed silent, his hands balling into fists even as he wondered at his own reaction. His father had shared women in the past. The baroness in 1749. The actress in 1936. And others, surely, that were so incidental that Nick had forgotten them. So why, now, did he have to fight the urge to punch his father in the face merely because he'd *looked* at Delilah. For the sin of sleeping with her, Nick would probably have to kill the man. Except, of course, his father wasn't a man and couldn't be killed.

Which went a long way toward explaining why he now stayed silent, fighting to keep his flaring temper under control.

When he didn't answer, Lucifer turned, looking at Nick with cold, dark eyes. "Toying with her, you said?"

"Of course, sir."

"I see . . ." He pressed his fingers together as he peered out the window. "You have an artist's temperament, Nicholas. Like your mother. So I understand you have some need to move slowly. To build, as it were, from the canvas out to the finished product."

"Exactly," Nick said, though his mind was reeling. His mother? He'd never known his mother, and it gave him a secret pleasure to know that this ability had come from her.

"But do not languish in your pleasure. I gave you a quest. Fail to meet it, and you will instead meet my wrath."

"I understand."

"I am sure you do," his father said. And then, with a swirl of cape and a burst of fire, he was gone, his departure as pyrotechnic as his entrance.

Nick stood there, unmoving, his eyes fixed on Delilah, no longer frozen in time. The crash and rattle of his father's departure had disturbed her sleep, and she rolled over, her hand reaching out as if searching for him. Unable to find him, she spooned against his pillow instead. His breath hitched in his throat, an unfamiliar wave of sentimentality washing over him.

She was even lovelier in sleep, her features soft, all traces of worry erased from her face. A true innocent, of the kind he'd had little experience with.

That couldn't concern him now, though. This woman was the key to everything he'd ever wanted. He wasn't certain why he'd chosen not to take a bit of her soul as he'd begun the painting. Conceit, perhaps. To see if he was capable of truly capturing her even without the use of his special magic.

Or perhaps pity. A small twinge of empathy for what this woman would lose at his hand.

The thought was unpleasant and he shook it off. Neither reason mattered. Certainly, he couldn't afford to indulge in anything that made him stray from his goal. For the first time in his life he had the opportunity to prove his worth to his father. To best his brothers. To sit on the throne of Hell. And to create a painting of such beauty and grandeur that the souls of the great artists who had come before him would weep.

The woman in his bed was the key. And as Nick stood watching her, he knew only one thing. He wanted what his father offered. And he would take what he needed from the girl to get it.

Chapter Seven

Lila awoke slowly, keeping her eyes closed as she ran through the previous night in her head. So delicious! And yet so decadent, too.

And now she was a little afraid to wake up. Afraid the spell would wear off and she'd wake up back in her apartment, late for work. Or, worse, she'd be in Nick's loft, but the connection she'd felt between them last night would be severed. He'd look at her with the eye of an artist and nothing more.

Honestly, she wasn't sure she could bear that.

Still, she couldn't lay here all day, the light weight of the sheet covering her bare hip and her breasts. One deep breath for courage, and then she opened her eye, peeking first through slits, her vision blurred from the peering through her lashes. *Nick's apartment.* At least the entire thing hadn't been a dream.

She took another breath, opened her eyes more fully, and sat up, one arm pressed against her chest to keep the sheet modestly in place. At first she didn't see him. Then she found him standing by the canvas. The one on which he'd been painting her last night.

His attention was fully on his work, and she watched him in silence, fascinated by the intense concentration reflected on his features. His jaw stayed firm, but his eyes flashed, as if he were engaged in some internal struggle, and only the perfect brushstroke would satisfy him.

Once again, doubt washed over her. Was he having second thoughts about using her as a model? She hoped not. Because although she'd started out hesitant, now she wanted nothing more than to watch her image revealed in pigment.

"Hey there, sleepyhead."

She jumped guiltily, then realized that he'd abandoned the canvas for her. Her cheeks heated, and she hoped he couldn't tell how excited she was by the thought of being his model. Vanity run amok, her father would say.

"Did I wake you?" He was coming toward her now, the scent of soap, turpentine, and oils seeming to precede him as he crossed the room to settle on the edge of the bed.

"No. I just woke up. I was watching you work. I like watching you work."

"Good," he said. "Because right now, watching *you* is my work."

"Should I go to the window?" she asked, feeling like a slacker as she started to swing her legs off the bed.

"No, no." He pressed a gentle hand against her shoulder, and she shivered from the touch. He noticed, and the smile he gave her shot straight to her toes. And then, when he leaned in for a kiss, Lila was certain that she was going to melt.

His mouth pressed hard under hers, his tongue demanding entrance. He sucked and nipped, taking as much as he gave and making her feel weak and woozy, as if he could possess her, body and soul, through nothing more substantial than a kiss.

When they finally broke the kiss, she pulled away with a sigh, feeling sleepy and sated. "Incredible," she said.

"Agreed." His smile was both appreciative and possessive. "You look beautiful."

"I've seen myself in the mornings, but I appreciate the lie all the same." She started to scoot off the bed, but he held her back. "Not yet. I like watching you like that. The way the light hits your cheeks. The way the sun tries to shine brighter than your hair."

She lifted a brow. "I've never been with an artist before," she said. "I'm not sure if you're trying to seduce me or simply planning on painting me."

"Can't the answer be both?" He kissed her briefly on the lips, then slid off the bed, his outstretched hand indicating that she was to stay. She didn't mind. She felt wild and sexy. Instead of being slightly embarrassing, the idea that he was watching her, studying her so intimately, made her feel all horny, and it was everything she could do not to slide her hands between her legs and touch herself under the sheet, even with him right there, undoubtedly aware of everything she was doing.

She squirmed a little, unable to shake the thought now that it had entered her head. She'd always been shy with lovers before, and this sudden urge to play the exhibitionist was both exciting and a little frightening.

"Are you okay?" He was watching her face, his brow furrowed.

She rolled her shoulders and sat up straighter, letting the sheet fall and pool around her waist. She leaned back against the pillows, the heat from the sun tickling her breasts and making her nipples stand at attention. She smiled at Nick, who was watching her with both interest and appreciation. Then she closed her eyes and lost herself to the moment, imagining that his brush against the canvas was stroking her body and igniting her soul.

A masterpiece. Nick's heart raced as he dabbed color on the canvas, dappling sunlight onto her hair and skin. Her shoulders were bare, her breasts glorious, and even though the focus of the portrait was the image of Delilah at the window, this vision was too beautiful to pass up.

He'd decided to do overlapping vignettes—images in softer style surrounding the focal point. And now he gave the canvas everything he could—his skill, his passion, and yes, just a hint of Delilah's soul.

He had almost hesitated, almost waited until the portrait was complete to infuse it with the woman. He wasn't entirely sure why he hesitated. Sympathy for the woman? Surely not. True, she delighted him more than any woman he'd known before. But that was more a reflection of who she was—the physical manifestation of the perfect model he'd always imagined painting—than of any foolish soft-hearted emotion he might feel toward the girl. He liked her. Yes, of course he did. But this wasn't about like or even love. This was about goals and power, fame and recognition. The girl was the key. And the more firmly he kept that in mind, the more forcefully he could push ridiculous sentimentality out of his head.

No, his hesitation to infuse the painting with her soul was pure selfishness. He wanted to know if he could bring the image to life. If he could do her beauty justice and create the masterpiece he saw in his mind without the assistance of his unique skills. In other words, was he truly the artist he claimed to be, or did he owe his fame to his father's legacy?

As he stroked sunlight into her hair, he told himself it didn't matter. He *was* his father's son, after all. And soon enough he would prove his worth to his father.

Ultimately, his father was the reason he hadn't given in to the urge to hesitate. Lucifer wasn't exactly known for behaving rationally or reasonably. If he returned again to check Nick's progress and saw that the canvas still lacked Delilah's soul, he might consider the quest forfeited, even if Nick still had days to go. In that event, not only would Nick be punished, but also the unthinkable would happen—his father would turn to Marcus to inherit. And that outcome was beyond unacceptable.

He shoved thoughts of his fractured family out of his head, focusing instead on his work. For more than an hour he lost himself in the heady scent of pigment and in the light that filled his loft. And, most important, in the woman on the bed in front of him.

During the entire session, she'd remained still, a near-rapturous expression on her face. Now she sat up suddenly, startled and alert.

"Delilah?"

She blinked. "What time is it?" Even as she spoke, her eyes sought out the clock. "Oh, shit. It's past eleven." She flew out of bed, standing there naked as she rubbed her hands over her face. "I can't believe I forgot!"

She turned to look at him, and he saw the instant she realized she was unclothed. Her cheeks turned pink, and she reached back, tugging the sheet off the bed and wrapping herself in it.

He smiled, amused, and her color bloomed even deeper.

"Silly, I know. It's not like you haven't seen me. But before you were painting me or . . . um . . ."

"Making love to you?"

"Well, yeah."

"I'd be happy to return to that task if it will make you more comfortable."

She shot him a warning look, but the twinkle in her eye reflected her amusement. "I'm being silly, I know. But I've been a little shy my whole life. What happened there, just now," she said, gesturing toward the bed. "I mean, the way I let that sheet fall like that. That wasn't me. I mean, it was me. But—"

"You're a model, Delilah," he said gently. "You were modeling for me."

An expression that could only be relief swept her face. "Of course. I—I was being silly. For a second there it felt almost like I was in a trance. How stupid is that, right?"

He shrugged, trying to quell the bubble of guilt building in his chest. "The job can be dull," he said. "Most models find themselves lost in their own thoughts after a while. It's the only way to sit there without becoming overwhelmingly bored."

"Of course. That must be it. But now I'm going to be incredibly late." She rushed toward her room, with Nick following behind.

"I called the agency last night," Nick said. "Remember? I explained the situation and arranged for a temp."

"Right," she said. "I remember. But that's not what I'm late for."

He raised an eyebrow, an uncomfortable wash of emotion

flooding through him. Jealousy? Surely not. What reason did he have to be jealous? Especially of something as trivial as her time.

No, the only emotion that made sense was frustration. Her time was his, after all. That was the deal they'd made.

"Beck and call," he said. "Remember our deal? The reason you're now living in my guest room."

She stopped, her head now poking out of the T-shirt she'd thrown on. "You're serious? But you've been painting me all morning. And this is important. I made a commitment. I can't just cancel it."

"This?"

"The literacy group at the arts center. Today's my day to work with some of the students. I can't let them down. They're depending on me."

"I see."

She looked at him, her eyes narrowed in concentration. "Do you?" He didn't answer, which was for the best as she didn't seem to expect a response. "Nick, you're an amazing painter. But haven't you ever wanted to share that gift? To help someone else learn to show their view of the world on canvas or paper?"

In truth, he never had. His upbringing had been sketchy at best. Raised haphazardly by his father since his mother's death in childbirth, the one consistency in his life had been a deep-seated knowledge that—above all else—he needed to take care of himself. The thought of wasting time helping someone else learn to paint had never occurred to him. Not in all his centuries.

"Are you suggesting I find someone else with an innate talent and mentor them?" That, perhaps, he could understand. Certainly he'd tutored under the best. Michelangelo, da Vinci. Not formally of course, but he'd learned what he could from them.

"Well, no," she said. "I mean, I think that would be a nice thing, and any artist would be lucky to study with you. But I meant someone new to the arts. Maybe someone without much talent at all. But who might enjoy the chance to learn a bit about it."

He blinked at her. Squandering his painting time to help someone else who might one day bring a masterpiece into the world . . . well, while he hated the idea of squandering his time, at least he could see the purpose of the exercise. But to steal time from himself merely so someone without an ounce of talent could learn to draw a bunny rabbit . . . well, that made no sense to him whatsoever.

He was about to say as much when he saw Delilah's eyes light up. "Why don't you come with me now?"

"Come with you?" The idea was so absurd he almost laughed. He wasn't interested in going with her. He was interested in keeping her from going at all.

"Sure. I know there's an art class going on right now. The room is right next door to the reading center. Watercolor, I think, although I haven't paid that much attention. It's always incredibly crowded, and I'm sure that Mr. Sims would be thrilled to have you volunteer. I think he's only got one right now, and they're both run frazzled trying to help all the students."

"You want me to volunteer?" he asked, desperate for clarification. "Just walk in, pick up a paintbrush, and start showing those folks how it's done?"

"Well, yeah."

The idea was absurd. He had no intention whatsoever of marching into an arts center and setting himself up as a damn teacher.

He was about to say as much, in fact, when she stepped forward and took his hand. "Please? I need to go anyway. Carrie and I have been volunteering together for months and I swore I'd be there. I made a commitment. And I'd really love to have the company." The corner of her mouth curled up. "Besides, I think you might enjoy it."

Nick rather doubted that, but he couldn't deny the hope in her eyes. Or, rather, he didn't want to. He pressed her fingers to his lips, kissed them gently, and nodded. "All right," he said. "Let's go."

Chapter Eight

"Excellent, Mr. Delacorte," Nick said. "Your composition has really improved since Wednesday." He indicated a portion of the canvas where Mr. Delacorte had drawn a rabbit peeking out from under a bush. Mundane, ridiculous, lacking in even the slightest tidbit of raw talent. And yet somehow still compelling simply because Mr. Delacorte had infused the painting with so much raw energy and desire.

And, in truth, he'd also managed to improve in just the three days that Nick had been working with him. That wasn't the amazing part, though. No, what had been really surprising wasn't Mr. Delacorte's improved skills, but how much Nick had enjoyed helping the squat little man along.

Not that he'd started the project with high expectations, but Delilah had been so eager, so excited when she'd introduced him to Mr. Sims. And, honestly, that first day had been more enjoyable than he'd expected.

Nick

He hadn't planned to go back, but Delilah had promised the reading group that she'd return, and from the moment he'd seen the fire in her eyes as he watched her work with the students, he knew he couldn't refuse her this anymore than he could refuse her in his bed after each session of painting.

They'd gone each day after that, and Mr. Delacorte's painting skills had increased dramatically. And Nick had to admit he took a proprietary pleasure in that fact.

Even more, he'd realized just how much he admired Delilah. Not as a beautiful model. And not because she'd revealed to him the joys of volunteering. He *did* enjoy the teaching, but he had no intention of clinging to that in some happy-go-lucky Pollyanna fashion. That was hardly Nick's style.

No, his admiration stemmed from her defiance of her father. She'd not only defied her father by coming to New York, but she'd combined that bit of rebellion with the dream of a career of which her father wholeheartedly disapproved. And while he knew that Delilah wished her father understood, she also seemed to have come to peace with the idea that she simply had to live her own life, risking her father's respect and love.

Of course, her inhibitions had slipped dramatically away over the last few days, so what she said now about her father was hardly telling. He smiled a little, thinking about their wild nights—and days—when they were away from the canvas. Her father was hardly the focus of their conversations. For that matter, conversation was hardly a priority lately.

But even before he'd started pushing aside her inhibitions so that he could get at her soul, he'd been astounded by the strength he'd found in her. A strength that made her stand up to her father, even while continuing to love him deeply.

He finished washing his brushes and then headed out of the classroom to find Delilah in the reading room.

"She's not here," Carrie said. "I thought she was with you."

"With me?"

"You're the only one around her being a bad influence, Mr. Front Page of the Tabloids."

Nick spread his arms, indicating the center. "I don't see any paparazzi around right now, Carrie. You want to explain what your problem with me is?"

Carrie crossed her arms over her chest and stared him down, her dark eyes flashing. "She's been acting differently ever since she's started modeling for you."

"Different how?"

"Wilder. Party girlish. It's almost like she's a different person."

"Maybe you're just jealous," he said coolly. "This is what she wanted, right? To be a model? Do you have what you've always wanted, Carrie?"

When she didn't answer, he pressed the point. "Don't deny Delilah her happiness just because you haven't found yours." He turned and walked out, clearly the victor in their minor skirmish, but the taste of success was bitter, not sweet.

He checked the rest of the facility, but couldn't find her. Finally, he went back to the reading center. To his relief, Carrie wasn't there. He found the director and asked if he knew where Delilah was.

"Hasn't been in for two solid days now," the older man said, his words a surprise considering Nick had walked to the center each day with Delilah by his side. "I assumed she was sick."

Nick frowned, but said nothing. He supposed that sick was one way to put it.

He headed out of the facility and scoped out the street. Not much nearby. Some shops. A few office buildings. A deli. And a pub.

He decided on the pub, although when he first stepped inside he had his doubts. Music blared from a jukebox, and combined with the sound of voices and pool balls clicking, the cacophony was so much Nick could hardly hear himself think.

He found her there, though, nursing a pint at a back booth, her skirt hiked up and her foot on the booth beside her. Her position revealed all, and gave the burly cretin in denim and a flannel shirt sitting next to her plenty to stare at. The view was so enticing, in fact, that the man was almost drooling.

"Take a hike," Nick said, sliding in on the other side of Delilah.

"Screw you," Paul Bunyan said, getting up and demonstrating to everyone in the bar that he fully fit the nickname that Nick had just saddled him with.

"I said leave," Nick said, and for the first time in centuries, he called upon his heritage to make his will be done. The man stared, then blinked, then turned and walked out the door.

Nick pushed the man from his mind, turning instead to Delilah. "Are you okay?"

"I was," she said, "until you scared my date off."

"Date?" he repeated. "You were going to go out with that guy?"

Her mouth curved up. "Well, maybe it's too much to say I was going to go out with him. But I wouldn't have minded letting him take me to the back. You know what I mean?"

Nick had a sick feeling in his stomach that he knew exactly what she meant. He also knew that the only reason those kinds of thoughts were in her head were because of him. He stood up, held out a hand for her. "Come on."

"Where are we going?"

"We're leaving," he said. "In case you forgot, the only reason we were at the arts center was because of you. We should be back at the loft, working on the portrait."

"Oh, right." A slow smile spread over her face, and she drew in a breath, her hands brushing the front of her shirt as she exhaled. "I love the way you touch me when you paint me."

"I don't touch you when I paint you," Nick said, trying to control a frustration that was building in him like wildfire.

"Sure you do. Maybe not with your hands, but you touch me." She leaned closer, her lips brushing his ear as she whispered. "I think about it all the time. I was sitting here, actually, thinking about you painting me when that guy came in. Since I didn't have you . . ." She trailed off with a shrug.

"You want me, but you'll settle."

"Never," she said. "But a girl does have urges." She took his hand, pressed it between her thighs, then sucked in a long, shuddering breath. Despite himself, Nick hardened and had to fight not to pull her close and sink deep into her right there.

"Do you think anyone's watching?" she whispered, voicing his thoughts even as she reached down, pulling the crotch of her panties aside so his finger could slip deep inside. "Do you think they can tell what we're up to?"

"I don't know," he said.

"I hope they can," she whispered.

"Delilah . . ."

She pulled away, and Nick wasn't sure if he was furious or relieved. Then she slid out of the booth. "Follow me."

He told himself he only followed to make sure she stayed out of trouble, but of course that wasn't the case. She went into the men's room, and after a second, he followed. He found her leaning against the sinks, her blouse unbuttoned.

He went to her because he wanted her. As plain and simple as that. But there was more to it, of course. He'd had a hand in this, erasing her inhibitions, opening the way for him to steal her soul. In a way this new Delilah was his creation, and while part of him desperately wanted to see the sweet girl he'd first brought home to his loft, he had to admit that another part of him wanted nothing less than the vixen in his arms.

"What are you waiting for?" she demanded, and since he didn't know the answer to that question, he reached up and ripped off her panties. As he did, she threw her head back and moaned with pleasure, the sound flowing through him like a hot pulse in his veins.

A rattle sounded behind him, and he looked up, barely able to concentrate on anything other than the woman in front of him. In the mirror, he saw the reflection of a kid, twentysomething, looking both scared and turned on. "Get the hell out of here," Nick said. "And lock the door."

The kid swallowed and nodded, then ran out. Delilah laughed. "Silly Nicky, he could have stayed and watched."

"No," Nick said, "he couldn't."

"Whatever you say," she said with a smile. "Until you finish that portrait, you're in charge of me, right?"

Nick wasn't at all sure about that. Certainly, he was losing control right then, his only thought a desperate need to be inside this woman. A woman he wanted more than any he'd known in all his centuries. Almost desperately, he pushed her skirt up around her waist, then lifted her so that her rear was pressed against the sink. She was already wet, and he slid into her with one hard thrust. Her legs wrapped around his waist, and she clung tight, her hips working in tandem with his as they moved in and out, their rhythm matching the low thrum of the bass reverb from the nearby jukebox until they both finally exploded, clinging together in a haze of heat and passion.

The banging at the bathroom door startled them apart. "Hey! You wanna let someone else get in there?"

He glanced toward the door, then back at Delilah. Their eyes met, and he grinned. "Come on," he said, helping her down. "Let's go give the folks out there something to talk about."

They got a few interested glances as they left the men's room, then headed straight for the street.

"Admit it," Delilah said, sliding her arm through his. "You liked that."

"I did," he said. "Sinking deep into a willing woman—what's not to like?"

"I'm just keeping score," she said.

He stopped walking, pulling her back to him. "Score?"

"That's two. Things that you like, I mean."

"And the first?"

"The arts center, of course. I told you that you'd like it, and you do."

He started walking again. "You're right. I do. And I thought you liked helping at the literacy center."

She shrugged. "Maybe I got bored."

"Mmm." He looked sideways at her. "I hope you're not bored modeling for me."

"Never," she said, aiming a genuine smile at him.

He matched her smile. "Glad it's not torture."

"Maybe it is," she said, stopping on the street and hooking her arms around his neck. She pulled up on her toes and brushed her lips over his. "Maybe I like torture."

"Do you now?" He cupped her rear in his hands and pressed her close, his body reacting immediately from the contact.

"Take me home, Nick. Take me home and torture me some more."

They hurried the last two blocks, stopping only at the corner deli to grab a couple of sandwiches and some sodas.

"Sixteen-fifty," the clerk said.

"My treat," Delilah said to Nick. "I've got this incredibly lucra- tive modeling job," she told the clerk. "I should splurge on sex toys and drugs, but sandwiches are more my speed."

"Oh," he said, looking so baffled Nick almost laughed. "Right." He took the twenty Delilah handed her, then returned four dollars and a couple of quarters. She took the sacks, and they headed back onto the street.

"He gave you the wrong change," Nick said.

"I know. A whole buck. It'll hardly break them. They charge too much for these sandwiches anyway."

She pressed a quick kiss to his cheek, then nodded toward the door. "Come on. I'll race you up."

Late-afternoon sun streamed through the windows as they burst into the loft at the same time. Beams of golden sunlight filled the otherwise dim room, giving it a dark beauty that Nick itched to paint.

"Fairy dust," she said.

"Excuse me?"

"You should dust more," she said, raising an eyebrow and obviously stifling a laugh. She waved a hand through a ray of sunlight, setting a flurry of dust particles dancing.

"I gave the maid the month off," he said. "She's the jealous type."

"Is she?" She understood the invitation for what it was, stepping into his arms and opening her mouth to his. Her kiss was raw and eager, and he felt himself harden from the soft firmness of her lips against his. She slid her hand down between them, cupping his cock and applying just enough pressure to drive him just a little bit crazy. "From what I've read in the tabloids, your maid's probably jealous of all of New York City."

"What can I say? I like variety."

"And yet I haven't seen even a hint of another woman in all the time I've been here. Could it be the tabloids lie? Or are you keeping the other women hidden?"

"Keep me satisfied, and I won't need any other women," he said. His tone was teasing. But as he spoke the words, he realized that he meant them. The realization chilled him, and he shook it off, willing himself to focus on the room, the light, and his model.

"The window," he said. "Let's get you in front of the window while the light's still good."

She hesitated for a moment, then went to stand there. She put her hand on the glass, chin up in the pose she'd held like a pro for days now. One beat, another. Then another. Time started to slip away as Nick lost himself in lines and colors. And, of course, in the bits of Delilah that he'd pulled free to illuminate his canvas.

Not too much—not yet. He'd had to start slowly, getting to know the woman he was capturing in the canvas. And over the last few days he'd done just that. Getting to know her even as, little by little, he started to fall for her.

It was an unwelcome realization, but one he couldn't deny. All he could do, in fact, was ignore it and lose himself in the miracle of creation. His art was all that mattered. This masterpiece that was coming to life in front of him. *That* was his only focus, his only concern.

He'd do well, Nick thought, to remember that.

"I was thinking," she said, pulling him from his thoughts. "I was thinking that maybe we should do something just a little bit different."

Her voice was low and sultry, flowing over him like warm honey. The sultry tones teased, tugging at his libido and making him as hard as steel. That was saying a lot, actually, when you considered that simply the way his brush traced the lines of her body had made him erect and on edge.

He took a deep breath, making sure that he'd wrested control away from his libido before answering. "What did you have in mind?"

"This," she said simply, then started to unbutton her blouse. It fell away, revealing her bra that she unhooked, then let slide to the floor. She reached up, her hands flat, her palms rubbing lightly over erect nipples. "You make me horny when you paint me," she said. "I think it's because I trust you. I've never been this uninhibited before. So the only explanation I have is that it must be you."

He swallowed, desperate to move away from the canvas and take her in his arms. "Is that good or bad?"

"Very good," she said with a come-hither smile. "Whatever you're doing to me, I like it."

"I'm glad," Nick said, but without the sincerity in his voice that he would have hoped for. What the hell was wrong with him? She was practically giving him permission to continue chipping away at her soul, stealing bits and pieces until it was all gone. He should be thrilled. Guilt free. Happy and sated with the promise of this woman, wild and uninhibited in his bed.

Instead, he just felt lost.

She moved away from the window, her head tilted to the side as she watched him. "I want more, Nick. I want you." She took his hand and pulled it toward her, capturing his fingers between her legs. They'd left her panties in the men's room trash can, and now his fingers found her damp and silky, and damned if his hesitations didn't evaporate in the face of his near-desperate desire.

He pulled her roughly to him, crushing her mouth under his even as his hands attacked her skirt, ripping open the zipper, then yanking it down over her hips. She squealed in pleasure, urging him to move faster, to rip her clothes, to do whatever it took to get inside her.

Seconds later, he was, and they bucked together in a wild frenzy, a storm of erotic intentions that filled him as much as his art ever had. She came with him, crying out as her body spasmed and her fingernails tore down his back. He ignored the pain, seeing only the expression of rapture on her face as she found release in his arms.

"I've been an idiot," she murmured later as they lay together on top of the sheets, the gentle breeze from an oscillating fan cooling their overheated bodies. "I thought modeling was the ultimate rebellion against my father."

"It's not?"

She shook her head. "Nope. You are."

He rolled over, propping himself up on his elbow so that he could see her face. "How do you mean?"

She lifted a shoulder, then rolled away so that she was talking to the wall rather than to him. "It's hard to put into words. But it's like what I really wanted was to take a risk." She rolled back, facing him again. "You're a risk, Nick. A big one. You make me feel wild and decadent, and that's something I never felt at home. It's like I go a little crazy when I'm near you. And especially when you paint me. Like I'm losing my footing. Turning into a bit of a bad girl. And I don't know. Maybe that's just what I needed."

"You like the way you're feeling?" he asked, weighing his words and trying not to entertain the little bit of hope fluttering around his head like a moth holding the promise of redemption. "What you're becoming?"

She licked her lips, her expression sultry. She lifted herself up, then climbed up to straddle him. "I love it," she said, writhing against him. She took his hand, lifted a finger to her mouth, and sucked. Like red-hot sin, fire shot from his finger to his cock. She reached down, stroking and urging him along, then lifted her hips and settled herself on him, moving so slowly that the sensation was pure torture.

She'd turned the tables on him somehow, taking control of a seduction that should have been solely in his hands. Never before had he been so controlled by a woman, but the truth was he didn't mind at all. He wanted to lose himself, both in her and to her. Most of all, he wanted to lose himself in a fog of passion so thick that he could forget that the woman he was falling for was quickly losing touch with herself, and that his brush was the weapon that would ultimately devour her soul.

"Fuck me," Lila whispered, not even shocked by the words that were coming out of her mouth. Not even a full week yet with Nick and she'd changed so much. So much more confidant, so much more daring. She felt sexy and alive . . . and at the same time desperately terrified that she was sliding into a chasm from which she'd never escape. As if all these exotic sensations were masking something else. As if good were hiding evil.

She shook herself, then ran her hands firmly down Nick's hard chest. That was her father talking and the last thing in the world she needed in bed with her was a head full of her father's thoughts.

Nick's hand had moved from her lips to her breast, and now she took it, sliding it down until his finger stroked her swollen clit, sending ripples of pleasure through her body. She arched back, letting the sensations flow through her, building and building until she was so close to the edge that just a feather touch would draw her over.

She held her breath, holding back the inevitable as she pulled herself off him, then leaned over to capture his mouth with a kiss.

"Paint me," she whispered. "Paint me while I come."

Chapter Nine

He was watching her. Painting her. Taking everything he saw and putting it into the pigment. Storing it on the canvas.

For days now, he'd been capturing her image, and now that the portrait was almost complete, Lila was so turned on she could hardly stand it.

Nick had been a little startled when she'd pulled away, then urged him to the canvas. That much had been obvious merely from the expression on his face. But Lila didn't care. All she wanted was this moment. The feeling of spinning out of control. More than sex, the vibrations that tore through her body when Nick painted her were so very . . . so very . . .

She shook her head and sighed. Honestly, there just weren't words.

"Right there," Nick said. "Hold it. The light from the street on your skin. It's incredible. I just need to—"

"No." She shook her head, wanting the sensation, but also wanting more and not sure how to get it. "No, you're right. The street. That's what I need." She tilted her head toward the chest of drawers where Nick kept his clothes. "Get dressed, Nicky baby. You're taking me out."

The taxi sped down Broadway toward the club that Lila had insisted they go to. And although Nick had cringed at the thought of visiting a club, he hadn't countermanded the direction.

Now, he sat back against the battered upholstery, watching her. He'd protested making this venture out into the world. He'd had his fill of clubs and the party scene centuries ago, his ventures out now designed only to keep him in the public eye and serve the celebrity status that had been foisted upon bachelor bad boy Nicholas Velnias.

Not that he found the nightlife distasteful. He didn't. But particularly when he was so close to the completion of a portrait, a venture out into the world would only serve to distract him.

And the truth was, he wanted this over. The painting was almost done, the final brushstrokes so close he could imagine the movements of his hand as the bristles caressed the canvas, the last bit of Delilah's soul swirling out to infuse a masterpiece that would surely one day hang in the Louvre.

Honestly, it was a moment to be savored. Which begged the question of why he wanted to rush through it, finish the painting, and then leave. Leave the girl. Leave New York. And, most especially, leave the painting at a gallery, not much caring if he ever saw it again.

He rubbed his temples, frustrated. Because the truth was he *didn't* want to leave the girl. But he didn't think he could stand to be around her now, knowing what she'd become. What he was making her become.

"Penny for your thoughts," she said, leaning against the side of the cab, the tight black Lycra of her skirt coming up mid-thigh, just low enough for modesty, and even that was debatable. She wore thigh-high leather boots with four-inch heels. And her sheer white blouse was paired with a lace red bra, revealing more than it concealed.

"I'm thinking how close we are to finishing the painting," he said.

"And then you'll be finished with me," she said with a little pout. "I don't think I like that."

"No?" As much as he wanted away, his heart gave a little jolt at the thought that she might want to stay with him.

"I like you, Nicky. I like the way you paint and the way you fuck." She glanced toward the driver as she spoke, without even a hint of a blush.

"Anything else?" he asked. "What about me do you like?" He leaned forward as he spoke and took her hands, surprised by his need to find some remaining hint of the woman she'd been inside her. Something he hadn't yet taken away and could hold in his heart even once he'd finally plucked it from her with the completion of the painting.

Her brow furrowed, almost as if she was confused. She blinked, and her eyes seemed to clear. Color rose in her cheeks, and she glanced out the back of the cab, not meeting his eyes. "I like the way you are when you're teaching at the center," she said. "And I like the way you looked at me that first time you sketched me. On the napkin, remember? As if I was the only thing real in the whole world and you could see everything good inside me. Being with you made me feel free and a little bit crazy, but in a good way. Now, though . . ."

She trailed off, and he saw a little shudder ripple through her body.

"Now, what?" he demanded.

"I don't know," she whispered. "I feel loose and wild and free, but at the same time it's like being trapped. Like there are things in me that were never meant to be, and I can't fight it. I'm getting sucked into a dark place, and I like it. But at the same time, I'm terrified."

He wanted to tell her she didn't have to go to the dark place. That she should run away from him. Run far and fast and leave him to deal with the wrath of his father.

But he didn't say anything. How could he? If he lost her—if he never finished the painting—he'd also lose his father's respect, not to mention the inheritance.

And so he said nothing. Even though her eyes were on him, imploring, he said nothing at all. And then he watched her eyes darken, her pupils dilate, and he knew the little bit of her that had risen to the surface had been sucked down inside once again. He'd pull that bit out tonight and be done with it. His father would come. It would be over.

And, frankly, Nick couldn't wait for the end.

Lila had no idea what sort of goody-two-shoes naiveté had possessed her in the cab, but once they reached the club she wanted to make absolutely certain it was gone. She let Nick slide out first, then leaned forward. The Plexiglas barrier in so many cabs was missing from this one, and she reached over, plucking back the fare that Nick had just paid. "Mad money," she said by way of explanation. "Now go, or you might get hurt," she added, backing her bluff with steel in her eyes.

He nodded, and she laughed as she slid out of the cab. Pathetic little man, not even able to stand up to a woman. She was about to say as much to Nick when she saw the expression on his face—surprise mixed with disappointment and disapproval. And something else, too. Guilt, maybe?

She wanted to lay into him, to tell him that she may have been naive once, but not anymore, and if he had any sympathy he could just save it for someone who cared.

She couldn't get the words out, though, because when she opened her mouth, all she wanted to do was plead for him to help her. *This isn't me!* she wanted to scream. And yet the words wouldn't come out. The fact that the words were there at all terrified her. Was she losing her mind?

She closed her eyes, counted to ten, and pushed her doubts away. She was at the club to have fun, and that's exactly what she intended to do.

They were ushered into the club right away, Nick's celebrity causing the door to open wide. Women gravitated toward him, edging close and whispering decadent things in his ear.

He steered them through the crush, finding a secluded table in the back. "Don't you like them?" she asked.

"I like you," he said.

"What's the matter, Nicky? You're so stiff. If you like one of them, that's fine. Pick one and bring her home with us."

He held up a hand, his face stern. "Just stop, okay? Just stop."

She shrugged. "Fine. It was just a suggestion." She fidgeted in her chair, caught a waitress's eye, and signaled for her. "Scotch," she said. "Straight up."

"Delilah . . ."

"Don't start, Nicky." She sighed and looked around, her foot tapping. "Damn, I feel antsy." She scanned the crowd, saw a small package change hands across the room, then leaned over and gave Nick a hard kiss. "Be right back," she said.

She eased her way through the crowd, then pressed her hand against the back of a blond guy with tousled hair and wild eyes. "Dance with me?"

He didn't answer, but pulled her onto the dance floor. They writhed and moved together, Lila shooting glances back toward Nick. She saw him once through the crowd, his eyes burning into her. Another twirl, and when she looked again, the table was empty. She blinked, wondering where he went.

"What's wrong?" the guy asked.

She shook her head.

"Were you really looking for a dance? Or were you more interested in my other services?" he asked, obviously referring to the little packages she knew he had hidden on him somewhere, and that could be hers for a price.

"What have you got?"

"For you? Anything." He took her hand and tugged her off the floor, then down a hallway and out into an alley.

The sultry night air seemed to envelope them, and she leaned against a brick wall, watching him do his pitch. "So whaddya think? Wanna try a little horse?"

"I don't have any cash on me," she said, wondering if she'd actually have the nerve to go through with it, and knowing, somehow, that she did. Hell, she wanted to go through with it. She wasn't that crazy about the person she'd been lately. Numbing her senses might be just the ticket.

He looked her up and down, his expression beyond lascivious. "No problem, sugar. I'm a big proponent of the barter system."

She brushed her hair out of her face, the movement little more than a delay. But why was she stalling? This man was right there, willing to offer her an escape for a price she could so easily pay. So why was some tiny voice in her head screaming that she didn't want what he had to offer? And that the price was way, way too high?

She closed her eyes, forcing the dissenting voice to shut up. She didn't want to be that girl again, did she? The sweet little girl from Alabama, so naive she practically tripped over her own feet as she craned her neck to look at the tall buildings. No, she didn't. But she also didn't want this man. She wanted Nick. But Nick wasn't there with her, and the little demon in her head was urging her, *Go on, don't stop. You wanted to go wild, didn't you?*

Did she?

Enough!

She forced herself not to think and to simply act. She took a step toward him, her fingers brushing his collar. "Barter, huh? I guess I'll have to figure out exactly what I have that you might want."

He leered. "I'm sure I can think of something."

"You look like the enterprising type."

He reached out and grabbed her roughly around the waist. It wasn't Nick, but she could close her eyes and still get lost in the sensations. And the point was the barter, anyway, right? A means to an end? A few moments where she pretended he was Nick, and then he'd give her the package and she could lose herself in a haze.

And so she closed her eyes and waited for him to touch her.

The touch never came. Instead she heard a howl, then a thud. Her eyes flew open, and the first thing she saw was the guy huddled on the floor, Nick standing over him, looking pissed off enough to kick the shit out of the guy.

"Nick!"

He whipped around to face her, his expression so hard and cold that she shrank back, silent. He yanked the guy up by his collar, whispered something that had fear rising in the guy's eyes, then shoved him through the door and back into the club.

Then he turned to her.

She pressed her back against the wall and met his eyes, trying to lift her chin in defiance, but not doing a very good job.

"What in Hades are you doing?" he roared.

"Back off, Nick! You may be painting me, but that doesn't mean you're in charge of me!"

"Not in charge of you? Who do you think made you like this?" Fury bubbled off of him, and he ran his hands through his hair, pacing the alley in front of her as if he couldn't quite believe he'd said that to her.

"What?" She shook her head, totally lost. "What are you talking about?"

"Is this the person you are, Delilah? Who you really want to be? A girl who's willing to go to bed with a stranger just to trade for a few hours of oblivion?"

Anger lashed through her. "You don't know what you're talking about. Maybe I liked him. Maybe that guy is just my speed."

"What? You like bad boys? Trust me, sweetheart, I'm as bad as it gets. You've been dancing with the devil and you didn't even know it."

His eyes burned into her as he spoke, and she shivered from a bone-deep cold despite the warm night. "What are you talking about?" she whispered.

"I've been stealing your soul, Delilah. Taking little bits and pieces for the portrait. And loosening your inhibitions along the way. It's almost all gone, but you probably already knew that. You're not the woman you used to be, are you?"

"I . . . what?" He was joking. He had to be. "Taking my soul? What kind of nonsense are you talking about?"

"For my father," he said. "I'm telling you the truth, Delilah. Dance with the devil and you will get burned."

Chapter Ten

Nick stared at her face, wondering if he'd gotten through to her. This wasn't about the painting any longer. He'd captured most of her soul in the canvas already. Hopefully that was enough to satisfy his father. Because he couldn't take any more.

Already, he was disgusted with himself. The anger he'd thrown toward her was really directed at him, and him alone. He'd taken something innocent and beautiful and turned it into something harsh, something ugly. His only hope now was that she'd hear the truth in his words and run. Run far and fast with what little bit of soul she had left. Run to her father, even, and see if he couldn't pull her back from the edge of Hell. Because Nick certainly couldn't rescue her. After all, he was the one who'd brought her here. And now, because he loved her, he had to let her go.

Loved her.

He did, too. And he hated with a passion what he'd done to her. What his father had made him do in the name of ambition.

He couldn't go through with it. He couldn't destroy what was left of the woman he loved. All he could do was urge her to get away. To escape. And let him face his father's fury on his own.

"You're serious?" she asked, staring at him like he was some sort of freak under glass. Well, he thought, maybe he was.

"As serious as sin, sweetheart." He took a deep breath, forcing himself to calm down. He took a step toward her and cupped her face in his hand. "Go," he said. "Just leave here. Go to your father. Get away while you still can. While there's still hope."

Something flickered in her eyes, something warm and alive. But then it faded, and a cold smile touched her lips. Instead of running, she pressed against him. "No way, Nicky. You're not getting rid of me that easily." She reached down to cup his crotch. "If you're the one who helped me along here, then I think that deserves a little thank-you."

"*Damn it*, Delilah," he yelled, jerking her hand away. "You're not listening to me!"

He grabbed her arm and started tugging her down the alley toward the street, ignoring her cries of protest. He hustled her into a cab, keeping a tight hand on her forearm in case she decided to bolt.

Back at the loft, he shoved her inside, then dragged her toward the painting. She jerked her arm roughly away and stood staring at it. "Beautiful, isn't it?" he said. "But it's a lie. It's a trick. Magic. The big mojo." He waggled his fingers. "I'm a hack as an artist, and you're the one suffering for it."

"I'm not suffering," she said, taking a step toward him. "Just calm down, Nick."

"I am *not* going to calm down. And I'm not going to be responsible for destroying you. I'm going to fix this," he said. "And if you won't run, I only know one way to do that."

And then, before she could protest, he tossed a mason jar filled with turpentine onto the canvas. Then he lit a match, and tossed that as well.

Flames erupted instantaneously, and she screamed, leaping toward the picture as if she'd beat them out with her own hands. He held her back, struggling to keep her away as they watched the painting blacken and crumble.

After a moment, the nature of her struggle changed. She bucked in his arms as her soul —now freed from the canvas—flowed back into her. And then her cries of protest changed to hysterical sobs. She sagged, crumpling to the ground and hugging her knees, rocking back and forth almost as if she was in a trance.

Nick let her go, taking the fire extinguisher and putting out the fire that had burned the canvas down to so much ash, the lingering scent reminding him of his father.

He knelt beside her, pressed a hand to her knee. She looked up at him, tears streaking her face. "What did you do to me?"

"I told you. I stole your soul. I'm sorry, but I did." The words were inadequate, and he knew it. But they were honest, and he hoped that counted for something.

He indicated the pile of ash. "You have it back now."

"Why? How?"

"For my father," he said, and then he told her the whole, sordid story. "I didn't have your courage," he said. "I didn't believe I could make it on my own. Without that particular skill to make my art stand out. And I couldn't stand up to my father. That simply wasn't an option."

"And so you used me. Even though you knew it would hurt me—would change me. You used me anyway."

"Yes."

"So that first night, when we made love. I was . . . that way with you because you'd worked some freaky magic on me?"

He shook his head. "No. I didn't start until later. The first night I was with you. Just like you are now. Pure Delilah."

She licked her lips, nodded uncertainly. "And then later you . . . you . . ." She twirled her hand. "Did your thing?"

"That's right."

"And you took my soul."

"Bits and pieces at a time, but yes. That's about it."

"But then you changed your mind."

He met her eyes, hoping that she could see into *his* soul. "Yes, I did."

"Why?"

He drew in a breath, hesitating, but in the end he had to speak the truth. "Because I love you."

She stayed perfectly still for a moment, and Nick held his breath, almost able to believe that it would be okay. He'd have to face his father's wrath, of course, but she'd be with him. And with Delilah he could see anything through.

He was wrong, of course. She wasn't with him. That much was clear when her hand whipped out, her palm catching him across the face in a slap that left his skin burning.

"You son of a bitch," she said. She climbed to her feet and ran into her room. He stayed rooted to the spot, listening to her pack. He wanted to go to her, to beg her to stay, but he knew he couldn't do that. He'd used her. He loved her, yes. But he'd used her. And in the worst possible way. He had no claim to her now. And besides, more than anything, he wanted her free. And that meant he wanted her away from him and, most especially, away from his father.

She came back into the room, the duffel slung over her arm. "Stay away from me, Nick," she said. "I don't ever want to see you again."

"I know," he said, then drew in a breath. "But I do love you, Delilah. I want you to remember that."

She made a noise, almost like a snort. "I don't care what you want me to remember," she said. "Because I'm going to do my damnedest to forget you. To forget everything."

A loud boom shook the apartment, and a whirlwind of flame appeared in the middle of the loft. Delilah's eyes went wide, and she stood rooted to the spot. Nick wasn't so impaired. He leaped to his feet, grabbed her arm, and yanked her toward the door. He pushed her through, yelling at her to run. To leave. And to never, ever look back.

And then he shut the door and turned to face his father, well aware that he deserved whatever punishment the devil might have in mind.

"Kelley-Hart. Publicity and Public Relations. How may I direct your call?" Lila answered the phone on autopilot, the same as she'd been doing for the last four days. Carrie had arranged for her to get her old job back, and she was grateful. At least it paid the bills while she applied for colleges and scholarships. Not that she'd started doing much applying yet. Mostly she'd just been sitting around, feeling numb.

She'd almost lost her soul!

She still couldn't quite get her head around that. Both that it had happened, and that Nick had saved her.

Of course, he'd set her up in the first place, but in the end he'd come through for her. She'd survived.

She couldn't help but wonder if he could say the same. She couldn't even imagine what it must have been like for him, facing down the devil and having to admit what he'd done. Sure, the devil was his father—how weird was that?—but still. In the end, would that help Nick at all?

The more she thought about it, the more ashamed she felt. Nick had saved her. Nick had *loved* her. And she'd left him to face his father alone. She'd abandoned the man she loved because she'd been too afraid of—

She cocked her head, startled by her own thoughts.

The man she loved?

The phone rang, but she ignored it. Did she really love him? Could she? The man had almost stolen her *soul*, for goodness sakes. But he had given it back, and surely that counted for something?

She frowned, her thoughts a mishmash. Even if she could forgive him, that didn't change the fact that he was the devil's son. Not exactly the kind of man she'd ever imagined bringing home to daddy.

But, of course, Nick could hardly help who his father was.

And did his family really matter? The question was whether she loved the man, not his heritage. And despite how furious she'd been when she'd learned the truth, the answer was that, yes, she did love him. Loved the way he'd made her laugh, and the way he'd made her see herself. The way *he'd* seen her. Loved the way he'd taken a chance at the arts center and then admitted to her that he liked it. And she even loved the way he'd teased out her wilder side. Not the dark, soulless part—*that* she'd just as soon forget—but the sexy, daring girl hiding just under the surface. The girl she'd been that very first night in his bed.

She'd felt alive with him, and now she knew why. She'd been falling in love. And no matter what he'd done to her, she couldn't escape that one simple fact—she loved the man.

Which entirely begged the question of what she was going to do now.

"Lila! The phones!" Carrie scooted up beside her, shot her a perturbed look, then answered a line herself. She answered them all, actually, then clicked on the after-hours recording even though it was only ten o'clock. "Let them think the phone system crashed," she said. "We need to talk."

"I'm in love with him," Lila said, as soon as they were ensconced in a conference room.

"You told me the whole situation was freaky and weird," Carrie said. "Something to do with his father."

"And it was," Lila said. "But I was angry. The truth now is that I miss him. And I don't know if I can go back. I'm not even sure how to find him."

She hadn't told Carrie the whole story, which meant her friend didn't realize that for all she knew, Nick's father had erased the man. Her stomach twisted guiltily. If he was gone, it would be all her fault. She could have saved him simply by offering herself. She hadn't, though. She'd run. Far and fast, and only now was she looking back, afraid of what she might see.

"That's what I wanted to tell you," Carrie said. "You've been moping around here for days. And even though I wasn't crazy about the way you were acting with him—"

"That was me," Lila said. "Not Nick."

"Whatever. The point is that I found him. Or, at least, I know he's in New York."

She handed Lila a printout from an article off the Internet, relaying how every Nicholas Velnias painting across the globe had suddenly burst into flames a few days ago, and the man himself had disappeared. There was no explanation for the strange event. The artist himself had reappeared in New York today at the Freystone Gallery, which had displayed much of his work. "The paintings were clearly deemed unworthy," he said. "Whatever the reason, I'm starting over." Despite reporters' demands for an explanation, none was given, and the media speculated that Velnias himself might not have an explanation behind the concurrent combustion of so many paintings.

"Odd, don't you think?" Carrie asked, one eyebrow lifted.

Lila frowned, wondering if Carrie suspected more about the situation than she let on. "Very odd," Lila admitted. She drew in a breath and looked her friend in the eye. "What do you think I should do?"

Carrie shrugged. "Don't know. But something like this must be traumatic for Velnias. He could probably use a friend right about now."

"I'm working right now," Lila said.

"My calendar's pretty clear today," Carrie answered. "I can probably handle the phones, too."

That was enough for Lila. She gave her friend a quick hug, grabbed her purse, and headed out the door. As the cab took her to Nick's loft, she rummaged in her purse, finally pulling out her day planner and the napkin tucked in tight at the back. Her image was still there. A Nicholas Velnias original. Perhaps the only one left in the world.

The only Velnias drawing that had no soul in it at all. And to Lila, it really was a masterpiece.

The knock on the door startled Nick. He looked up from the blank canvas, wondering if he should answer it or ignore it. He decided to answer. It wasn't as if he was busy. For days now he'd been trying to paint, and for days he'd made not even one mark on a canvas. His confidence was shattered and, as far as he knew, his father had taken his talent when he'd taken everything else.

He pulled the door open, then felt his heart skip in his chest as he saw the woman standing there.

"Hello, Nick."

"Delilah."

Her smile seemed to light the room. "Can I come in?"

He stepped back, letting her enter, then stood there, his heart filled with wonder—and hope—at seeing her again.

"Why are you—"

"I was so worried when I read—"

They stopped, realizing they were talking over each other.

"You first," he said.

"You disappeared," she said. "And then I heard about the paintings burning. And, well, I was worried about you."

"I'm flattered," he said, his heart lifting even more when she smiled.

"Will you tell me what happened?"

"I was punished," he said flatly, not really wanting to remember. "But nothing I won't survive." He frowned. "Actually, I *won't* survive it. He took my immortality. One day, I'm going to die just like everybody else."

"Oh." She licked her lips. "I hadn't really thought about how . . . different . . . you were."

"I'm not different at all anymore. Every skill I inherited from my father is gone. And every painting I created that had even the tiniest bit of my magic in it, destroyed."

"I'm so sorry. Your work was beautiful."

"Don't be sorry," he said. "The paintings were stunning, but they were false. As false as my idiot notions of being an artist."

"He took your skill at painting, too?"

Nick tried to smile but couldn't quite manage. Instead, he gestured toward the blank canvas. "I don't know. According to my father, my mother was an artist. So perhaps I still have some bit of skill inherited from her. Something he couldn't erase from me. But I don't know. I can't seem to bring myself to begin again. It's hard to believe you have any skill at all when every bit of work you ever completed bursts into flames at exactly 12:06 a.m."

"Not everything," she said.

"What?"

"Everything didn't burn."

He shook his head, not at all certain what she was talking about.

"The sketch," she said. "Of me. I still have it." She rummaged in her purse, finally pulled out a tattered cocktail napkin. And there she was. Delilah's beautiful face rendered in charcoal and smiling up at him, as if silently urging him to try again.

"You kept this?" A stupid question, really, since of course she had. He was holding it, wasn't he?

"I tried to throw it away after I rushed out of here that day," she admitted. "But I couldn't bring myself to."

"Why?"

"At the time, I wasn't sure."

"But now?"

"Now, I know why. I kept it so that you could see it. So that you'd know that you have real talent."

"I see." Disappointment filled him. "That's all?"

She shook her head. "No. I also kept it because I love you."

"Delilah . . ." He reached for her, color flooding back into his world as she took his hand.

"I hated you there for a while, I really did. But mostly I love you. And the napkin was the only thing I thought I could have of you."

"You can have more if you want," he said. "You can have all of me."

A smile tripped across her mouth. "Yeah? I don't know. I'm really only inclined to date master artists," she teased. "If you want to paint me, though . . ." She gestured toward the blank canvas. "Maybe prove you're worthy of me?"

He grinned, the weight on his heart suddenly lifting. And, more important, the tightness in his fingers evaporating. He *did* want to paint her. More, he was certain that he could. The finished product might not ever hang in the Louvre, but he was certain that, no matter what, to him it would be a masterpiece.

She kissed him, hard. And Nick drank in the taste of her like a dying man drinking from an oasis. He might have stolen her soul, but she'd stolen his heart. And as far as Nick was concerned, it belonged to her. Forever.

MARCUS

Dee Davis

Chapter One

Chateau Lavermont, French Riviera

Danielle Coussy slept soundly, her mouth open slightly, her breath slipping in and out of her body on a soft hiss. Even in repose, she was a beautiful woman. Married four times, she was a bit long in the tooth, but plastic surgery had done wonders for her wear-and-tear-ability. All that to say that screwing her hadn't been too much of a burden. A bit on the tame side perhaps, but considering the end result, well worth the effort.

Marcus Diablo carefully pulled his arms free and slipped out of the bed, Danielle's only reaction a soft sigh. He stood for a moment, staring down at her, his eyes drinking in the sweet curves of her breasts. Just for a moment, he considered abandoning his goal and sliding back between her legs. It was a tempting thought, but only a passing one.

Slipping into pants and shirt, he moved on silent feet to the doorway, the rococo frame elaborate even for a French chateau as grand as Lavermont. He actually remembered the place in its heyday—when France was on top of the world, and known for its lavish elegance and decadent society. How he missed those days.

Still, there were treasures in France. One just had to work a little harder to find them. Smiling, he walked into the hallway, the clock chiming three. The servants would be up in just over an hour. It was time to make his move.

With a last glance through the door at the still-sleeping woman, Marcus turned to make his way down the main stairway, careful to keep to the left on the fifteenth stair. It had taken weeks to learn everything he needed to know—the habits of not only Lavermont's mistress but her staff as well. He'd also managed to work out the codes for security at both the chateau and the massive gatehouse that protected it.

Considering the advanced security available, it was woefully out of date. But then this was the French Riviera and everything was more relaxed. He stopped on the second-floor landing, his gaze sweeping right and then left, ascertaining that the coast was still clear. Satisfied, he took the last of the stairs two at a time, excitement building. It was always the same. Centuries passed and still he loved the thrill of the chase, closing in on a thing of beauty with the intent to possess. It mattered not if it was a woman or a priceless work of art. The ecstasy was the same.

He entered the library and shut the massive door behind him, careful to avoid any sound. The room was enormous, all the walls lined with books, most of them ancient, all of them rare, and none of them ever touched by anything other than the occasional duster.

A cardinal sin in Marcus's opinion. Although "sin" might not exactly be the right word.

He grinned and stopped in the middle of the room, forcing himself to ignore a Monet and then a van Gogh. He was not here for paintings, no matter how exquisite. Perhaps another time. He turned and moved purposefully toward an ornate corner cabinet between a window and the west wall, pulling on a pair of latex gloves.

The top tier of the structure was designed to look like a separate box. But it was in fact an illusion, and reaching up under the cabinet's top drawer, he triggered the mechanism that opened it.

For a moment, he simply stood and stared. The tiny golden statue was everything he'd dreamed it might be. Venus in all her glory. Stolen from Louis XVI, the statue had disappeared from public view centuries before. Some experts even thought that the statue had been melted down for the metal.

But Marcus always persevered when it was something he wanted, and though it had taken nearly a hundred years, he had finally found her.

And now, she belonged to him.

Slowly he reached for the tiny Etruscan treasure and stroked the shimmering line of her breast and hip. Now here was a woman to bed. Still smiling, he slipped the statue into his pocket, reveling in the weight of her against his thigh.

Sad that a statue was more of a turn-on than the woman upstairs, but then six hundred years of fucking was bound to diminish the act a bit. Practice certainly made perfect, but there wasn't anything much he hadn't experienced. *Been there, done that* was a major understatement.

His whole life was a bit like that. Same old, same old. Except when he was acquiring something wonderful. Like Venus. He brushed his hand against the statue in his pocket and, after resetting the little box, turned to go.

All in all it had been an uneventful heist. But then it wasn't over yet. Striding through the main hall, he entered the security code and made his way out the front door. It was a bit brazen, but Danielle was sound asleep and her staff only bleary-eyed, if even that.

His Jaguar was parked to the side of the circular drive. He'd refused Danielle's offer of parking it in the stable-turned-garage, citing the fact that he must return to Paris early the next morning. Actually he was headed for the Marina Baie des Anges and his yacht anchored nearby. But the lie would serve him well when she realized what he had done.

He slid into the car, carefully wrapped Venus in a soft cloth, then placed her in a leather pouch, securing the package underneath the false bottom of his glove compartment. Then he started the car, shifting quickly into gear, knowing full well that the noise of the engine might arouse the household. Hopefully they would react as all well-paid servants and turn a deaf ear, by now more than used to Danielle's gentlemen callers and their nocturnal leave-taking.

The gate loomed ahead of him in the fast coming light of dawn. If things held true to form, the gatekeeper would still be abed, his plump wife warm and willing. All Marcus had to do was enter the code and he was free.

He slowed the Jag, approaching the gatehouse with caution. No sense in being careless. The keypad was on the left and he rolled down his window, his mind reaching for the proper sequence of numbers.

A wizened face appeared in front of him. The gatekeeper.

Blast and damn.

Marcus forced a pleasant smile, his hand tightening on the pistol in his hand. He hated the thought of injuring the man. He'd spent too much of his life killing. Nowadays he preferred to manage his heists with as little bloodshed as possible. Unfortunately, that wasn't always an option.

"*Bonjour*, Francois," Marcus said, his French slightly archaic but perfectly passable even in this day and age. "You're certainly out and about early."

"One could say the same for you, monsieur." The Frenchman's eyes narrowed as he stared down through the open window. It was only up close that Marcus realized he was carrying a rifle.

"Out hunting, are you?" Marcus forced a pleasant smile.

The man's eyes narrowed further. "There are poachers about." The statement might be pointed or Marcus might be anticipating things that did not in fact exist. It had always been a weakness of his—making trouble where there was none.

"Well, I'm sure you'll keep them all in line." Marcus fingered the steering wheel with his left hand, his right hand beside him, ostensibly to shift gears, but in fact he was holding the gun well out of Francois's sight. No sense tipping the old boy off. "I'm afraid I'm late for a meeting. Danielle gave me the password, but if you'd be kind enough, I'll just let you open the gate. Save me the trouble." He smiled again, waiting to see what the old man would do.

The Frenchman stood for a moment studying Marcus, his distrust evident, but then with a characteristic shrug, he walked to the keypad and opened the gate. *"Au revoir."* He nodded his head, and Marcus gunned the car, slipping through the wrought-iron opening before the gate had even completed its motion.

The road ahead was steep and curved, chasing along the sea toward the private cove where *Apollyon* was harbored. He pressed on the gas pedal, letting the car have its head. It wasn't as much of a challenge as sailing but there was a certain thrill in speed. And these days he'd take his pleasure where he found it.

All in all, the entire endeavor had been much too easy. Security systems were not as much fun as rapiers and guardsmen. In the old days looting had been much more pleasureful. Marcus sighed, taking a turn on squealing wheels, the countryside rushing by at dizzying speed.

Immortality wasn't as seductive as everyone thought. There were definite drawbacks. He sighed again, and took a second turn, this one swinging so close to the rocky cliff he could clearly see the beach below.

A short straightaway allowed for even more speed. He could see the yacht off to his left. Just a few more kilometers and he'd be there. Unfortunately, he was not traveling alone. Danielle's Ferrari appeared in his rearview mirror, her bodyguard driving. Eduard wasn't the type to take the car out for an idle spin, so Marcus could only assume that he'd been discovered.

Or maybe Danielle was simply trying to keep tabs on her latest boy toy. Either way, he wasn't about to let the man take him without a chase. Hell, he wasn't about to let the man take him, period. Gunning the Jag, Marcus concentrated on the road now, his senses heightened as he settled into the thrill of the chase.

True, he preferred to be the hunter, but he'd been on the other side of the coin often enough to relish the rush of being stalked.

Besides, Eduard only had a chance as long as Marcus played fair, and Marcus only played fair as long as he was winning.

Eduard was rapidly closing the distance between them, the Ferrari's powerful engine a seemingly solid match for the Jag. Marcus swerved the car back and forth in a squeal of rubber that stirred up enough dust to momentarily slow his pursuer. Taking advantage of Eduard's setback, Marcus gunned the engine again, the sports car responding with a new burst of speed.

A few meters later, Marcus spun the wheel left, the car now following a faintly marked track straight down to the cove. Eduard made the turn as well, but not without breaking, which gave Marcus an even greater advantage.

The road was rutted and strewn with stones making the going bone-jarringly difficult at this speed, but Marcus kept his foot to the floor, ignoring the scraping undercarriage. He could always buy a new car; he could not, however, obtain a new Venus.

The Ferrari bounced behind him, and then suddenly slid to a halt. Marcus felt a surge of elation as Danielle's car faded from his rearview mirror, but it was instantly replaced with concern. Eduard had given up all too easily. Something was afoot.

But what?

Marcus took the final hill of the track full speed, the Jag cresting the top, flying out and landing hard on its axles. But it continued on, finally swerving to a half-crescent stop at the edge of the cove, a spray of pebbles and sand filling the air.

Reaching over to the glove compartment, Marcus sprang the lock and pulled the leather pouch from its nesting place. Almost there.

He jumped out of the car, carrying pistol and pouch, his gaze sweeping the track behind him for signs of Eduard. The only sound that broke the silence was the distant moaning of the seagulls. No engine noise, no gunfire. Nothing.

Still afraid to relax his guard, Marcus ran for the edge of the water and the dinghy beached there, using the rocks for cover. Once on board, he stowed the statue safely in his coat pocket, and reached back to start the outboard motor.

Two pulls and the engine sprang to life, the little boat already hurling out toward its bigger sister anchored at the mouth of the tiny harbor. As always, Marcus felt better on the water, in his element so to speak, although his father would no doubt take issue with the idea, never understanding his third son's affinity for water.

The sea air cleansed his lungs and he began to relax. Danielle had stolen the statue herself, so there was no chance of her turning him in. And once he'd reached open sea, she'd never find the Venus again. It was as simple as that.

As he neared the rocks that guarded the cove, a new noise broke through the heavy morning stillness. A motor. Marcus's gaze raked the area, trying to find the source, the decibel level indicating something more than a local fisherman, a speedboat perhaps.

It was too early for tourists, which left only one conclusion—Eduard had called in reinforcements. As if in testimony of the fact, a silver-striped jet boat appeared from just off his starboard side, closing quickly.

He opened the throttle, physically urging the little dinghy forward. His boat was no match for the monster closing on him, and his only hope was to use his size to his advantage. The opening to the cove was studded with rocks. They thrust upward like sharp fingers, threatening anyone who dared to enter or exit.

Marcus had memorized their position before he'd ventured into the cove, knowing that he might need their protection should he be followed. With a sharp right turn, he edged between two mono-liths. His pursuer slid into the opening as well, maneuvering his boat with the ease of an experienced sailor.

Again Marcus turned sharply, this time avoiding the razor-sharp edge submerged off his bow. He jerked the wheel again to the right around another rock and then yet another, the jet boat still tight on his tail.

Apollyon loomed dead ahead, less than a hundred yards, but the boat behind him was obviously piloted by someone who knew these waters well. Which meant that he, too, would clear the rocks and then close the distance in no time.

Marcus had been in tighter situations and still escaped, but this one was pushing the envelope. A bullet zinged overhead. The bas-tard was shooting at him. Risking a look behind, he saw that there were two men aboard, which meant the gunman had all the time in the world and no distractions.

Not that he was going to accomplish anything. But in the time it took Marcus to regenerate, it was quite possible that he would lose control of the statue. And that simply wasn't acceptable.

He pulled up to the side of the yacht, ducking another round of bullets, and cursing the damage to *Apollyon*'s paint job. Taking quick aim, he got off a round of his own, successfully clipping the gunman's right arm. That ought to help even the odds a bit.

Marcus yelled for Faust and a ladder, already tying off the dinghy to give him stability. The other boat was closing fast, and based on the reports grazing the hull, the gunman was managing to shoot despite his wound.

The ladder dropped and Marcus started to climb upward, re-leasing the dinghy as soon as his feet cleared the third rung of the ladder. The little boat twirled in circles for a moment, then started back toward the speedboat. There was a moment's confusion, and then suddenly *Apollyon* simply disappeared.

If Marcus hadn't known what was happening, he'd have fallen, but he'd been his father's son for going on seven centuries and he knew the devil's work even when he couldn't see it.

"Father," Marcus roared, stepping out onto the deck. "What the hell do you think you're doing?" There was the sound of a muffled explosion, as Marcus's dinghy hit the jet boat, exploding on contact just as Marcus had planned for it to do. "I could have handled them myself."

"Seems to me like you did." Marcus's father materialized slowly, head to toe, along with the rest of the yacht. The sea was quiet now, the only remnants of the speedboat a wash of burning refuge. "Nice touch. Although I'll never understand why it is you go to all the trouble to steal something when all you have to do is wish for it and it's yours."

Marcus shrugged. "Your way takes all the fun out of it."

"Need I remind you that my way is ultimately your way whether *you* like it or not." His father's tone was laced with both anger and laughter. It was an old bone of contention.

"So what are you doing here?" Marcus sighed, eyeing his father with suspicion. The old devil never came to see him unless he wanted something.

"I have a proposition."

Marcus raised an eyebrow, trying to contain his smile. His father's entire life's work was built on propositioning, and more often than not he got his way. Except with Marcus. "I'm not interested."

"Even if the prize is taking over my empire?"

"You know I'm not interested in your enterprises. Too damn much responsibility. I like answering only to myself."

"And you think I answer to someone?"

Marcus resisted the urge to look skyward and instead ignored the question. "I told you I'm not interested. Why don't you ask Jack or Nick. They're far more likely to be seduced by your offer. Especially Jack."

"I have." His father's voice was quiet, regretful, and Marcus jerked up to meet his father's gaze. "They failed me."

"No shit?" Marcus wasn't sure which was the more prevalent feeling, elation or surprise. He had nothing against his brothers, but they were hardly a close family. And push come to shove, and it often did, they'd almost always bested him. The idea that maybe he had a shot at coming out on top appealed greatly.

His father shrugged. "I'm afraid you're my last hope."

Now there was a compliment. Marcus forced a smile. "So what is it exactly you want me to do?"

"I need you to procure something for me."

At least finding things was his specialty. "Something my brothers couldn't find?"

"No." His father shook his head, his eyes still sad. "They were charged with different tasks."

"But they failed." Marcus was trying not to gloat.

"They chose a different path, as it were." Lucifer shrugged, all remnants of sorrow erased. "But I'm trusting you not to let me down."

It was tempting. A quest, a chance to make son of the year, and best of all the opportunity for one-upping his brothers.

"So what is it exactly you want me to get?" Marcus asked.

"The Devil's Delight."

Marcus's heart lurched. He was good, but he wasn't that good. The Devil's Delight was the stuff of dreams. The kind of thing that every collector would kill to possess. But in truth no one had ever actually seen the thing. It lived only in legend.

"Oh, it exists." His father's voice was soft, possibly even reverent, if that hadn't been impossible. "I've held it in my hands, but a traitor stole it eons ago. And now I need it back. Interested?"

Marcus swallowed his excitement; no sense in tipping his hand. "Depends."

"On?" His father asked, cutting right to the chase.

"I work on my own, with no involvement from you."

"Done."

"And I do things my way. Without calling on your minions or my powers."

His father sighed. "Also done."

"Fine," Marcus said, holding out his hand. "Then I'm in."

They shook on it and Marcus laughed at the notion that he'd just made a bargain with the devil. He might have been concerned except for the fact that said devil was his father.

"When do I start?"

Chapter Two

St. Emilion Monastery, Avignon, France

The chapel at St. Emilion was dark, the only light faded silver swathes spilling from the clear-story windows, the antipodean shadows only adding to the Gothic gloom. Celeste Abbot moved on silent feet, her mind's eye recreating the floor plan she'd so carefully studied.

The church was a work of art in and of itself, but she ignored the stonework, arches, and stained glass, keeping her mind instead on the task at hand. Assuming her sources were correct, the object she sought lay in the sacristy just behind the altar. There was no high-tech security in the sanctuary, but she was certain there would be something at the doorway or within the robing room itself.

Sotheby's had fought long and hard to obtain the right to auction Theloneous Gerard's possessions. Simple though they might be, they had historical significance. And not insignificant value. The man had been the abbot of the monastery during Nazi occupation. And because of his alleged cooperation had acquired certain protections, as well as a couple of Renoirs that under normal circumstances wouldn't have found their way to an abbey.

But it wasn't the Renoirs she was interested in.

It was the journal.

Celeste smiled as she made her way down the center aisle, a statue of St. George standing watch over her progress. Although it was only an effigy, in the half light the saint seemed almost real.

The altar was simple, but she recognized the silver work of Odiot in the candlesticks and the smooth turns of Jean Goujon in the marble rendering of Mary. Priceless works of art that should never have found their way here. But they had. And if the rumors were to be believed, there had once been much more.

The monks of St. Emilion had supposedly amassed an astonishing collection of art over the past three or four centuries—their acquisitions said to rival that of some of the greatest museums—the pièce de résistance a perfect ruby called the Devil's Delight. Unfortunately, the only remaining pieces were here in the chapel, the rest of the treasure, if indeed it ever existed, lost with the passing of its last keeper.

Which explained the interest in Theloneous's belongings. Particularly the journal. There was every possibility that person who purchased Theloneous's diary would hold the key to finding the ruby, or at least the treasure. Except, of course, that the pages would never make it to auction. Not if she had anything to do with it.

Her father's obsession with finding the ruby had ruled most of her adult life, and the emergence of the journal presented the first real possibility of finding a clue to the stone's whereabouts in years.

There was no way she was taking the chance on it falling into someone else's hands. Sotheby's would just have to live without it.

She moved deeper into the church, the moonlight making the stained-glass figures shimmer and shift as she passed. She shivered, not sure exactly why, maybe just the chill in the cavernous sanctuary. Or maybe someone was walking on her grave.

The thought actually brought comfort. She could even hear her grandmother's voice. The remembered sound was soft and Southern. *Home.* She hadn't been back to Savannah for years, her father preferring Europe as a base for his quest. They moved often. Nomads in a modern world. It was fascinating, she'd never deny the fact, but she longed sometimes for the simple house on Cedar with its rambling front porch and moss-laden cypress trees.

She shook her head, clearing her thoughts. There was work to be done. Pausing at the head of the altar, she crossed herself, the gesture ingrained from Sundays spent with her grandmother at All Saints Episcopal Church. It had been a lifetime ago, but some things you never forgot.

It only took a minute to traverse the dais, and she paused at the carved door set into the paneling behind the altar. She pulled a flashlight out of her pocket and ran the pencil-thin line along the crevices that marked the boundaries of the door. There was no wiring evident but she held her breath anyway as she reached out a gloved hand to turn the handle.

Silence continued uninterrupted. Maybe she'd been wrong about security. Or maybe she simply hadn't encountered it yet. Relieved, she stepped into the shadow of the room, closing the door behind her. Immediately she was plunged into complete blackness, the dark almost a living, breathing thing. She'd broken into many places in her efforts to help her father. Had even stolen things when the occasion demanded. But she'd never gotten used to it. Never felt completely comfortable in the dark waiting for the other shoe to fall.

She switched on the flashlight, moving slowly to illuminate the tiny room, stopping at the first corner. Two crates stood side by side, the Sotheby's name stenciled in black on each of them.

Bingo.

She crossed over to them, careful not to brush against a table towering with books. No sense in sending out her own alarm. The crates weren't all that large, and she knelt in front of the first, delighted to find that it hadn't been sealed shut. Inside were two padded compartments, each containing a painting. The Renoirs. It was tempting to pull them out for a quick peek, but she'd already taken too much time.

Double-checking to be certain nothing else was couched between the compartments, she moved over to the second crate. Like the first, the lid had not yet been secured, but unlike the other crate, this one was not compartmentalized. In fact, things appeared to been have stacked without rhyme or reason.

She reached in to remove a sheaf of papers, flipping through them to quickly scan the contents. Nothing. Putting them carefully to the side, she pulled out an exquisite miniature, obviously Dutch, set it aside, and picked up a silver crucifix. It was intricately wrought, the fine workmanship marking it as sixteenth century. She closed her hand, her fingers stroking the smooth metal, and then opened it again, putting the cross next to the miniature.

Her father would be delighted with it, but she wasn't here for silver work. The remaining contents of the crate were quickly searched and discarded. The journal wasn't there. She stood up, running a hand through her hair, the arc of the flashlight cutting through the dark room as she searched for more crates.

"Looking for something?" The lazy heat of his voice twined around her like a cat or a lover, probably a bit of both.

"I should have known." She turned the flashlight toward the sound of the voice, almost expecting to find the room empty. The man was a shadow. "How long have you been here?"

"Just long enough to secure the journal." Marcus Diablo smiled, his green eyes glittering in the light.

"So why wait for me?" She knew the answer, but she wanted to hear him say it. Or deny it.

"I need your help."

"You mean my father's help."

He shrugged, his smile potent. "It's all the same, isn't it?"

There was an insult in there, she was certain of it, but somehow he had a way of sugarcoating the knife. But at least he was being honest with her. Unlike the last time. "Let me have the journal." She held out her hand, her gaze locking with his.

"I hardly think that's likely. After all, the last time we were together, you didn't exactly wait around for me."

The last time they were together was a moment she tried very hard not to dwell on. "What was I supposed to do? Hand the Degas over to you on a silver platter? You seduced me in the hopes that I'd tell you where it was."

"I seduced you because I wanted to bury myself inside you." Somehow they'd shifted positions, standing only inches apart. "The Degas was a bonus. Besides, seduction is a two-way street."

"A lane and a boulevard, maybe. They're hardly the same thing." They were breathing in tandem now. She could see the muscles in his chest bunch with each inhalation.

"But a perfect fit, no?" His teeth were white in the shadows.

She shook her head, fighting for clarity. He was doing it again. Seducing her. And she'd sworn never to let that happen again. Once had been enough.

Okay, maybe that part was a lie. But wonderful things could still be dangerous.

"I want the journal. It's my father's life work to find the Devil's Delight. You know that. This isn't the same as a painting or a statue."

"It's his heart's desire. Yes, I know." His frown held a hint of disapproval. "Unfortunately, I have a client who desires it as well."

"And your client trumps my father?" She inched forward, still holding his gaze.

"In this case"—his expression changed, his face hardening like one of the marbles he so often procured—"yes. My client trumps everyone."

"I don't think so." With lightning speed honed from years of practice, she grabbed the journal and pivoted to run, her emotions tumbling between regret and elation. To her credit, she made it as far as the sacristy door.

"Going somewhere?" His body pinned hers to the wall, every hard muscle pressing into her flesh with the searing precision of a carved relief, two halves that were ordained to fit together.

"Let me go." She started to struggle, then stopped, the motion causing far more damage to her senses than simply holding still.

"Why?" His smile was crooked. "This is much more fun." He dipped his head, his lips brushing against hers. It was meant as a tease, but something in his touch ignited a fire inside her, and without thinking she responded, the kiss deepening to something far more than what he'd intended.

She closed her eyes, letting passion carry her away, his remembered smell and taste combining into a potent aphrodisiac. His fingers cupped her breast, the thin fabric of her shirt doing little to buffer the sensation. His tongue was possessive, stroking and thrusting in a way calculated to bring pleasure.

Calculated.

Gathering her wits, she pushed back, but she was too late. He'd already retrieved the journal. "You son of a bitch." She swung her hand, intent on knocking the smirk from his face, but he caught her wrist, still smiling.

"Come on, Celeste," he said, holding her firmly now, "no name calling. It isn't ladylike."

"Well, I'm not a lady," she responded, immediately regretting her words when she saw the glint in his eye.

"Believe me"— he leaned closer, his breath warm on her cheek—"I'm more than aware of that fact." He kissed her again, then released her, the sudden motion almost causing her to lose balance.

"So what happens now?" she asked, regaining at least a modicum of composure. Except for the fact that he was breathing a little faster, there was no sign that Marcus had been affected by their interchange at all. "You walk out of here with the journal?"

"That would have a certain quid pro quo, you have to admit." The last time they'd done this, she'd walked away with not only the Degas, but a fabulous Willendorf Venus as well.

"I only took the Venus because you used me to get to the Degas."

"You took it because that's what you do. Same as me."

"There's a difference. I do it for my father. And I always try to obtain things through legitimate sources first."

"Right." He nodded as if that made sense. "Definitely puts you on higher ground."

"Damn it, Marcus. You know how much this means to my father."

"We've covered that territory before." They'd reached a stand-off. And apparently she was on the losing side of the proposition since he had the journal, and she did not.

"I could turn you in," she threatened.

"You could, but you won't."

"Why?"

"Because then someone else would have Theloneous's journal. And if that wasn't a problem, you wouldn't be here right now, would you?"

"Well, better the authorities to have it than you."

"Fine. Call them. I'll get my comeuppance. And the journal will disappear forever into the hands of some avid religious collector. Which of course means that if there's something in it that could lead to the Devil's Delight—that will be lost, too."

"So either way I lose."

"Maybe not." He stepped back, the distance between them not as welcome as she'd have thought. "At least not for certain."

"What do you mean?" She tilted her head, frowning at him. There was simply no trusting the man, but she couldn't seem to help herself.

"Well, the only person I know capable of truly understanding what's in the book is your father."

She nodded, waiting.

"And so, as I said before, I could use his help."

She tried but couldn't contain her snort of derision. Her father was not likely to volunteer to help Marcus.

"Either I take it on my own, or we work together temporarily. You can handle the old man."

She opened her mouth to tell him where to go but apparently her mouth didn't get the memo. "Temporarily?"

"Right. We figure out what clues, if any, are buried inside Theloneous's journal. There isn't actually any real proof he had the Devil's Delight."

She started to argue, but he waved her silent.

"Assuming there's something there. We'll both have it."

"And then?"

"Then we go our separate ways." He shrugged, as if it were nothing. And of course it was. But still, she didn't like the way he seemed to be able to pop in and out of her life as if it was of no consequence. "And may the best man win."

"Or woman," she said, stubbornly wanting the last word.

"Yes, we mustn't forget that." He'd closed the distance between them again. "A kiss to seal the deal?"

She tipped her head up, ready to protest, but one look at his eyes and she forgot all about that. His mouth was hard and hot. Nothing at all tentative in the kiss.

She knew she ought to protest. For self-preservation if nothing else. But she couldn't.

Truth was, she didn't want to.

Not even a little bit.

Chapter Three

The soft rocking of the *Apollyon* was soothing after the tension at the monastery. Celeste had wanted to present the journal to her father at their hotel, but Marcus far preferred to be on familiar territory. Especially after time spent in the monastery. Although he had nothing against men of the cloth, his history, not to mention his heritage, certainly didn't lend itself to his feeling comfortable in pious surroundings.

Or maybe it was just being near Celeste again.

Either way the important thing now was for him to keep the advantage, and to do that he needed to keep his wits about him. Celeste Abbot had a way about her unlike any other woman he'd ever met. She managed to seep inside a man, a little at a time, twining her way into his heart in a totally unacceptable manner. And having withstood the onslaught once, he wasn't really eager to try to do it again.

Which didn't hold a hell of a lot of water when one considered that he'd practically bedded her there in the chapel. Blame it on baser instincts.

Those he had in spades.

"Finding anything?" he asked for the thousandth time, leaning over Cedrik Abbot's shoulder to stare down at the manuscript.

Theloneous's writing was torturously small and the ink was faded, in some places so much so that it was totally illegible. And, as if that weren't frustration enough, the monk had favored Latin, but hadn't been very good at it. So on top of everything else, what little meaning could be gleaned from the writing was thrown into question when a word was misspelled or misused. All of which was making Marcus want to chuck the entire thing off the bow of the yacht.

Of course that wouldn't help him find the Devil's Delight, and so he kept his peace by pacing the length of the lounge at regular intervals.

"Will you be still?" Celeste hissed. "It's hard enough to think on a rocking boat, without your making it worse with your infernal pacing and endless questions."

"It's a yacht. Not a boat. Damnation, woman, it's practically the biggest ship I've ever had the privilege to command." The minute the words were out he regretted them. They were true, of course, but sounded ridiculous out of context, and there was no way in the world he was going to explain to Celeste Abbot and her father that he'd spent most of his very long life as a pirate.

"Both of you be quiet. Your incessant bickering is making this more difficult than it needs to be." Cedrik Abbot was an overbearing academic sort. Usually the type of man Marcus despised. But there was a singleness of purpose about the old goat that required at least a modicum of respect. What Cedrik Abbot wanted, for the most part, he got.

Celeste shot him a look, then crossed her arms and turned her back to look out the window at the gentle swell of the Mediterranean.

Torn between wanting to throttle her or her father, or maybe both of them, Marcus settled instead for a strong measure of whiskey, aged, single malt, straight from the banks of the River Dee. Swallowing it in a single gulp, he relished the heat of the fiery liquid as it slid down his throat. Beware of saints and fools, his father had always said. The former because they were tricky, the latter because they usually were great friends with the former.

He eyed the old man hunched over the journal. Cedrik Abbot was neither a fool nor a saint, and yet, Marcus recognized him as a viable opponent. He'd tangled with tougher men, but Cedrik was shrewd. And determined. The combination was very dangerous indeed. And he had a powerful weapon in his daughter. One he used with great frequency.

"There's definitely a reference here to the fact that the monastery housed a great treasure. Of course that could simply be confirmation of the art collection. But it goes on to refer specifically to 'that which is above all value.' Then it goes on to say that the abbot of St. Emilion is bound to protect the treasure at all costs."

"So the second reference could be to the Devil's Delight," Celeste said, turning from the window.

"Well, he doesn't say it outright. In fact, he doesn't say anything at all clearly. But if one reads between the lines, so to speak, there seem to be passages that could be referring to the Devil's Delight."

According to legend, the Devil's Delight was a twenty-four-carat ruby of perfect color and transparency. Some claimed it had been formed from a drop of Christ's blood. Others said that it was the stone that God gave to Aaron. Either way, according to Marcus's father, it had been stolen from him long ago, and that fact alone made it more than an ordinary gemstone.

There were vague references to it in ancient texts—Greek, Roman, Egyptian, and even Sanskrit. Various rulers throughout the early ages, including Alexander, Constantine, and Attila, claimed to have possessed the stone, but it never seemed to stay in one location for any length of time.

Those who owned it believed the stone gave them power. But others, primarily those who coveted it, believed that once it was possessed the owner was cursed, his goals and desires twisted into something heinous. And further they believed that if the ruby was possessed out of greed the owner's soul became the property of the devil. Hence the stone's name, and no doubt Marcus's father's motivation for wanting it to surface again.

After the thirteenth century, when the stone was allegedly stolen from the Vatican by a group of monks sworn to protect the sanctity of the church and its holy fathers, there was no further evidence of the ruby's whereabouts. Enter the monastery at Avignon and Theloneous Gerard. It had long been held that the guardians of the stone, such that they were, centered at St. Emilion. But there was no proof.

Until now. Marcus blew out a breath, pulling his thoughts to the present. "So what do the other passages say exactly?"

"There's mention of Aaron. Specifically that which once belonged to Amram's firstborn."

"That could be anything." Marcus fought to control his temper, wondering why in the hell he'd thought working with Celeste and her father could possibly yield anything more than frustration—on a variety of levels.

"Yes." Cedrik nodded. "I'd have to agree with you. But there's more. He also references the *lord of gems*, which refers to God's hierarchy of stones. Rubies at the top. And then he goes on to talk about the dark becoming the color of fire."

"Rubies have long been connected with heat and fire," Celeste inserted.

"All of which added together," Cedrik continued, "would seem to confirm that the monks of St. Emilion were in fact harboring the Devil's Delight."

"So where is it now?" Celeste asked, coming to stand behind her father, her proximity to Marcus sending his synapses into overdrive.

"He doesn't say." Cedrik frowned. "Only that he had betrayed his order, committing an egregious sin. I think this journal is meant as a confession, but the passages are rambling at best, nonsensical at worst. I'm having trouble following the thread. There's mention of capitulating to the enemy. Hitler maybe. It's hard to be certain. The writing is nearly illegible."

"Well, the reference makes sense. Theloneous was abbot during the Nazi occupation. So he'd probably see Hitler as an enemy."

"So how did he capitulate?" Marcus asked—despite his longevity his knowledge of history was sorely lacking. For the most part he'd seen upheaval as nothing more than an opportunity for further plunder.

"It's well documented that he was a collaborator," Celeste said. "So maybe this egregious sin involves selling or giving the Devil's Delight to the Nazis?"

"But it's not solid confirmation. Maybe he's just talking about the art collection. He mentions that in there, too, right? Or maybe the bastard was crazy and the ramblings in the journal mean nothing at all." Marcus blew out a breath, his frustration building to the breaking point. He needed answers and he needed them now.

"The only way to determine the truth is to finish the translation, but I can't do that with the two of you hovering." Cedrik motioned them away, then seemed to think better of it. " Do you have a computer on this ship?"

Marcus noted the deference the man gave the word "ship." At least one of the Abbots listened. "Of course there's a computer." Marcus had little use for the thing, but Faust was quite handy with it. "Faust?"

His longtime friend emerged from the doorway, leaving no doubt that he'd been listening at the transom. Faust was an immortal, too. But unlike Marcus he had no known familial connection to any deity. Rather his state of forever seemed to be more a quirk of nature. The two of them had met in the middle of a fight on the high seas, each mortally wounding the other. When it became apparent that neither of them was affected by the other's blow, they had struck up a grudging relationship, one that had deepened into real friendship over the centuries.

"Would you mind showing Mr. Abbot where the computer is?"

Faust nodded, his submissive posture negated by the twinkle in his eyes. If possible Faust loved a good adventure even more than Marcus, and although he disapproved of Marcus kowtowing to his father, he still couldn't resist the thrill of the hunt.

Cedrik picked up the journal and followed Faust from the room. Marcus turned back toward Celeste, surprised to see that she was no longer in the room. Instead she stood at the railing, the moon silvering her hair.

Pouring them each a drink, he walked outside, the soft breeze filling his senses. He loved the water. Loved the freedom and the endless possibilities it presented. He walked over to Celeste and handed her the glass.

"Baccarat. Seventeenth century," she said, turning the faceted crystal in her hand.

"Good eye." He'd taken the glasses off of a French galleon, simply because they'd appealed. It was only with time that they'd gained value.

"And the scotch?"

Also plunder, but this time of a more contemporary vintage, and it had been a wager, not out-and-out theft. "It's the Prince of Wales's private stock."

"You certainly don't have a problem with living large, do you?"

"I fail to see the value in living any other way. And fortunately it's never been much of a problem." There was a time just after Napoleon fell. Marcus had chosen the wrong side, and almost found himself at the end of a hangman's noose. Not that that had been the issue in and of itself. It was more the liquidation of his assets—most particularly his ship. A sweet little schooner named *Sea Breeze*.

"Not a bad way to go, I guess," Celeste said. "As long as the price isn't too high."

"The price is always high. The key is to be willing to pay it." He leaned against the railing, looking out at the moonlight dappling the water. "It's all about choices, really."

"I suppose so," she said. "But aren't there times when there isn't a choice? Or if there is, it isn't really a viable one?"

He thought about it a moment, sipping his scotch, the yacht

seemingly weightless in the gentle swell of the sea. "There's always a choice. Maybe not one you want to see or make, but that doesn't change the fact that it's there."

They stood in silence for a moment and Marcus was surprised at how companionable it felt. Over the years he'd learned to isolate himself from others—at least, emotionally—knowing that the pain of living on without them would be far more painful than any joy coming from human connection. Immortality had its downside.

And of course there was always the risk that someone intimate would discover who exactly he was. Mortals were not capable of dealing with his heritage, particularly when it came to his father. He'd learned that lesson the hard way—centuries ago. And he wasn't about to repeat it.

The problem was that Celeste had an uncanny way of breaking through his barriers. She had almost done it before, but he'd quickly extracted himself from the situation and never looked back. It was a choice well made, and fate was not going to have another go. Time had taught him well when it came to self-preservation.

Women were a distraction, nothing more. An enjoyable one, to be sure, but there was simply no point in settling when there were so many to sample.

"Do you have a family?" Celeste said, breaking into his thoughts.

Not one that he was willing to talk about. "No." He shook his head to emphasize the point. "My mother died when I was born, and my father never really had that much time for me. I guess you could say I pretty much raised myself."

"No brothers or sisters?"

A lot of them actually, but he never gave them much thought, content pretty much to exist on his own. "I think my father had other children. But not with my mother."

"That's kind of sad."

"It wasn't a big deal." For some reason her sympathy made him angry. "I never had it any differently. So there's been nothing to miss."

"Still, it's nice to have family."

"Unless they smother you."

He saw her hands clench on the railing and knew that he'd hit home. Her father kept her on a short leash. And even if it was done from love, there wasn't anything admirable in the fact. "My father and I are very close. There's really just the two of us now."

"And your mother?"

"Same story as yours. I lost her when I was born. My grandmother raised me until I was old enough to travel with my father."

"Where is she now?"

"Dead."

Sooner or later everyone died. As an immortal, he thought it a bitter pill. "I'm sorry."

"No. It's all right. We had a wonderful life together. I'm just grateful for the time I had." She stared out at the water, the wind lifting strands of her hair. "But I do miss her sometimes."

Silence descended again, this one awkward. Talking was overrated as far as Marcus could see. Especially with a woman. Negotiating polite conversation was akin to sailing through mined waters in a fog-shrouded sea.

But he needed her continued help—or rather, her father's—if he was to succeed on his father's mission. And the idea of besting his brothers was too appealing to dismiss for the sake of avoiding uncomfortable ruminations. Besides, she wasn't exactly hard on the eyes. And it certainly didn't take much to remember what she'd felt like beneath him, moving with a fluidity that had almost made them seem one.

"You think it really exists?" she asked, looking up at him, her blue eyes as unfathomable as the ocean.

"The Devil's Delight?" He fought to make sense of her words, his body taking a completely different tact. "Yes. I believe it's out there somewhere. It's just a matter of tracking it down."

"For your client."

"Yes."

She frowned, her expression puzzled. "Of course I could be wrong, but I somehow got impression that you don't usually work for anyone but yourself. So why would you let something so rare pass into someone else's hands?"

"Let's just say he made me an offer too good to refuse."

"And if I made you a better offer?"

"Well"—he let his eyes travel slowly from her head to her toes and then back again—"it's tempting, but I'm afraid you can't possibly top what he's put on the table."

She studied him for a moment, then tilted her head, the moonlight caressing her hair and skin. "It isn't about possession with you, is it? Everything is in the hunt."

He stared down into the water and then looked up again. She saw far more than he'd have thought possible. "There's something to that, I suppose. But make no mistake, I do love beautiful things." He stepped closer, framing her face with his hands, using libido to hide his cascading emotions.

She licked her lips, her tongue darting out and then in again, as if it were afraid. But then maybe it should be. He laughed at his whimsy and bent to kiss her, drinking her in along with the moonlight and the breeze.

She murmured softly in protest, but opened her mouth, her tongue dueling with his, giving and taking all at the same time. Their connection was effortless, almost as if there were other forces at work—guiding them.

But Marcus had made his father promise that there would be no hocus-pocus. And beyond that Marcus didn't believe in such things. Chemistry was nothing more than a calculation of combination. And what more basic combination was there than a man and a woman?

He stroked her hair, pulling her tighter against him, reveling in the feel of her body pressed to his. He slid one palm down her back to cup her buttocks, the feel of her quivering response enough to make him lose control. With a groan, he twined his fingers in her hair, using his tongue and teeth to arouse her even further.

Maybe there was something to this possessing thing after all. Just at the moment he wanted nothing more than to know that she belonged to him.

The sound of Faust clearing his throat shattered the moment and they sprang apart, Celeste gripping the railing, refusing to meet his eyes.

"Sorry to interrupt, Captain," Faust said, the title old habit. "But you're wanted inside. Apparently the old monk used the ruby to buy his way into a position of power during the war. And Abbot thinks he's figured out who took it as payment."

Chapter Four

"I've got two names," her father said, pointing at the open laptop. Celeste stood at the far corner of the little library. The room was small but cozy in a leather, whiskey, and man kind of way. The walls were primarily covered with books, but there was the odd piece of artwork. A tiny Rodin and a beautiful gold Venus that could only be Etruscan.

A recent acquisition, if she was remembering the scuttle. Something about Danielle Coussy. The woman had never had a chance. Celeste wiped her mouth with the back of her hand, Marcus's touch still burning on her lips.

Marcus was not a pledge-his-troth kind of guy. Love them, use them, and leave them was more his style. And she had been there and done that. On the other hand, at least if she were to get involved with him again, she'd not be caught holding any silly illusions.

"Celeste," her father chastised. "You're not listening."

Marcus hid a grin behind the curve of his hand, but she saw it nevertheless, unsure whether he was laughing at her father or at her. Probably both. Anger replaced passion, the leap not too surprising, since at least where Marcus was concerned the two emotions seemed to walk hand in hand. There was just something so different about him. Something that called to her and infuriated her all at the same time.

"I'm listening, Father." Celeste forced an insipid smile and avoided Marcus's gaze. "Do tell us what you've found."

"There were two men who headed up the Nazi occupation in Avignon. One was SS, the other regular army. And if we accept the idea that the monks at St. Emilion had possession of the ruby, then we move on to Theloneous's confession that he committed the sin of sins and broke his pledge to protect it."

"Conceivably by giving it to the Nazis," Marcus said, frowning at her father.

"It would indeed be a most egregious sin." Her father nodded. "And it is established fact that Theloneous was a collaborator. So—"

"It would follow that the men he did business with during World War II could be the next link in the chain of possession," Celeste finished for him.

"Following that logic, the most likely candidate would be the SS officer." Marcus was twirling his glass of whiskey, the smoky liquid almost golden as it hit the lamplight. "Do you have a name?"

"I do." Cedrik held out a piece of paper. "Heinrich Erikson."

Celeste moved to stand next to Marcus's chair, looking down at the printout, trying to avoid thinking about the strong hands that held it. "He's so young."

"There is no minimum age for evil," Marcus said, his eyes on the photo. "But this isn't our man."

"How do you know?" Cedrik said, frowning.

"Heinrich Erikson is dead. Died just before the end of the war."

"And you know this because?" Celeste found that she, too, was frowning.

"He was friends with my father. *Good friends.* If he'd had the ruby, I'd have known about it."

There was far more to it than that. Celeste could tell by the look on his face, but she wasn't about to question him here. Not in front of her father. Maybe not at all. Marcus wouldn't be the type of man to share his secrets easily. She shook her head, pulling her thoughts away from the charismatic man beside her. "You said there were two, right?" she asked, her gaze meeting her father's. "Maybe it's the second man."

"I don't know." Cedrik sighed. "He doesn't seem the type. He never gained any kind of prominence in the Reich as far as I can tell. And if Theloneous gave him the ruby, surely he'd have given it to Hitler?"

"If you had it, you wouldn't give it away for anything. Why should this man be any different?" Celeste sat in the chair next to Marcus, her hand only inches away from his.

"So what's his name?" Marcus asked, standing up to refill his glass. Celeste found herself holding her breath, hoping that he'd settle back in the chair next to hers, but instead he walked over to perch on the edge of a rosewood desk. She swallowed her disappointment, reminding herself that this was all a game to him. Check and checkmate. Winner take all. She'd do well to remember the fact.

"Hans Weisbaum," her father said, reading off of the computer screen. "He's Austrian."

"Well, that could explain a lot," Celeste said. "I mean there was certainly no love lost between the Germans and the Austrians. They may have fought with Hitler, but most of them didn't like it very much. Maybe Hans kept the Devil's Delight as a one-up against the Third Reich."

"Or maybe he just liked it," Cedrik said with a shrug. "Beauty has a way of getting under the skin."

"Some more than most," Marcus said, the heat of his gaze sending her nerves dancing.

"Is he still alive?" Celeste asked, her voice coming out on a quiver.

Marcus's slow smile signaled he knew he'd gotten to her.

"I don't know," her father said, blissfully unaware of the undercurrents zinging around the room. "Unfortunately, as I said, he was a small player. Except for his brief command in Avignon, he seems to have pretty much disappeared."

"No death record, I take it?" Marcus crossed his arms, studying the older man.

Cedrik shook his head. "Nothing like that. Which I think is a good sign. I do know that there was family farm near Hallstadt. It's just southeast of Salzburg."

"Actually, I know the place." Marcus said. "Stayed there once with a friend. It was a hell of a party. But it was also a very long time ago."

Maybe Celeste was imagining things, but there seemed to be more to what he was saying than the words belied. Something somber—maybe even a little sad. Or maybe she was seeing shadows where there were none.

"Any chance the old man's still there?" Marcus asked.

"Every possibility. The Austrians are a proud lot and tend not to wander too far from home. My guess is that if he's still alive, he's probably still working the family farm."

"But surely if he had the ruby, he wouldn't have gone back to the farm?" Celeste had never understood the need to hold onto something merely for the sake of owning it. It simply wasn't in her nature. Or maybe it was her own small way of rebelling against her father. Hard to sort those kinds of feelings out. And quite frankly she wasn't all that interested in soul-searching anyway.

"He might not have had a choice," Marcus said. "After the war, it wouldn't have been safe for Hans to try and sell something like the Devil's Delight. First off, it would have marked him as a Nazi, which he most likely would have wanted to avoid. And second off, it would have also made him a thief. And the war crimes tribunals were not something to be taken lightly. No, my guess is that if he had the stone, he would have kept the fact secret."

"But things changed, surely. I mean he wouldn't have needed to keep it secret forever," Celeste said, her gaze encompassing both Marcus and her father.

"No. Marcus is right," Cedrik said. "He would've had too much to explain. And while I do agree that for a while things got better, they've certainly taken a turn for the worse these days. I mean everyone wants retribution. And if you don't have provenance you're going to have a hard time selling anything that could have been plundered during the war."

"But there's the black market. We use it all the time."

"Yes, but we're insiders. As is Marcus. Despite the fact that we play loose with the rules, we still have our own code, and it wouldn't be easy for a man like Weisbaum to gain access to our circle."

"That's reverse snobbery, and you know it. Besides all he'd

have to do is mention the Devil's Delight and half the collectors in the world would be sniffing around faster than he could say the word 'ruby.'"

"You're probably right, but that just supports the idea that Hans kept his secret. As you pointed out, if the ruby had surfaced, we'd have heard rumors. And we haven't." Marcus stood up and walked over to the drinks table to pour himself another whiskey. "I think Cedrik is onto something."

"So what do we do now?" Celeste asked, trying to sound as if she didn't really care. "It's not as if we're really working together. I mean after all, we want the stone and you want the stone, and at the end of the day, only one of us can have it."

"I can think of any number of reasons why it might be interesting to work together." He raised an eyebrow, managing to look ruthless and desirable all at the same time. "But our agreement was that once we figured out what the journal had to offer, we'd go our separate ways."

"Right. So how do you want to handle that?" She swallowed the disappointment flooding through her. "My father counts to three and we both dive off the side of the boat?"

"It's an idea. But I'm sure we can come up with something more civilized." He'd moved closer, ignoring the fact that her father was still in the room.

"It seems to me"—Cedrik's voice was better than a cold shower—"that it'd would be simpler if the two of you worked together, at least until you manage to actually find Herr Weisbaum."

"Having doubts about your daughter's abilities?" Marcus asked, his tone every bit as cool as Cedrik's.

"Not at all. I simply don't see why our little partnership needs to end just now. For all we know we're on the wrong track altogether. So while you all work on the Weisbaum angle, I'll have another go at the journal."

Marcus's eyes narrowed in speculation as he studied the older man. "And what's to stop you from pursuing the ruby on your own, while your daughter keeps me running in circles?"

"Nothing." Her father smiled, but the gesture lacked humor. "You'll just have to trust me."

"Not likely," Marcus said. "But if you'll agree to stay here with Faust, then maybe I'll agree to let Celeste tag along."

"Tag along?" She tried but couldn't stop the protest. "What do you mean by that?"

"Just what I said, princess. You're not bad at what you do. But I'm better. And so either you tag along, or I'll leave you behind. Your choice. But make no mistake, Cedrik." He switched his attention to her father, dismissing her in the process. "In the end, I intend to win the day."

"Don't underestimate me, boy. I may be an old man, but I'm not dead."

They were glaring at each other now, engaged in a testosterone-driven pissing match. Celeste blew out a breath.

Men.

Slipping out of the open doorway, she walked up the passageway and out onto the deck. The moon had set, leaving the yacht cloaked in shadow. She could see the lights of the coast glittering against the black line of the sea. It wasn't that far. Less than a mile. And she was in good shape.

It would serve them both right if she dove over the side and started the search for Hans Weisbaum on her own. She leaned over the railing, the water below lapping softly against the hull. The idea had originated in anger, but now, suddenly, it seemed appealing. The water was warm and the shore truly wasn't that far away. All she had to do was swim to the shore, make her way to her hotel, gather some clothes and supplies, and hit the road.

It was a bit impulsive, but it beat playing the pawn.

She kicked off her shoes, peering behind her to see if there was any sign of her father or Marcus. Light spilled from the windows, but there was no sign of life. She slipped out of her pants, then her shirt, the night air cold against her bare skin.

She had a moment's hesitation, but pushed it aside, the image of mocking green eyes urging her onward. *Tag along, my ass.*

She scrambled up onto the diving platform at the stern of the yacht, holding the railing for balance. Sucking in a breath, she lifted her arms, and tensed her muscles to launch herself downward into the water.

But just as her calves tightened for the dive, a hard muscled arm slipped around her waist.

"Going somewhere?" Marcus lifted her up and over the railing as if she weighed no more than a feather. He pulled her close, purposely sliding her body along his before letting her go. She stumbled, but quickly regained her footing, anger mixing with emotions she had no intention of trying to identify.

Ever.

"It seemed a nice night for a swim." It sounded lame. But at least her voice wasn't shaking. "Where's my father?" She looked toward the cabin light, not certain whether she was relieved or annoyed that he hadn't followed Marcus out on deck.

"Let's just say we came to a meeting of the minds."

"How wonderful for you both." She moved toward the pile of

her clothing, managing to scoop up her shirt before he managed to stop her. "So why not just let me go? You made it perfectly clear what you think of my abilities."

"Well, for one thing there are currents out there that make it harder to swim to shore than it looks."

"I'm a good swimmer." She jerked free and pulled on her shirt, fumbling with the buttons.

"I'm sure you are." He reached over to help, the act of closing the buttons somehow more sexually charged than if he'd been undressing her. "But that doesn't change the fact that it's dangerous to swim at night. Besides, I would have caught up with you by morning."

"Because you're so much better than I am."

"No. Because while you were out here contemplating a skinny dip, your father gave me the location of the farm."

"You're unbelievable. You'll do anything to get what you want. Even manipulate an old man."

His eyes flashed. "I didn't manipulate anyone. Cedrik Abbot never does anything he doesn't want to. I'm not sure I completely understand why it is he thinks we should continue to work together. But he does. And since for the time being it suits my purposes, I agreed. All of which you would know if you'd bothered to stick around."

"I was protecting my father."

"You were running scared."

"Of what?" She shifted so that they were standing nose to nose, her anger spurring her momentum. "You?" She choked on the word, knowing immediately that she'd stepped into a trap.

"Maybe." His hand snaked around her waist, pulling her close again. "Or maybe I'm not the only one good at manipulations."

He bent his head, and she lifted her hand to push him away, but apparently her fingers weren't with the program because they twined around the soft cotton of his shirt, urging him closer.

The kiss when it came was like an explosion. Heat rocketed through her with the power of fission. What was it with this man? He touched her and everything that mattered disintegrated in the path of her overwhelming desire for him.

He trailed kisses along the line of her jaw and the soft skin of her neck. She trembled at the touch and felt him smile. He moved lower, his tongue circling one taut nipple beneath the thin gauze of her shirt. Even with the material protecting her, she could feel the heat.

She arched her back, offering herself to him, knowing that it was probably a mistake, but too much on sensory overdrive to care. His hand slid inside the shirt and underneath the satin of her bra, his fingers tightening on her nipple, pleasure mixing with pain, her body tensing in anticipation.

His mouth moved to her bare breast, drawing the nipple and aureole deep inside his mouth, the moist suction threatening to send her over the edge. With a groan he swung her into his arms and carried her back into the companionway, down the hall until he reached a door at the end. Kicking it open, he carried her inside and then laid her down on the bed.

Celeste started to reach for him, but then stopped, surprised to see the anger reflected in the sea green of his eyes.

"Get some sleep," he said, his voice still hoarse with passion. "We've got a lot to do tomorrow." With that he turned on his heel and left the room, the sound of a key turning in the lock signaling the end of the encounter.

She curled into a ball, fighting angry tears, trying to figure out exactly what had just happened. One minute he was all over her, passion threatening to consume them both, and the next, he's locking her away like she was some sort of medieval chattel.

She leaped off the bed and tried the door handle, rattling it until her arm hurt. Next she tried the porthole that served as a window. It was firmly fastened, and even after she'd slammed it with the back of a chair, it refused to crack.

Exhausted, she down on the end of the bed, wondering if any gem, no matter how rare, could possibly be worth dealing with Marcus Diablo.

And what scared her the most was that the answer was yes—only the reality was that it didn't have anything at all to do with the Devil's Delight.

Marcus stood at the railing, staring out into the midnight wash of the sea. Traces of light like phantom trails glimmered green against the breaking waves, a chemical reaction that never failed to capture his imagination.

"You all right?" Faust had materialized as usual without a hint of his coming. "I heard you yelling."

"She makes me crazy."

"Some women are like that." There was a quiet smile in his friend's voice, and Marcus tightened his hand on the railing.

"I suppose. But not with me. There are too many secrets, Faust. And we've seen firsthand what happens when someone finds out the truth."

"You're speaking of Adelaide."

Adelaide Dumont had been the daughter of a preacher. An

innocent beauty whose heart had been as big as the sky. Marcus had fallen head over heels. He'd been young—at least by immortal standards—and he hadn't realized it was possible to feel so strongly for another person.

They'd spent a glorious summer together, doing all the stupid things young lovers do. Reading, talking, dreaming, and of course making love. And then he'd made a horrible mistake. He'd told her his secret, believing that the love they shared would make her understand.

But she didn't. In truth, she couldn't. Looking back on it now, he should have known. Should have predicted. But it was so normal for him—his parentage, his immortality—he'd only thought to share it with her, to open his heart completely. He'd never thought of how it would seem to her.

They'd found her in the vicarage, her father's dueling pistol still in her hand.

"It wasn't your fault, Marcus. She just couldn't deal with the enormity of it all."

"She couldn't handle the fact that I'm the devil's spawn. It's as simple as that. I was the very personification of the evil her father spent his lifetime railing against."

"No. That's not true. Maybe Adelaide saw it that way. But that doesn't make it true."

"And it doesn't change the fact that I will never allow a woman to get that close to me again."

"But if the woman really loved you . . ."

"You're saying that Adelaide didn't?"

"You were both very young." Faust's expression was unreadable in the shadows, but Marcus could still hear the concern in his voice.

Marcus

"The degree of maturity has nothing to do with it, Faust, nor the depth of affection. The end result will always be the same."

"Then why did you agree to work with her?" They weren't talking about Adelaide anymore.

"Because I need her father's help." Marcus sighed. "And because a part of me isn't ready to let her walk away."

Even though in the end, that's exactly what he'd have to do.

Chapter Five

"Adelaide," Marcus screamed, the world gone suddenly black. *"Adelaide."*

The dark seeped around him like a woolen cloak threatening to smother him. He fought against it, willing himself to see. It was a dream, he knew that, but it still had the power to hurt him. He had to wake up.

Struggling with the weight of the night, he pulled himself from sleep, struggling to light a candle. Anything to keep the night at bay. He patted at the nightstand trying to find the flint, but his fingers encountered nothing. Frantic now, he searched with both hands, finally locating it, but no amount of striking seemed to work, the darkness growing deeper with every second.

It's only a dream, his mind whispered. But he struggled to light the candle nevertheless. Finally, in desperation he reached for the candle itself. As if in touching the wax he'd somehow be able to conjure the light.

But instead his hand hit brass. Smooth, polished brass. Confused, he swung around to the side of the bed, his mind clearing.

There was no candle.

Only a lamp.

He reached for the switch and the cabin instantly flooded with light. Sweat trickled down his temple, and he brushed it away with an impatient hand. He needed air. Padding naked toward the door, he stopped, remembering that he was not alone, and reached behind him for a pair of sweats.

The air in the passageway was cooler, and as the last vestiges of the dream faded, Marcus fought his anger. Why the hell did he have to relive it all over and over again? Wasn't it enough that he'd gone through it once?

The light in the library beckoned. It was his sanctuary. Except for the hidden galleries at his estate in Monaco, it was the only place he truly found solace. He stepped into the room, stopping short at the sight of Celeste curled in a leather wing chair, still wearing nothing but her shirt.

She had her back turned to him, her attention on the book she held in her hand, an original copy of a work by Galileo.

"How the hell did you get out?" He had the satisfaction of seeing her jump, his anger disproportionate to the crime. But he couldn't help himself. The last thing he needed right now was to see her, half naked, sitting in his library as if she belonged there.

Her startled look turned sheepish, as she twisted to face him, a long, thin filament in her hand.

"Underwire."

He frowned not following the train of her thought.

"From my bra?" She motioned to her chest, now startlingly devoid of secondary reinforcements. As if reading his thoughts, she lifted the book to cover her chest, her cheeks flushed with color. "I don't like being imprisoned."

"I wasn't locking you in, I was . . ." The words were out before he could stop them, but he managed at least to cut off the ending. "Pretty resourceful of you," he concluded, trying to keep control of his rioting emotions.

"I've learned a few things along the way." There was definitely underlying meaning in her statement, but he wasn't ready to consider the fact.

"What are you reading?" He nodded toward the book.

"I'm not reading actually. It's in some archaic form of Italian. But the illustrations are amazing. Is this original? It must be worth a fortune."

"I suppose so. I never really thought about it. I've just always liked what the man has to say." He had been considered a fringe lunatic in his day, but even then Marcus had seen the wisdom in his observations.

"You can read this?"

He shrugged, knowing he was treading on treacherous ground. "I speak several languages." Most of them archaic, but there was no need to share the fact.

She frowned, clearly not pleased with his answer, but not willing to push. "You've got an amazing collection here." She waved at the books. "And most of them have your name in them."

"They're my books." It was his turn to frown as he struggled to follow the line of her thought.

"Yes, but, in most of them the ink is quite old. As old as the books actually. And some of them are inscriptions—from the original author." She waited, her look speculative.

He clenched a fist, forcing a calm he didn't feel. "Marcus is a family name, Celeste. The older inscriptions belong to my ancestors. I come from a long line of collectors."

"And a couple pirates, judging from those." She pointed at the bound ship's logs on one of the shelves.

"You've been busy."

"Just interested." She tilted her head, studying him. "I can see you on the high seas."

"There's not much of a place for pirates anymore." He tried but couldn't keep a wistful note from his voice. "Everything is about control these days. At least according to those"—he waved at his logs—"it used to be all about freedom."

"There are still ways to find freedom, Marcus. One just has to look a little harder, that's all." She closed the book, her eyes still narrowed in thought. "Besides, you're not that different from your predecessors."

"How so?" he asked, curious despite himself.

"You can plunder with the best of them. Just look at all the things in this room." She waved toward the Rodin sculpture and his recently acquired Venus. "And I know for a fact that this is only the tip of the proverbial iceberg." Her eyes darkened with memory. She'd been to his estate. Seen his collection. Hell, she'd stolen from it. "If you're any indication, I'd say modern piracy is alive and doing well. Your ancestors would be proud."

"You're not doing so badly yourself. Any pirates in your background?"

"Nope, just good old Georgia farmers, with a couple of bluestockings thrown in for good measure." She traced the gold leaf on the cover of the book with one finger, her mind obviously still working on the similarities between Marcus and his imagined ancestors.

"Why are you still here?" he asked, in an attempt to change the subject before she started connecting the dots. "I'd have thought you'd have hit the water the minute you gained your freedom."

She stared down at the pages of the book. "I figured you were right. That my best shot at finding the ruby was to work with you. At least until the right opportunity presents itself."

"A temporary truce?" He wasn't sure he was ready for it, but she was right: Having her along for the ride might prove useful.

She nodded, her eyes still wary. "As long as you don't try to lock me up again."

"I guess it depends on whether you're going to keep trying to run away."

"I wasn't running away. I told you that."

"Right." He nodded, leaning back against his desk, knowing full well that he was goading her.

"Look, I'm not the one who started something they couldn't finish."

He pushed off the desk, crossing over to her in one fluid stride. "I am perfectly capable of finishing what I start, princess. But I'm also equally capable of recognizing when I'm about to make a mistake."

Hurt flashed in her eyes, but was gone before he had time for regret, anger filling the void. "And what the hell makes you think I would have allowed you to continue? You do have a certain kind of charm. I'll admit that." She jumped to her feet, the distance between them only inches now. "But there are two groups of men in the world. The ones a woman can love. And the ones she only wants to sleep with. And believe, me, Marcus, no one would ever mistake you for the happily-ever-after type."

It was exactly what he'd told Faust he wanted. No entanglements. But hearing it from her lips was like a slap in the face.

Hell and damnation.

They stood for a moment staring at each other, the tension between them ratcheting tighter than a mainsail in a gale-force wind.

Her gaze collided with his, her eyes hungry. And with a little sigh, she threw herself at him, her skin soft against his bare chest. Then her lips found his, her kiss a wicked combination of come-on and surrender. And there was not a force on earth powerful enough for him to resist the attraction. He wanted her. Had wanted her from the moment he'd seen her again.

He opened his mouth, welcoming her inside, reveling in the thrust of his tongue against hers. They parried and dueled, using touch as a silent language, neither advancing or retreating but instead joining together in a tempestuous dance of emotion and sensation.

His hands moved in slow, languid circles across her back, the silky feel of her skin adding fuel to his rising passion. She moved closer, pressing against him until he could feel his throbbing erection against her thigh.

With a groan, he pushed her backward toward the desk, lifting her so that her legs straddled the corner, his mouth crushing hers, drinking her in, his need for her laid bare. She threaded her hands through his hair, pulling him closer, clearly wanting him as much as he wanted her.

Trailing hot kisses down her neck, he pushed back the filmy fabric of her shirt, baring her breasts. Dipping his head, he took one nipple into his mouth, biting softly, her answering moan sending liquid heat coursing through his groin. He circled her aureole with his tongue, then drew it further into his mouth, sucking until she pleaded with him for more.

Happy to comply, he slid his fingers under the elastic of her panties, teasing the soft skin at the juncture of her thighs.

"Please," she whispered, her voice shaking with need. *"Please."*

Slowly he slid a finger between the satiny folds of her labia, unerringly finding the nub marking the center of her desire. He circled it lazily, still sucking at her breast, her hair draped around his head like a curtain.

Then with a final kiss, he shifted back to her mouth, two fingers sliding deep inside her, his tongue mimicking the rhythm. He fed on her pleasure, the movement of her body against his as she strove to find release.

His mouth and hands possessed her, wanting nothing more now than to give her pleasure, to take her somewhere she had never been before.

She cried in frustration when he released her, but he just smiled, his eyes locked with hers as he knelt beside the desk, pushing open her knees. Her eyes widened, but then with a sigh she opened for him, her tongue moistening her lips as she leaned back to brace herself on her elbows.

He slid down her panties, lifted her left leg over his shoulder, and softly kissed the tender skin of her inner thighs. With a soft cry, she reached for him, urging him forward.

She tasted like the sea, sweet and salty, and he relished the power he felt in taking her to the edge of the precipice. He drove his tongue deep inside her, feeling her contract against him, his penis throbbing in anticipation.

He tasted her, drinking her in, pulling her soul from her body into his. The darkness surrounded them, comforting this time, her hands caressing him as he moved his tongue in and out, in and out, driving her higher and higher, until she lifted off the table, crying his name.

He stood then, gathering her trembling body in his arms, realizing that he too was shivering. But hers was from climax, his was from white-hot need. She rained kisses on his face as he carried her to his cabin, her body rubbing tantalizingly against his erection as they walked.

He pushed open the door and carried her into the room, letting her body slide against his as he released her, the simple touch nearly sending him into climax. The lamplight turned her hair to gold, and she stood for a moment, her eyes wide with question. Then as if some internal battle had been decided, she slid out of her shirt.

For a moment he considered refusing. Knowing that if he allowed himself this pleasure, there would be hell to pay. But she was so beautiful, and he ached for her in a way he had not ached for a woman in so damn many years.

Pushing the door shut, he turned back to her, waiting, knowing the next move had to be hers. She took a step toward him, reaching down to pull his sweats from his hips, her fingers trembling.

He covered his hand with hers. "You're sure."

She nodded.

"You were right, Celeste," he reminded her. "I'm not that kind of man."

"I know," she whispered, reaching up to brush her lips against his. It was a covenant of sorts, though he wasn't completely certain what it was he was agreeing to.

But in truth, he didn't care. And with a groan he pulled her hard against him, accepting what she offered, raising the ante with the fervor of his kiss.

They backed into the room, arms locked around each other, tongues tangling together with need. She slid her hands along the muscles of his chest, the contact setting his synapses on fire.

She teased him then, running her tongue along the edge of his nipple, laughing softly when it tightened under her touch. Then she dropped her hand, stroking first the ridge of his stomach and then the hard length of his penis, squeezing and stroking in a way that threatened to unman him on the spot.

"Bloody hell." The words ripped out of him on a sigh.

And she laughed again, the sound musical. She tightened her hold, the strokes longer now, faster. And he pulled away, swinging her into his arms again, his mouth branding her with his kiss.

He reached the bed and they fell back against the sheets, legs tangling together, as they rolled until she was on top, straddling him. She leaned down, her hair tickling his neck, her lips caressing the rough beginnings of his beard. Then she was everywhere, kissing and exploring, leaving nothing untouched, unloved.

Trembling with the sheer power of the feelings she evoked, he rolled over, pinning her beneath him, wanting nothing more than to feel himself deep within her heat. Catching her gaze, he waited, poised above her.

And she nodded, opening to him, and with one swift move he buried himself deep inside her, the contact beyond all imagination.

There was passion reflected in the depths of her eyes, passion and something else, something so tender it almost took his breath away. Slowly, almost languorously at first, he began to move, each slow thrust tormenting and delighting them both.

With a moan, she arched upward, driving him deeper, and the fury erupted, the storm reaching crescendo. They moved together faster and harder, each stroke ratcheting them upward.

Marcus

Marcus closed his eyes, and let himself go, surrendering to the moment. Together they moved in a sensual spiral higher and higher until they found release, the climax more amazing than anything he'd ever believed possible.

And in that moment of ecstasy, he held onto the fact that it was his name she called, his body she clung to—his soul she held in her hands.

Chapter Six

"Looks like we're almost there." Marcus stopped near an outcropping of rock, pointing ahead to a farmhouse hugging the side of mountain.

"Well, it certainly doesn't look like the home of a jewel thief." Celeste stopped, too, fighting for breath. This was practically the first time they'd stopped all day. They'd crossed three borders and a mountain range in record time, although having a private plane and then a Jaguar had certainly facilitated their speed.

Celeste couldn't help but be impressed with Marcus's efficiency. Had she tried to reach Austria on her own, she had to admit it would have taken considerably longer and certainly have been done in less comfort. However, the Jag was now sitting at the bottom of the mountain in front of an old barn, the road to the farmhouse too rutted to risk the low-slung vehicle.

Hiking, it seemed, was to be the order of the day.

Marcus started out again, taking the slope as if it were nothing, and she pushed on after him, determined to keep up at all costs. Despite the fact that she'd spent most of the day with the man, they'd hardly talked. At least not about anything consequential. Not that she was surprised. After all Marcus had made it perfectly clear last night that their liaison was temporary.

And even if he hadn't told her as much, his actions would have confirmed the fact. This morning she'd woken to an empty bed. Granted he'd taken the time to retrieve her clothes, leaving them folded neatly on a chair. She'd never claimed he was a cruel man. Just a brutally honest one. But it was clear he'd already moved on, his thoughts centered not on her, but on the quest for the ruby.

She'd found him with her father, discussing the possible hiding places Hans Weisbaum could have devised, the two of them caught up in the chase like little boys playing in their backyard. Only Faust had acknowledged her presence, and that was more disconcerting than anything. The man studied her with an intensity that suggested he was trying to read her mind.

Or see inside her soul.

The whole thing had made her uncomfortable, and if it hadn't been for a need to keep up with what was happening, she'd have been tempted to abandon ship once and for all. But she'd known she was competitive since the day Susie Wheeler had dared her to walk across a pipe spanning the Chatham River. She'd broken her arm and damn near drowned, but she'd persevered and made it across.

Nothing much had changed since then, and she was still determined to come out on top. Which meant she had to get the ruby.

Damn Marcus Diablo and whatever it was she was starting to feel for him.

So in truth his lack of emotional involvement was all for the best.

Her father had been searching for the Devil's Delight all of his adult life. Long before Celeste had become his second in command. She'd never understood totally why this particular piece meant so much to him. Perhaps it was the legend, or maybe just the rarity of the jewel itself. Perfect rubies of that size were almost nonexistent. It certainly wasn't about sharing it with the world. That much she was certain of.

Her father had designed a jewel-encrusted case that had been waiting for its occupant for more than twenty years now. The centerpiece of his collection. A collection that, by necessity, had to be hidden away, since he had no provenance for at least 60 percent of the pieces. But there was obvious joy in his possession.

She'd thought Marcus was the same. But despite the fact that he did own several priceless pieces, she had the feeling that she'd nailed it when she'd accused him of loving the hunt more than acquisition itself.

She shook her head and pulled her thoughts to the present. Whatever motivated Marcus Diablo wasn't her concern. Just a few more days and all of this would be over. Her father would have the Devil's Delight, and she'd be able to put Marcus out of her mind for good.

The little voice in her head mocked her, but she ignored it. Mind over matter. Or in this case determination over desire.

She'd done it once. She'd do it again.

"You okay?" Marcus asked, turning so suddenly she almost crashed into him.

"I'm fine. Sorry, just got a little distracted. I didn't mean to hold things up."

"Look"—he reached out to cup her face with his hand—"I didn't mean to leave you high and dry this morning. I just thought that maybe it would be better for you if your father didn't know we'd spent the night together."

"I wasn't thinking about last night." She sounded waspish, but it couldn't be helped. It was the only way she could think of to fight off an unsettling urge to cry. The man had a way of disarming her at the most unexpected moments. "I was thinking about the ruby."

"I see." His face shuttered and his hand dropped. For a moment she almost thought she'd hurt his feelings. But then he shrugged and turned back to continue the trek up to the farmhouse.

The building was typical of the region, a cinderblock rectangle, stuccoed white with a gabled roof. Geraniums decorated every window, the vivid color distracting the eye from the run-down appearance of the structure. Slightly to the left was a wooden barn attached to the house by a single-story passageway. In winter the passage would allow the farmer access to his stock without having to deal with the snow and ice.

Now, however, the soft clanking of cowbells filled the meadows, the brightly colored wildflowers dancing in the breeze. It was bucolic, like a Turner painting. Only the cows were Austrian, not English. Still it was a lovely sight.

"When we get there, it might be best to let me do the talking," Marcus said, slowing to fall into step with her.

"Because you're so much better with the English language?"

"Actually we might need to speak German, but I was really

thinking that this part of the world isn't as emancipated as some. And usually men here prefer dealing with other men."

"Wonderful. Just the thing to make my day. A chauvinist ex-Nazi on top of an enigmatic art thief with issues. Aren't I the lucky girl?" The minute the words were out she wished them back, but it was too late.

Fortunately, Marcus only laughed, the sound making several of the cows raise their heads to check out the newcomers.

Five minutes, and an almost vertical climb, later they reached the front steps of the house, giant pots of some sort of blue alpine flower flanking each side of the massive door. The flowers seemed so cheerful that Celeste was almost taken aback by the scowling aproned woman who emerged from the door.

She had the robust look of a country girl, bright red cheeks and braided hair, but her girlish days had long since passed, her once blond hair speckled heavily with gray, her well-rounded cheeks filling out her wrinkles. It was impossible to guess her age. Life could be harsh in the mountains. But Celeste guessed she was somewhere between forty-five and fifty.

"Was wollen Sie?" she asked, demanding to know why they were here. If this had been Montana, she'd have been holding a shotgun.

"Kennen Sie Hans Weisbaum?" Marcus asked, with a smile that could melt half the ice in Antarctica. The farm woman didn't blink.

"Ja. Er war mein Vater. Warum fragen Sie?"

Celeste tried to translate, fairly certain that the woman had identified Weisbaum as her father, but the rest of it was simply too fast to follow.

"Sprechen Sie Englisch?" Marcus asked. And Celeste found herself praying the woman would say yes. Without English, Marcus would be at a decided advantage since his German was obviously fluent.

"Ja." The woman nodded, her expression softening slightly.

"My name is Marcus and this is my colleague Celeste."

For some reason the word "colleague" grated on her nerves, but she pushed it aside. Now was not the time to get into it with Marcus.

"Why is it you wish to speak with my father?" the farm woman asked, pulling Celeste's thoughts back to the matter at hand.

"We are here on an urgent matter. Something to do with property he might have."

She frowned, her shoulders tightening again. "My father is dead, and whatever he may have been involved with, I assure you it died with him."

For a backwoods farm woman, the lady was pretty darn good with English.

"Fraulein Weisbaum."

"Frau Mueller," she corrected.

"Frau Mueller," Marcus continued, "we are not interested in anything your father may or may not have done. What we are trying to do is find a very valuable artifact, and we were led to believe your father might have been able to help us." He laid his hand upon her arm with the innate sensuality of a man who knew women—really well.

The thawing of Frau Mueller took less than six seconds. She looked down at his hand, then back at his face, her stern expression crumpling into dismay. "You are talking of the great stone, no?"

It couldn't be that easy. Celeste tried to keep her expression neutral, but astonishment was hard to contain.

"The Devil's Delight," Marcus said, almost on a whisper, his thumb massaging her forearm ever so slightly. Celeste couldn't decide if she was impressed or nauseated. A little of both probably.

"I do not like to speak the name. Please, come inside." She shot a look around the empty hillside as if she thought it might be full of armed intruders, and then motioned them through the door. Actually she motioned Marcus. Celeste was left to follow on her own.

The great room was rustic, but charming in its own way. A carved staircase led up to rooms on the second and third floors. Flames flickered in an open hearth, the warmth making the room seem stuffy, but still adding a sense of cheerfulness.

Two chairs were angled to face the fireplace, with a wooden bench sitting perpendicular in front of the window. Frau Mueller and Marcus took the chairs, leaving Celeste to the bench.

"You understand I do not know where it is," Frau Mueller was saying. "In point of fact I have never seen it. But I do know that it brought my father—my family—nothing but trouble."

"He brought it home with him from the war?"

"*Ja.*" She nodded, her face full of regret. "From the priest, he got it. My mother, she told him it would bring us bad luck. To take a holy thing is a sin." She looked to Marcus for confirmation, and he nodded his agreement. "They fought about it often. It was hard not to overhear. She died a month later."

"What happened?" Celeste asked, unable to stop herself.

Marcus shot her a look and then returned his attention to Frau Mueller. "If it's not too painful, Frau Mueller, we'd really like to know." He was back to massaging her arm.

"Please, call me Helga," she said, dabbing her eyes with the corner of her apron. "It was all so long ago."

"Anything to do with the ruby could be helpful, Helga," he urged, his voice purposefully soothing.

"She was walking up to the high pasture. Taking my father his lunch. But she fell and broke her neck."

"But that sounds like an accident," Celeste said, frowning at them both, feeling a lot like she'd dropped into some sort of Wagnerian parody.

"Perhaps. Except that my mother grew up on this mountain. And the place where she fell . . ." Frau Mueller paused for effect. "It was perfectly flat."

"And your father believed it was the ruby that caused her death," Marcus prompted.

"Not at first. But then other things kept happening. Our herd sickened. And my brother died. One thing after another. Our lives were intolerable. But still my father would not give it up."

"He kept it here?" For the first time Celeste heard a note of excitement in Marcus's voice.

"In the beginning, *ja*, he kept it here. But soon he realized that he would lose everything if he didn't get it out of the house. I begged him to sell it. Or to give it away. Even throw it into the lake. But he could not let it go. It possessed him. Controlled him to the point that he cared for nothing else."

"But you said he moved it."

"Yes. I got very ill. It was a horrible fever. The doctors could do nothing. And my father was afraid for me. I was all he had left. So he took the stone away. And slowly I recovered." She patted her leg and for the first time Celeste noticed the brace there.

"So he got rid of it?" Part of her was relieved, it sounded

horrible, but another part of her was disappointed. Despite the seeming danger, she knew her father would never quit until he too possessed the stone.

"Not, how do you say, um"—she struggled for the words—"for permanent. He merely took it from the farm. And since I did not ever see or touch the thing, I believe I was allowed to recover."

"How do you know your father kept it?"

"Because his luck did not change. Only mine. And indirectly, because of me, that of the farm." She waved her hand at the rolling meadowland outside the window. "He suffered greatly. From a rare form of cancer. It ate away at him for close to twenty years. And no matter how he tried, he could not find forgiveness for what he had done."

"But he tried?" Marcus was leaning forward now, his interest no longer feigned.

"I don't believe he ever let go of the ruby. He admitted to me that he still had it, once toward the end of his life, in a fit of delirium. But he would never talk of it again, and I didn't dare raise the question as I did not want to bring the curse down upon my family."

"No one else in the family has seen the same misfortune then?"

"There is no one left but me and my husband. The illness I had robbed me of the chance for *kinder*, I mean to say—children. But I know that my father spoke the truth. He still had the stone. He must have hidden it somewhere."

"You said something about seeking forgiveness?" Marcus asked, reaching out for her hand, this time in true sympathy.

"Yes. He tried to seek absolution."

"In the church?" Celeste asked. Maybe there was a priest who knew where the stone was.

"No." She shook her head. "He was afraid to go to there. But I know that he tried to right his transgression in other ways. He spent the last part of his life decorating the skulls of the dead, and tending the *beinhaus* in Hallstadt."

"Beinhaus?" Celeste asked, uncertain of the translation.

Frau Mueller looked to Marcus for help.

"In English we call it a charnel house."

Celeste shivered, an old memory surfacing.

"You all right?" Marcus asked, and if she hadn't known better, she'd have said he was actually concerned.

"Just never understood the tradition."

"It is common sense." Frau Mueller shrugged. "In Hallstadt, there is only so much land for burial. After so much time, we must— *bewegung,*" she said, looking again to Marcus for translation.

"The word is 'move.'"

"Ja. So." She nodded. "We must move them."

"Dig them up you mean." Celeste tried but couldn't contain her frown.

"It is our way." She crossed her arms as if daring Celeste to argue. "It is not as if we abandon them. They are placed in the charnel house."

"So the heads are . . . ?"

"All people who lived and died in or near Hallstadt. There are many centuries represented. It is a tribute to them, the painting."

"And your father helped to create the tribute."

"Yes. But with him it became almost as much of an obsession as his desire to keep the ruby. He had always loved the place. He often told stories of playing there as a child. And I'd like to believe that at least in part he found peace in tending the dead. But I do not know for certain that this is true."

Celeste thought it a macabre way to seek redemption, but then she didn't believe in curses, so from her point of view the whole endeavor was pointless. Accidents happened and people contracted horrible illness. Owning a glassy piece of corundum was not a sin. No matter the size or the stories connected with it. Still, she couldn't help feeling sorry for Frau Mueller.

"Is this your father?" She held up a picture of an old man standing in front of what looked to be a pile of skulls. Lovely.

"*Ja.*" The woman reached for the frame. "That was taken in Hallstadt. Not too long before he died. He gave it to me. For the memories."

"Is that the charnel house?" Marcus asked.

"*Ja.* See." She pointed proudly at a skull just above her father's shoulder. "*Das* is his work."

"It's lovely," Celeste managed, suppressing a shiver of revulsion.

"Do you mind if we borrow this, Helga?" Marcus asked, the silky tone back in his voice.

"Take it," she said. "Maybe if you find the ruby, my father can at last rest in peace."

"Is he buried at the charnel house?" Celeste asked.

"No." Frau Mueller shook her head. "When the church began to allow cremation, we were given a better option. My father's ashes were scattered to the mountains he loved." She looked out of the window, tears cresting in her eyes.

"I think that we have taken enough of your time, Helga,"

Marcus said, taking the photo. "I promise I'll see that this is returned."

"Just find the Devil's Delight. It is aptly named. And when you find it"—she widened her gaze, for the first time including Celeste—"you would do well to destroy it, before it has the chance to destroy you."

Chapter Seven

"You don't actually believe that the stone is cursed, do you?" Celeste asked, not bothering to keep the disdain from her voice.

Perched on the cliffs that edged one of the most beautiful lakes in Austria, Hallstadt had clung to the side of the mountains in the Salzkammergut for almost five thousand years. By the time they'd reached it, the village was shutting down for the night. Fortunately, they'd had no trouble finding a *gasthaus*, the plan being to hole up for the night and dissect the information they had so far, trying to come up with some kind of lead.

A four-story ochre affair complete with the requisite geraniums hanging from tiny balconies, the inn was clean and hospitable in the way only Austrians seemed capable of replicating. Their rooms were adjacent to one another, but considering the fact that Celeste didn't trust herself around the man, she'd insisted on the lounge.

Nursing a *viertel* of wine, she waited for Marcus's response, surprised that he didn't immediately agree. "You don't believe it, do you?"

"I learned a long time ago never to discount anything. But do I think the ruby is inherently dangerous? No. At least not to me." He swirled the beer in his stein, contemplating the foamy liquid inside.

"Well, don't think for a minute that you're going to psyche me out of trying to find the Devil's Delight. Because it's not going to happen."

"I'm not trying to frighten you, Celeste. I'm just stating the truth."

"The ruby can't hurt *you*."

"It can't." His sigh was disproportionate to the overall tone of the discussion and she frowned.

"Are you all right?"

"I'm fine." He took a sip of his beer. "Just a little tired. It's been a long day. And we don't have a whole hell of a lot to show for it."

"Well, we know that Weisbaum got his hands on the ruby and that he brought it to Austria."

"But we don't know where it is now." He stood up and walked over to look out of the window. Lightning flashed to the east, back-lighting the mountains. "There's a storm coming."

Somehow it suited her mood. "We can be pretty sure the stone hasn't gone far, though. Weisbaum spent most of his time here and at the farm. If he was as obsessed with the ruby as his daughter led us to believe, I'm betting he didn't let it get too far out of sight."

"That still leaves a lot of ground to cover." He turned to face her again, a clap of thunder shaking the house. The owners had disappeared, leaving them to their privacy. It was too early for tourists, so they pretty much had the place to themselves.

"Well, there's got to be a clue in something she said."

"He seems to have developed a latent interest in redemption." Marcus leaned back against the windowsill, the lightning highlighting the blue-black of his hair.

"But not enough to get rid of the stone." She stared down at the photograph in her hand, willing Herr Weisbaum to tell her his secret.

"So where does that leave us?" Marcus finished his beer, setting the stein next to the pitcher the hostess had left.

"Well, he worked at the charnel house." She tilted her glass, trying to put the puzzle pieces together. "So maybe that narrows our focus. Although it seems a pretty public place."

"It's certainly contained," he agreed. "But maybe that's a clue. The man did spend a hell of a lot of time there."

"Painting skulls." Thunder underscored her words.

"As Helga said, it's tradition. And in its way it's a demonstration of love. Even if it seems a bit ghoulish by our standards."

"Maybe so. But once when I was little, my father took me to a place like that, somewhere here in Austria, I think. Anyway everything inside was made of bones. *Human* bones. There was even a chandelier of sorts, made out of thighs and pelvises." She crossed her arms, shivering. "I got sick and ran out. My father made fun of me. Called me weak. God, I don't know why I'm telling you this."

"Because it hurt you." He'd moved so that he was standing by her chair, looking down at her, his green eyes looking eerie in the half light. "And for the record, 'weak' is the last word I'd use to describe you, Celeste."

Except when it came to the man standing in front of her, she actually agreed, but she'd had to work long and hard to achieve the state. The lights flickered with a bright flash of lightning, the celestial spear followed almost immediately by a crash of thunder.

Celeste stood up and walked to the window, purposely increasing the distance between them. "So tomorrow we'll go to the charnel house? See if there's something up there."

"You really up to it?"

"You just told me I wasn't weak. I'll manage. Besides I'm not a kid anymore."

"Believe me, I'm more than aware of that fact." Marcus came to stand behind her, watching the storm as it unleashed its fury.

The wind whipped across the yard, spraying gravel against the window, and she jumped back startled, his arms closing around her waist to steady her. She started to pull free, but before she could move the lights went out, plunging the lounge into darkness.

His grip tightened, and reflexively she turned to face him. The storm gathered fury, rain lashing the window, lightning flickering through the room with the power of a strobe. One second Marcus's face was illuminated, their eyes locked in silent communication, and then the image was gone, his heat the only physical proof she had that he was still standing there.

But heat was more than enough.

Framing her face with his hands, he bent his head, his mouth slanting over hers, the moment before contact seeming to last an eternity, and then when his lips touched hers, it was as if something inside her combusted, a fire blazing with the fury of the storm outside.

It was almost as if it were only the two of them, bound together by the kiss. Nothing else was real. There was only this moment, this man. She threaded her hands through his hair, pulling him closer, opening her mouth, delighting in the taste of him.

He dropped his hands, one sliding to the small of her back, urging her closer still, the other cupping her breast, rolling her nipple between his thumb and forefinger, the exquisite pressure triggering ripples of heat, pooling between her legs.

With a groan, he swept her into his arms, taking the stairs as if she weighed nothing. In seconds they were in his room, the storm outside still rattling the windows, sheets of rain beating against the glass.

He dropped his arms, his body sliding against hers, the friction unbearable. She tore at his shirt, mindless of buttons. In turn, he pulled off her sweater, making short work of her bra, and then pressed her to him, his lips on her eyes, her cheeks, her ears, and her neck, licking, stroking, each rasp of his tongue setting her nerves on fire.

She grabbed his head then, forcing a kiss, her tongue sliding deep into his mouth, wanting to possess him as he had possessed her. They moved backward until her body was braced against the wall, his penis hard against her belly. Fumbling in her need, she tore at his zipper, sliding it down with trembling hands. Breaking contact for only a moment, he removed his pants, and watched silently as she slid out of her panties, her skirt joining them on the wooden floor.

The bed was only a few steps away, but they couldn't wait, and he pressed her back against the wall, lifting her up so that she could twine her legs around him, opening herself for him as he thrust into her. The door leading to the balcony blew open with the force of the storm, cold rain drenching them as he thrust harder and harder, the two of them struggling for rhythm, striving for release.

Pleasure surpassed itself until it bordered on pain, every muscle responding to her need for release. He kissed her face and breasts, biting her nipples, and using his hands on her hips to push himself deeper—and then deeper still.

She screamed his name, certain now that she was riding the thunder, and then the world split into white-hot light and she forgot where he ended and she began, wanting only for the pleasure to go on forever.

Shaking now from the sheer joy of it, she drifted slowly back to reality, his body hot in contrast to the cool of the rain. The thunder faded as he held her against the wall, his breathing ragged, their bodies still connected.

Then gently, he carried her to the bed, as if she were the most precious thing in his universe. And she smiled up at him, watching through layers of contentment as he secured the door, and then lay down beside her.

His kisses now were almost reverent, as he cherished what he had moments before so violently taken. His hands and his tongue moved over her in a leisurely exploration that sent spirals of sensation dancing through her, her body reawakening to his touch, the banked heat beginning to build again.

He kissed her shoulders and the soft skin along the inside of her arms, stopping to leisurely suck on each of her fingers. Then he kissed his way across her belly, giving equal attention to the hand resting there, then up the other arm with tiny kisses that led to her ear, his tongue tracing the whorl, then drawing her earlobe into his mouth, the gentle sucking sending her squirming against the bed.

With a smile, he slid lower, kissing the tender skin of her feet and ankles, moving ever so slowly upward, ratcheting up her need with every stroke, every kiss, his hands clearing the way— massaging, kneading, exposing nerves she hadn't even known she possessed.

And then just when she thought she couldn't possibly feel any more—when she was certain he'd satiated every part of her—he pushed her legs apart, his hair tickling the skin high on the inside of her thighs. One minute she closed her eyes in anticipation and the next she was arching off the bed, his hands holding her hips in place as he sucked her clitoris, each stroke of his tongue sending her closer and closer to the edge.

She threaded her fingers through his hair, urging him onward, her mind splintering with her rising desire. Color formed behind her eyelids, burning hot, and she almost forgot to breathe. She was close, so close . . . and then he was gone.

The cold air taunted her.

She opened her mouth to protest, but he was there again, on top of her. She lifted, opening, wanting nothing more than to be a part of him, her need for him overriding everything else. And then he was there, inside her, and they were moving together, the friction unbearable, her pleasure and his coming together into a crescendo of light and sound and magic unlike anything she'd ever experienced, for a moment she was afraid, frozen on the edge of nothingness.

And then she could feel his fingers linking with hers, feel his body moving inside her, and she let go, the world disappearing into the fury of their climax against the soft rumble of the dying storm.

The room had grown cold with the passing of the storm and Celeste shifted sleepily under the comforter, reaching for Marcus's warmth. When her hands encountered nothing but down, she opened her eyes, frustration quickly turning to alarm.

Marcus's side of the bed was empty.

She'd been duped again.

Moving with a haste that belied the fact she'd been sleeping only moments before, she started to gather her clothes, then abandoned the idea in favor of the neatly folded ones in her room. Marcus had undoubtedly gone to search for the ruby, taking advantage of the fact that she'd been lulled into a passion-induced coma. She cursed herself for her stupidity, wondering if it was already too late.

Maybe he'd managed to figure out where Hans had hidden the stone. Or maybe he'd known all along. She ran through the things that Frau Mueller had said as she pulled on jeans and a sweater. The only conceivable place was the charnel house. But nothing beyond Hans's seeming obsession with making restitution seemed to point to the little cemetery.

Still it was a starting point, and if she was lucky, maybe she'd catch Marcus before he had the chance to find the Devil's Delight. She bent down to tie the laces on her boots, and then tiptoed back out into the hallway. The door to Marcus's room was still open.

And the room was empty.

How could she have been so stupid?

She moved quickly down the stairs, trying to remember exactly where the charnel house was. She'd found it on the map, but hadn't bothered to translate its location from paper to reality. Another mistake.

And to top it off, Marcus would have the car. Which meant that she would have the further disadvantage of having to find transportation should it turn out that he'd already left Hallstadt.

At the bottom of the stairs, she hesitated for a moment, her heart twisting at the thought that what had seemed so beautiful had in fact been nothing more than a sham. Fool me once . . . the saying went. Well, she'd definitely been played. And there was no question of blaming anyone but herself. She'd known better. Walked into it with her eyes open, and damn it all to hell, she'd let need override common sense.

Her father would never forgive her if she let the Devil's Delight slip through her fingers. *Never.* Squaring her shoulders, she headed for the front door. She'd be damned if she'd let Marcus Diablo get the better of her.

"Going somewhere?" The familiar voice rasped through the dark like black velvet.

"Marcus." She spun around, trying to find him in the shadows. As if on cue, the clouds shifted and a shaft of moonlight illuminated him. He was sitting in the wing chair, barefoot and barechested, his jeans not even fastened properly.

She swallowed, just the sight of him sending her pheromones into overdrive.

He hadn't gone anywhere.

"Running out on me, again?" There was a mocking note in his voice that she hadn't heard before.

"No. I . . . No." She stuttered, trying to think, trying to pull herself together. She'd been so certain that he had deserted her.

"Well, you could have fooled me." His eyes traveled from her head to her toes, taking in the heavy sweater, the boots—definitely traveling gear.

"I woke up and you . . . you were gone." She hated that she sounded apologetic. He was the one who'd gone missing. Not her. And yet here she was defending herself. "Damn it, Marcus, I thought *you'd* run out on me."

"Well, that hardly seems likely now, does it?" He laughed, waving a hand at his bare chest. And what a chest it was.

"I didn't know."

"You could have checked before running off with guns cocked and loaded."

"I'm not . . ." She stopped, anger rising. "What did you expect me to think? It's not like you haven't made it perfectly clear that I'm—what did you call it—a tagalong? That we're only working together because my father forced it. That I am nothing more than a momentary distraction, a sexual conquest to be used and discarded." The last came out before she could stop herself.

He was across the room in the second, eyes flashing. "I'll admit I have used women to get what I want. I'll even admit that the first time I slept with you it was with one eye on the prize; however, tonight was not about anything but the two of us. I don't know what the hell it is between us. But it's there and you can't deny it any more than I can. It takes two to make love, Celeste, and at least by my recollection, you were right there with me."

"But you told me yourself there's no future in it."

"There isn't." His face shuttered, all expression lost, and she fought the urge to reach out and touch him, to try to bring it back. "There can't be. I'm not the kind of man who can settle down."

"Well, maybe I'm not the kind of woman who wants to."

"All women want a future, Celeste. And I can't give that to you. It's as simple as that."

"So, what? You take the ruby and you're out of my life?"

"Something like that." He shrugged, running a hand through his hair, the gesture making him seem less hardened, younger— almost vulnerable. "Look, I don't want to discuss this. I didn't run out on you. That's the point. I couldn't sleep so I came down here to look at the photograph Helga gave us."

"In the dark."

His teeth were white against the stubble of his beard. "Yeah. I've got superpowered vision. Didn't I tell you?"

"That's not funny." And it wasn't, although she couldn't exactly put her finger on why. There was just something about him that made her feel like anything was possible. She shook her head and reached for the lamp, the light blinding for a moment until her eyes adjusted.

He looked even more devastating in the light, and she swallowed the urge to tell him to go put a shirt on. Surely she could handle her libido enough to keep from letting his half-dressed state distract her—again.

"I had the lamp on earlier. I just turned it off so that I could think."

"About?"

His eyes met hers, his gaze intense. "Everything."

The word hung between them for a moment, and she debated trying to get him to say more, but knew it would most likely be a fruitless exercise. Marcus wasn't the kind of man to discuss his feelings. He'd said there couldn't be a future. And whether she agreed or not, she knew that no amount of argument would change the fact.

And in all honesty, she wasn't certain what she'd argue for. She'd never really thought of her life beyond her work with her father. There'd been men of course, but no one of consequence.

And then Marcus had come along all brash and self-contained, and he'd swept her literally off her feet. But then, just as easily, he'd deceived her and left her high and dry—although she'd turned the tables quite nicely, thank you very much.

But still she hadn't been able to stop herself from wishing it had played out differently. And now he was back. Only nothing had changed. Except that the thought of him walking away again left her feeling so empty inside.

None of which she was going to share with him.

"So did you come up with anything? About where Hans might have hidden the ruby, I mean?" It was a coward's way out. But there was something compelling in the idea of self-protection.

"No." He shook his head, accepting the change of subject. She swallowed her disappointment. "Just that the charnel house seems as logical a place as any. The photograph doesn't really reveal anything. And I even studied it with a magnifying glass on the off chance that there was something."

She'd done the same earlier and come to a similar conclusion. But she picked the photo up again and stared at it, willing inspiration to hit. The picture showed a somber-looking Hans Weisbaum standing in front of an artfully arranged pyramid of bones.

On closer examination, one could see that some of the skulls were artfully painted with rose garlands, strands of ivy, and the occasional black cross, the deceased's name and date of death stenciled in black script. M. J. Schmidt, 1879. Liesl Gasterman, 1899. Sandor Balog, 1965. Michael Stuben, 1654. T. G., 1981. L. Prager, 1922. F. M. Heinnman, 1785. And the list went on. Memories contained in the calcified remains of what was once human. Edgar Allan Poe with a folk-art twist.

"The photograph shows only a small part of the charnel house," she said, setting the picture back on the table. "Maybe there's something else there that will give us a clue."

"No time like the present." Marcus stood up.

"But it's not even daylight yet."

"It will be soon. And the rain's stopped. So unless you're afraid of ghosts, I don't think we have anything to worry about."

"I don't believe in ghosts or cursed stones, or any kind of magic for that matter. I believe in what I can see. The rest of it, I'll leave for the clerics and psychics."

"All lumped together." He laughed, but his eyes didn't reflect the emotion, and she wondered what she could have said to upset him, then dismissed the notion altogether. She was just being oversensitive. Which wasn't all that surprising, considering the situation.

"Something like that." She shrugged. "But if we're going to go to the charnel house, I think maybe you need to dress a little more appropriately?"

He looked down at himself, and then bowed, the movement courtly and mocking all at the same time. "Right then, clothes for milady. I'd hate to offend your sensibilities."

She opened her mouth to retort, but he was already gone.

Marcus

Maybe Marcus Diablo *was* a pirate. Or at least had his ancestor's blood flowing in his veins. Either way she had the sudden premonition that she was playing with fire.

And even an idiot knew that was the fast track for getting burned.

Chapter Eight

"There's nothing here." Celeste said, sinking down to the ground, her head in her hands.

They'd been over the place three times, with nothing to show for it. The charnel house hadn't been locked, which in a small village in Austria wasn't really all that surprising. There was a respect for the dead here. That and a healthy fear of the authorities. Other countries could take a lesson.

Marcus joined her on the gravel-covered floor. "There's got to be something we're missing." He let his eyes travel around the length of the room. It was small and simple, the stone façade without adornment except for a large crucifix.

Three walls were covered with rows of skulls resting on femurs and tibias packed together in such a way as to provide a shelf of sorts. The back wall held an additional level of painted heads, resting on a crude wooden shelf, votive candles adding an eerie light as dawn broke over the mountains outside.

"Hans must have been standing there in the photograph." Celeste pointed to the left-hand corner of the *beinhaus*. He was surprised at how well she seemed to be handling it all considering her aversion for human remains. He supposed he should have given her more credit. She had been anything but incompetent the first time he'd met her. It's just that in trying to put her out of his mind, somehow he'd forgotten all of that.

He wasn't allowing himself to examine the depth of his feelings for the woman; it wouldn't serve any purpose, but admitting that he admired her surely couldn't hurt. Although that's as far as it could go. In the end, he was going to betray her trust. He was going take the ruby.

He'd accepted his father's challenge because of the prospect of besting his brothers. And the idea still held great appeal. But if he were honest, he'd also have to admit that he'd accepted because his father had asked so very little of him in his life. And now because of that he intended to keep his end of the bargain. Even if it meant hurting Celeste in the process.

In truth, some things were just not meant to be. And even if the chemistry was amazing, hell, even if he cared about her, there were limitations that simply couldn't be overcome. His parentage for one. The fact of his immortality another.

He'd tried to be normal once, centuries ago, and that had ended in disaster. Since then he'd managed to avoid entanglements that threatened his heart. Hell, he'd thought the thing long dead.

Turns out he'd been wrong.

But that didn't change anything.

"Earth to Marcus," Celeste prompted, her breath crystallizing in the morning air.

He shook his head, clearing his thoughts. "Sorry," he said with a sardonic smile. "Too much late-night activity."

She blushed and ducked her head as he pulled the snapshot out of his pocket. Celeste was a strange combination of sophistication and innocence, the combination seductive in a way he would never have predicted. He stared down at the picture, then at the area of the charnel house Celeste had indicated. "I think you're right about where he was standing. But I'm not sure what that tells us."

"Probably nothing," she sighed, taking the picture from him. "But if there is anything here, then I'm betting the photograph is a clue. Frau Mueller said that Hans gave it to her for memory. An odd way of putting it surely."

"Could just be that she got her English mixed up."

"Maybe. Or maybe he was trying to make a point. Telling her there was something special about the photograph. Or the part of the charnel house pictured there."

"It's certainly possible, although we haven't seen anything here to support the fact." Marcus frowned, jumping to his feet. "But it's worth looking again." He walked over to the corner of the room, bending so that he could more closely examine the skulls there.

They came in all sizes, some pristine white, others blackened or yellowed with age. And they all shared something that would forever elude Marcus—closure. An ending of sorts. Perhaps life would seem sweeter when one knew it could be taken at any moment. Or then again, maybe not.

"Marcus?" Celeste's voice held a note of excitement. "When did Frau Mueller say the church began allowing cremation?"

"Sometime in the sixties." He turned to face her. "What's that got to do with anything?"

"There's a skull here in the photograph dated 1981. With the initials T. G."

Marcus frowned. "Theloneous Gerard. It couldn't be that simple."

"Is it there?" She'd risen to her feet and had come to stand beside him, her gaze locked on the rows of skulls.

"I don't see it. Let's try counting from the votive in the picture and see if that helps."

Celeste counted silently, her finger bobbing as she moved along the line. "No luck."

"All right. Let's try it from the other side. Maybe we're wrong about where he was standing. Or he wants us to try the inverse of the photograph."

They counted again this time from the right, and again came up empty-handed.

"Maybe it's been moved?" Her earlier enthusiasm had faded. "I mean it's been years since the picture was taken. If someone saw the fake, they'd have moved it, right?"

"Yes." Marcus nodded, his mind turning over the puzzle. "Which makes the whole thing sort of an odd gamble. I mean why mark something in a photograph that he could be fairly certain would eventually be discovered and removed? That doesn't make sense."

"So then what does it mean?" Celeste asked, clearly exasperated.

"Hang on." He held up a hand, counting again along the left side, until he got to the place the 1981 skull should have been. "You were right."

Celeste moved closer, her nearness setting off synaptic explosions that had nothing at all to do with Hans Weisbaum and his riddles. Marcus sucked in a breath, steeling himself to the task at hand.

"Look. The date on this skull is 1891." He waited for her to see the relevance.

"Oh, my God, it's a palindrome of sorts: 1891—1981."

"Exactly." He wasn't sure exactly why he was so pleased that she'd gotten it, but he was. "And it gets better. Look at the name."

"Gerta Thode." She smiled. "Theloneous Gerard. The initials are backward, but they work."

"Could be a false lead, but it seems probable. Do you want to do the honors, or shall I?"

To her credit she actually seemed to think about it a moment, then shivered and stepped back. "You do it."

Marcus reached down and carefully grasped the skull, pulling upward in an effort not to disturb the others surrounding it. Nothing happened. He held the skull up, turning it in the early morning light, searching the various orifices for signs of a note or perhaps carving of some sort. But there was nothing seemingly out of the ordinary. Only the requisite ivy leaves curling around the letters and numbers.

"It looks old, so it must be the real thing," Celeste said. "But it can't be a coincidence that Hans replaced it in the photograph. There has to be something more. Maybe the name is meant to throw us off. A blinding glimpse of the obvious."

"All right." Marcus lowered the skull to study it more closely. Celeste edged closer as well, looking at it from around his shoulder. He contained a smile. "It won't bite."

"I know that," she snapped, but still didn't move. For a woman who had declared her fervent disbelief in ghosts and curses she seemed to entertain a rather sizable belief in the power of the dead. Her hand was hot on his arm, and he resisted the urge to move away and break the contact. "Look at the tendrils on the ivy," she said, her grip tightening. It's as if they've been modified." She moved around him, her curiosity overriding her fear. "The paint is darker here, see?"

He looked at where she pointed on the skull, and sure enough the tendrils that curled around the date were a different color of green. He squinted and then tilted the skull, trying to make the most of the light coming from the doorway. "They looks like L's and R's."

"Left and right." She frowned, concentrating, then smiled, excitement sparkling in her eyes. " I think it's a combination."

"To what?"

"The skulls. Put Gerta back." She motioned to the gap where the skull had been resting.

"Gerta?" he asked, suppressing a smile.

"Well, we can't keep calling her 'the skull.' And it *is* her name."

"Fine. I'll put her back." He gently laid the skull back into its row.

"Okay. So the first tendril is an L. And the first number is a one. So I'm thinking we move one skull to the left. Michael." She pronounced the name with a German flourish.

"All right. So the next tendril is an R. According to your theory we'd move right eight skulls to . . . ," he said, counting carefully over from Michael, "Friedrich."

Celeste consulted Gerta's skull again. "The next one is an L. So left nine. That puts us one to the left of Michael. Sandor." She patted him on the head, apparently having completely forgotten her reticence.

"So what's the last one?"

Celeste bent down to study the skull. "Left again."

Marcus moved down the line, passing Sandor and stopping at his neighbor Liesl Gasterman. The skull looked much like all the others, except that it seemed more bleached than either of its neighbors.

"So pick it up," Celeste urged, standing at his elbow, enthusiasm coloring her voice.

Marcus reached out for the skull, closed his hand over the top and lifted upward. "It's not moving." He tried again, but it seemed Liesl was stuck in place.

"Try pushing," Celeste suggested.

He pressed downward. There was an audible click, but nothing happened. "It's still not moving."

"Maybe *it* didn't," Celeste said, all playfulness disappearing from her voice, "but *that* did." She pointed to a two-foot section of the thigh bones supporting the skulls. The section was in fact a façade, the partial bones meant to camouflage the opening behind. Pressing Liesl's skull had swung the "door" outward.

Marcus walked over to the bone door and pulled it wider, revealing a hole with a rickety-looking wooden ladder descending down into the dark.

"Great. A hole into Hell," Celeste said, staring down into the dank darkness.

"Or a treasure chamber." Marcus moved toward the opening, turning on this flashlight.

"You're not going down there?" Celeste protested. "It could be a trap. Or a grave." She shivered again.

"I suspect it's the catacombs. There have to be more skulls than what we're seeing here. Or maybe it's just a tunnel between the graves outside. Either way it's obvious that Hans rigged this door. And if he went to all that trouble, then my guess is there's a reason."

"Beyond his preoccupation with the dead." Celeste still didn't look convinced.

"Look, you stay here, and I'll go down and check it out."

"And take the ruby? No way." She shook her head to emphasize her point. "I haven't come this far to let you win by default."

"All right then." He grinned. "Ladies first."

She actually took a step back, but then squared her shoulders and moved toward the hole. "Fine. I'll go." She reached into the pocket of her coat and pulled out her flashlight. The beam dipped down into the dark and then disappeared.

"You're sure?"

"I'm not afraid, if that's what you're implying." Her shoulders tightened, the tension a direct contradiction of her words, as she sat on the edge, then twisted around so that her feet were on the ladder. "See you at the bottom," she said, her voice light, the glow of her flashlight fading as she disappeared into the hole.

If nothing else, he had to admire her courage.

Although if he were being completely honest, he'd have to admit admiring a hell of a lot more than that.

The ladder ended about four feet from the ground, the wood rotting away in the damp. Celeste pointed the flashlight downward, but couldn't really see much except what looked to be a mud floor. Praying that she wasn't jumping onto some ancient citizen of

Hallstadt, she let go of the ladder, bending her knees as she hit the ground to absorb the impact. Turning in a circle, she illuminated the area, delighted to see nothing more than a passage leading off to the right.

Marcus dropped down behind her, his presence filling the cavern. He'd always seemed larger than life to her, and somehow down here the image was only amplified. Still, she had to admit she was glad he was here. It was one thing to deny things that go bump in the night in the light of the day. Standing underneath a cemetery was another thing altogether.

"So looks like we follow the passage," Marcus said, his breath stirring the hairs on the back of her neck.

She nodded, shining the flashlight down the passage but still not moving.

He took her hand, his fingers tightening around hers. "It's just a passageway."

Any other man would have pushed past her. Or made fun of her. But he did neither, merely stood there waiting for her to find her courage, and somehow that made it easier to move forward.

The corridor was really no more than a tunnel, moisture-slick rock and dirt glistening in the light from their flashlights. They moved forward without incident for about thirty yards, and then suddenly the tunnel made a ninety-degree turn to the right, the floor sloping sharply downward.

The opening was shored up with rocks, as if the tunnel they'd just traversed had been dug specifically to intersect with the one shooting off from it. The remnants of an arch, dead ahead, was filled with ancient rubble.

"Looks like this used to be an entrance of some sort," Marcus said, pushing past her to examine the old doorway. "I think I was right. This is an old catacomb. Hans must have known about it. And built the connecting tunnel."

"So much for redemption."

"Maybe it's not all it's cracked up to be." Marcus shrugged and started down the new tunnel, not giving her time for rebuttal.

After about ten feet, the tunnel widened to a full-fledged passageway, cobble stones replacing the muddy floor. Marcus moved into the space first, sending the flashlight beam in a wide arc across the open area.

Celeste wished he hadn't. The walls here weren't actually walls at all, but cubbyholes of sorts. Human cubbyholes. Or rather indentations holding human remains. In the shadowy light many looked as if they were sleeping. Curled on their sides, hands splayed. But others . . . others looked as if they hadn't gone willingly. A trick of the light and decay no doubt, but the image was the kind that burned into your brain.

"Let's just keep moving, please." Amazingly her voice was steady. And she took strength from the fact, pushing past Marcus, intent on taking the lead, but his hand on her arm stopped her.

"They're long dead, Celeste. They can't hurt you."

"I know that." She jerked her arm away and pressed past him, alarmed that his touch had been far more disturbing than the bodies on either side of her. She was in way over her head.

They continued on for another twenty or thirty yards, and then suddenly the crypt ended in a stone archway. They stepped through it into a small chamber, their flashlights illuminating the remains of what had probably once been an altar. The center of the wall held a sandstone inlay, an oval inside of it containing a fresco. It was faded in places almost making it unrecognizable, but the gleam of a sword, the faded image of a knight, and the green of what could be a dragon's tail seemed to indicate St. George.

"Dead end," Celeste said, shining her flashlight around the room. "There's no other way out. So, what now?"

"Hans didn't dig that tunnel for nothing. There has to be something here that will lead us to the ruby."

"Well, the stone has been linked to the devil obviously, and more obscurely to Aaron and to Jesus," Celeste said, turning in a slow circle trying to find more artwork. "But I don't see anything here connected to any of them."

Marcus was standing by the altar, running his hands over the remaining stones. "No trick doors, either. At least not that I'm seeing. Maybe we need to go back to the beginning and start examining the niches. It could be the ruby is hidden with one of the bodies."

Celeste started to protest, the idea making her physically ill, but before she could finish the thought, another popped into its place.

"The monks at Avignon. They had a patron saint. I saw an effigy in the chapel when I was breaking in."

He turned toward her, shaking his head, clearly not following her train of thought.

"St. George. The patron saint of Theloneous Gerard's order is *St. George.*"

They turned together, Marcus's flashlight illuminating the fresco. In the direct light, the raised sword glimmered brightly, pointing downward at a spot in the floor. The cobblestone there was dusty, but through the glazing of dirt the painted cross was clear.

Marcus smiled. It seemed that X marked the spot.

Very apropos.

"So what do we do?" Celeste asked, already walking over to the stone. "Press it?"

"It wouldn't be that simple or someone simply walking by could trigger the thing." He knelt down beside the painted cobblestone, tracing the cross with his finger. There were no indentations. Nothing to indicate the stone was anything beyond decorative, but the sword had clearly pointed it out. And the mere fact that it was different from all the others had to signify something. "There must be another cross here somewhere. Something similar to this one. We find it, and I'm betting we find the ruby."

"But there's nothing on the walls at all, except for St. George."

Marcus stood up and walked over to the altar, carefully inspecting the sandstone that surrounded the fresco.

"Anything?" She came to stand behind him, her chin by his shoulder, her breath warm against his ear.

"Not yet. There's nothing visible here at all. But maybe it's not supposed to be something we'd see." To demonstrate he spread his hands across the wall, sliding his fingers over the stone, trying to discern an indentation of some kind.

She nodded her understanding and moved to the other side of the sandstone inlay, letting her fingers trail over the roughened surface. They worked quietly, in partial darkness, the only sound their soft breathing.

Marcus finished first, reaching the edge of the fresco having found nothing more than a couple of pockmarks and one tiny fissure that resembled nothing at all. "How's it going with you?"

"Nothing so far. The surface is actually remarkably smooth. How old do you figure it is?" she asked.

"Judging from the artwork, I'd say medieval, but the fresco could have been added later. I'm guessing that the catacombs predate the present charnel house. In fact, since the tunnel between the two seems to be fairly new, I'd hazard a guess that the original entrance was in here."

Celeste looked up in response to his remark, then frowned. "Actually I think maybe I saw it, or what was left of it." She pointed with her flashlight to a tumble of rock in the far corner. The top of the rubble reached up fifteen feet or so to the ceiling and the faint remains of what might have originally been an opening, now obscured by the fall of rock. "Could that be it?"

Marcus moved his flashlight to give better illumination, mica in the stone glistening in the light. "Could be. Maybe it led to an older charnel house. One they abandoned."

"Hang on," Celeste said, moving over to the fallen stones. "I think there's something up there." She waved with her flashlight at a spot near the ceiling on the back wall. "Can you see it?"

He squinted, and was just able to make out what looked to be a slash of black against the rocks.

"I'm going to see if I can get closer." She was already scrambling up the fallen rocks, loose debris raining down on the floor below.

"Be careful. There's no telling how stable those rocks are." As if to prove his point, the rubble shifted, and Celeste slipped. Marcus was beside the rocks in two strides, but she had regained her footing and was still determinedly trying to get higher.

"Can you shine your flashlight up there, please?" she asked. "I need mine to see where I'm going."

He moved the beam of light so that the tiny spot of black was highlighted. She was only a couple of feet away now.

"I've got it." She leaned over, the rock pile rattling ominously and then quieting. "It's a cross, Marcus. Same as the one on the floor. Only it's made of stone. Marble maybe."

He moved closer, tipping his head back so that he could see, the light indeed highlighting what appeared to be a cross.

"It looks like there's something written on it. But I can't make it out." Celeste shifted her weight from right foot to left as she tried to move closer to the cross. The movement sent more rock skittering to the floor, this time the entire pile of debris sliding downward in an avalanche of stone.

One minute Celeste was teetering at the top and the next the she had disappeared into a swirling cloud of scree. Marcus ran forward, yelling her name, the beam from the flashlight unable to cut through the heavy dust filling the air.

Large chunks of the ceiling rained down on his head, hitting with a force that significantly slowed his progress. He felt something slice into the skin above his brow, the warmth of the resulting blood flowing down his face. But he didn't even stop to assess the damage. It wasn't as if he were truly in danger. What mattered now was finding Celeste.

Another rock slammed into his back, the resulting force knocking him off of his feet, the flashlight tumbling from his hand, its light extinguished. Marcus pushed away the rubble, fighting to hold onto consciousness as more rocks pummeled his head and shoulders. Darkness pushed at the edges of his vision, the dust so heavy it was choking him.

He fought to his knees, but the world was spinning now, and he recognized the signs of regeneration. For a cut or a bruise the process produced only mild dizziness, but for something more lethal, he often passed out. Usually just for a moment or two. But he didn't have that kind of time.

Celeste needed him now.

He tried to push to his feet, but his mind and his body were not of accord, the blackness spreading across his vision. The last thought he had, before sliding into unconsciousness, was that if he'd been another kind of man, he'd have prayed. Prayed for Celeste.

But damn it all to hell, he wasn't that kind of man.

Chapter Nine

The rock fall stopped almost as suddenly as it had started, the dark absolute. Celeste gingerly shifted, checking body parts, making sure that everything was working. She'd somehow managed to ride the falling rock, staying on top of it so that she'd sort of surfed her way down to the bottom.

She was scratched and bruised, and her elbow was bleeding like crazy, but there didn't seem to be anything seriously wrong with her. "Marcus?" she called, her voice sounding tiny after the crashing stones. "Are you all right?"

She remembered hearing him scream her name, but then nothing more. "Marcus?"

No answer came out of the dark, but she quashed the panic that rose inside her. He had to be all right. She needed him in her life. Needed him to goad her, to laugh at her—to make love to her.

Fighting to stay calm, she felt the rocks around her, praying for a miracle, and it seemed that God was on her side. She closed her hand around the cold metal of her flashlight and flipped the switch, blessed light illuminating the particles of dust still filling the air.

"Marcus? Can you see the light? I need you to make a noise and let me know where you are. Marcus?"

The chamber was deadly quiet, the only sound her blood pounding in her ears. "Marcus, say something. *Please*. Help me find you."

She struggled to her feet, her legs shaking but holding firm. One step and then two, she dodged her way around the fallen debris, moving the flashlight in slow arcs across the floor. There was nothing on the first pass, or the second, her heart ratcheting up with each swipe of the light. But then on the third, she saw a hand.

Scrambling over the debris, she blindly started pulling rocks off of him, using strength she hadn't even known she had. Her muscles ached from the effort, her palms scraped as she moved stone after stone until he was free.

Dropping to the floor beside him, she felt his wrist for a pulse, but couldn't find one. His hands and face were covered with blood, and she fought tears as she cradled his head in her lap. Using her sleeve she tried to wipe the blood away, but there was too much, and the deep gash at his hairline just kept pumping more.

But pumping was good. It meant a heartbeat.

She pressed her finger against his throat, moving it until she found the pulse she so desperately sought.

He was alive.

He was still alive.

Tears of relief fell unheeded, their tracks cutting through the dust and blood still on his face. "Marcus," she said, her voice stronger now. "Open your eyes. Come on. Please. Open your eyes."

She brushed back his hair to tend to the gash, surprised to find that the bleeding had slowed to a trickle, as if it had already begun to heal. Or maybe she'd just misjudged it. Even the smallest head wound bled like crazy. Either way it was no longer her main concern. Waking him was.

"Marcus?" She stroked his hair again, staring down into his face. "Come on, sweetheart, open your eyes."

She felt the movement before she saw it. His muscles bunching and tightening as if waking from sleep. Then his eyes flickered open. "Celeste?"

"I'm right here."

"You called me 'sweetheart.'"

Color flooded her face. Considering she'd thought him dead not five minutes ago, he looked remarkable fit. And despite the absurdity of the notion, she found herself angry. "I was worried. I just said the first thing that came into my head."

He grinned, then sobered, and despite her protest, sat up, visually searching her for signs of injury. "All you are right?"

"I'm fine. You're the one who was knocked out. Not me."

"I never should have let you climb up there in the first place." His hands were everywhere, gently probing and squeezing, checking her for injury. "Are you sure you're all right?"

"Damn it, Marcus, I told you, I'm fine. You're the one with the gash on your head. When I found you I couldn't even find a pulse." Restating it send chills running through her. "I thought . . . I thought you were dead."

His arms slid around her, and she buried her face in his chest, reveling in his warmth and the steady sound of his heartbeat.

"I'm fine, princess. Just a few cuts and bruises. We were both very lucky."

Celeste nodded, and then pushed away, embarrassed at her show of weakness. "I didn't mean to overreact, I was just so afraid."

"Me, too." The simple words held all kinds of meaning, but now wasn't the time to try to interpret them. She reached up to smooth back his hair, to make sure the gash really had stopped bleeding, but he covered her hand with his, leaning forward to kiss her, the touch so gentle it was almost a whisper.

As if he were paying homage.

And then he moved again, pushing to his feet, holding out a hand to help her up. She took it and once they were standing, pointed the flashlight toward the arch leading to the catacombs.

Remarkably, except for a small scattering of rocks, it was free of debris.

"Looks like the bulk of the damage was to this end of the room." Marcus turned back to survey the rubble behind him.

Celeste turned, too, aiming the beam of light at the corner where the cross had been, but the corner was gone. The cave-in re-formed that part of the room so that any sign of the wall there had been obliterated. It was impossible to tell if it had been destroyed or was merely buried behind the mountain of rock. Either way it was totally inaccessible.

"We've lost it." Despite the dire nature of the situation, her disappointment was acute. They'd come all this way. Survived the cave-in only to lose the prize.

"Maybe not." Marcus's voice sounded uncharacteristically awed, and she turned to question him, the words dying on her lips as her gaze followed his.

The little altar had also miraculously survived the melee. Even the fresco of St. George was still intact. The only apparent change was that the entire structure had slid about four feet or so to the left, along the wall. But it wasn't the altar's state of grace that had caused Marcus's tone. It was St. George and his still-silvery sword, the tip now firmly pointing at the dark opening in the wall behind where the alter had once stood.

The opening was narrow. Only a couple of feet, the short passageway on the other side, not more than a half a foot wider than that. Like everything else in the catacombs, it had been constructed long ago—and then forgotten.

Until Hans Weisbaum had rediscovered it.

The batteries on the remaining flashlight were dimming perceptibly. Marcus had been glad of the fact just after the cave-in. The shadows had helped to hide his regeneration from her. She'd noticed how quickly the blood had stopped, but she hadn't had enough light to see that the wound had in fact disappeared altogether. It was worrisome, but in the height of her anxiety, she'd no doubt written it off to her panic.

He knew he was lying by omission. But he also knew what the result would be should she learn of his ability to heal his wounds. Especially lethal ones. Reflexively he reached for the small of his back, the faintest twinge of pain reminding him that were it not for his father's genes he would be dead many times over.

And he wondered not for the first time what it would feel like to know that there would be an end. Mankind spent so much time trying to prolong life. If only they knew how desperately lonely it could be.

He shook his head, wondering when he'd become such a philosopher. But he knew the answer. Or at least the reason. She was standing right in front of him. All women were dangerous. But the ones like Celeste were the worst. They dug their way into to a man's soul and immediately started cleaning house.

Well, his house was in perfect order. He wasn't interested in changing things. And even if he was—

Well, he couldn't.

Glancing around, he saw, with relief, a set of torches at either side of the door.

"You think those will work?" Celeste asked, eyeing the resin-soaked jute.

"I don't see why not. It's perfectly dry down here. And if they do work it'll be a damn sight better than the flashlight."

As if in agreement, the bulb flickered and then dimmed even further.

Marcus produced matches and in short order had the torches burning, the brighter light making the new passageway seem larger. They traversed it in short order, stopping at the opening at the other end. Behind them the other room had disappeared into the darkness, and standing next to her, Marcus felt Celeste shiver.

But then she squared her shoulders, and without a second look stepped through the opening into the room ahead. Containing a smile, Marcus followed, holding his torch high to illuminate the room.

A natural cavern, the space was about ten feet wide and almost as deep, with no visible ceiling above, although the darkness indicated it was up there somewhere.

"Where are we?" Celeste whispered.

"Somewhere underneath Hallstadt, inside the mountain. My guess is that this cave served as an ancient burial site. Or maybe even a sacred place. Look over there." He waved the torch in the direction of the closest wall. "See the carving. Definitely old."

"The ruby could be anywhere." She turned in a circle, the light following her as she moved. "If it's here at all."

"It's here. Hans Weisbaum as good as pointed the way himself."

"All right." She nodded, accepting his pronouncement without argument. "So where do we start?"

"Look for niches. Anything that might lead to a second room or a small hiding place. I'll check the carving. Maybe George and his dragon are in here somewhere, too."

It wasn't until they'd reached the far side of the cavern that they hit pay dirt—an anteroom, barely five feet square and just tall enough for the two of them to stand upright. But inside, painted with copious detail, was a second fresco of St. George.

This one clearly not old at all.

"You think Hans painted it?" Celeste asked, running her fingers over the painted rock, searching for a lever or an opening of some kind.

"Seems possible. We know he had artistic ability. And we know that he was determined to lead us somewhere."

"Starting with the photograph." She frowned. "But it doesn't really make sense, does it? I mean one would think he'd want to hide the ruby so that no one else could find it. So why the clues?"

"Maybe because he believed his daughter would want it someday. He did leave her the photograph. Or maybe he just couldn't stand the thought of the Devil's Delight being lost, so he left his own sort of map." He reached out to trace the figure with his finger. "There's no sword."

Celeste frowned, her disappointment showing. "Or anything else that appears to be highlighted differently from the rest."

Marcus turned slowly, letting his eyes run the gamut from floor

DEE DAVIS

to ceiling, finally stopping to face the opposite wall. It was un-
adorned, flaws in the rock making it seem to move in the flickering
torch light. He stepped closer, studying the shadows, something
about them feeling off.

"Celeste, I think there's something here," he said, more to himself really than to her. The wall was deceptive. What appeared to be
solid rock was really two overlapping layers of stone, the fissure in
between them running almost parallel to the opposite wall. Impossible to see unless one was specifically looking.

He turned to study St. George behind him. Sure enough, the
edge of the man's sword was just visible from this angle, an inten-
tional use of torchlight, the sword held perpendicular to the man's
body—the tip pointing directly at the fissure.

Marcus squeezed into the crack, inching his way forward,
aware that Celeste had followed behind him when the light of her
torch joined his. It was tough going, but only for a couple of feet,
and then the fissure opened into another antechamber, this one
about twenty feet long and half again as wide, the far end still
shrouded in shadow despite their torchlight.

"Oh, my God." Celeste's voice held a note of reverence, mixed
with awe. "This is amazing."

It was beyond amazing actually. A collection worthy of some
of the finest museums in the world. Hans Weisbaum, it seemed,
had taken quite a bit more from France than just the Devil's Delight.

Just on cursory examination, Marcus recognized Vermeer, Pi-
casso, Van Eyck, Botticelli, and Cezanne. There was a Donatello
on a pedestal in one corner. And an intricately rendered nude that
could only be a Michelangelo.

There were paintings and statues everywhere—probably at least forty or fifty—all of them seemingly works of great value.

"This is Holbein," Celeste said, stopping in front of a huge canvas depicting an Elizabethan couple. "I don't think it's ever been catalogued. How in the world did he manage all of this?"

"My guess is that you're looking at the treasure of St. Emilion."

"You're saying that Theloneous gave it all to Hans?"

He shook his head. "No. I think he gave Hans the ruby in payment for making sure all of this was kept safe."

"From the looters. That would explain why Hans left the clues. Once he was dead, he wanted it found. This is what it must be like to find a pirate's treasure," she marveled, her eyes wide as she took in the beauty of the art surrounding them.

Marcus, however, had seen his share of plunder, and instead of allowing himself to stop and absorb the beauty, he focused on the prize. The Devil's Delight.

It had to be here somewhere. He searched the left half of the chamber and then the center, with nothing to show but additional works by the likes of Tintoretto, Goya, and Matisse, finds in and of themselves surely, but not the prize he was seeking.

Celeste, it seemed, had also recovered her objectivity, methodically looking behind each of the paintings for a hidden cache. *Smart girl.*

But Marcus was betting on the far end of the improvised gallery. Unlike the other walls, this one was devoid of art. The glimmer of mica and crystals was the only decoration. It could be that Hans had simply run out of treasure. Or it could be that there was something more precious hidden there.

He was about six feet from the wall, when a shadow or maybe

a sixth sense caused him to look down, his booted feet resting on the edge of a chasm that seemed to drop straight down into the bowels of the earth.

He bent and held his torch over the hole, but there was no bottom to be seen, the dark encompassing a lower chamber no doubt, or maybe an ancient river bed. Following along the edge he realized that it ran the entire length of the cavern, separating the room effectively into two parts.

"I think I see it," Celeste said, slipping past him, her torch indeed illuminating something on the far side.

He reached on instinct, his heart in his throat, his hand closing around her wrist just as she stepped off into the void. Yanking her backward, he stumbled, then held firm, the two of them safely on solid ground. "Are you all right?"

"I'm fine, I think." She grimaced as she moved her shoulder. "Beats the alternative. I never even saw the gap. If you hadn't been there—" She shuddered at the thought.

"But I was." He resisted the urge to pull her into his arms, to feel for himself that she was all right. "And everything's fine now."

"Except that the ruby is over there. And we're over here." She held up the torch again, a blood-red glimmer refracting from a hollow in the wall across from them.

"Maybe there's a way across. I can't believe that Hans would desert us now." Marcus walked the along the edge of the rift, searching for something that might constitute a bridge. About three feet from the far wall, he found it. A protrusion that on first glance looked like the end of a root, but in reality was twisted hemp. Calling for Celeste, he placed his torch in a bracket on the wall and then lay on his stomach and reached down for the rope.

"What have you found?" Celeste asked, holding her torch so that he could better see.

"I'm not certain, but I'm guessing a bridge." He pulled the rope hand over hand, until the knotted jute began to come into sight.

"It *is* a bridge. Or at least a rudimentary version thereof," Celeste said, excitement coloring her voice. "See. It's attached on the far side."

Marcus pulled it taut and secured it to an iron ring apparently driven into the side of the chasm for just such a purpose. "Right then, I'll cross first, shall I? Then if it's safe, you can follow."

She opened her mouth to argue, shot a look down at the crevice, and changed her mind. "All right, you go. But be careful."

It wasn't as hard as it looked, no worse than climbing the rigging of a schooner to reach the crow's nest. But there were a couple of dicey moments when the rope groaned and tipped dizzily downward.

But in just moments, he was safe on the other side. "Hang on," he yelled. "There's a torch on this side, too. Let me light it and then you can come across."

After placing her torch in a bracket, she started across the divide, the little bridge swaying back and forth drunkenly.

"You're doing fine. Just keep coming."

About halfway across, there was a pop as one of the knots broke, the right side of the bridge listing downward as a result. Celeste lost her footing and for a moment dangled over the edge, then with a quick swing of her feet, she managed to right herself, darting across the rest of the bridge with a grace that belied the wildly wobbling structure.

He grabbed her as she stepped off of it, not giving a damn

DEE DAVIS

about anything other than reassuring himself that she was all in one piece.

"You're smothering me," she said, pulling back, laughter lighting her voice.

"I just don't want to lose you." The words were out before he had the chance to think about their meaning.

"Not a chance," she said, her eyes suddenly sobering.

They stood for a moment, and then turned together toward the back wall and the indentation where they'd seen the sparkle of crystal.

They moved forward together, the area in front of them flooding with dancing light as the torch hit first the burnished gold of a small altar, and then the multifaceted red glow of the Devil's Delight.

308

Chapter Ten

Celeste couldn't take her eyes off of it. It was almost as if it were calling to her, reaching out with crimson fingers of light to draw her forward. A ridiculous notion but nevertheless it was there.

She took a step toward it, but Marcus physically stopped her, his arm an unmovable barrier to her goal. "Don't touch it," he said, the sound of his voice cutting through the hypnotic effect of the stone. "It might be booby-trapped."

She shook her head, feeling as if she were shaking off something physical. "So what do we do next?"

"I'll try and dislodge it."

"Like Indiana Jones?"

Marcus frowned, as if he had no idea what she was talking about. Apparently his love of art didn't extend to Spielberg.

"You know," she said, containing a laugh, "move the stone and replace it with a rock or something—to keep it balanced?"

He considered the idea for a moment, clearly still not getting the reference, then bent down to pick up a rock roughly the size of his fist. "It's worth a try."

Moving carefully he stepped up onto the natural dais and extended both hands toward the ruby, the rock in his right. Celeste held her breath as he eyed the stone.

"There's a bracket here. Made of gold. The ruby is sitting on it." He inched forward for a closer look. "The way it's sitting I'd say that the weight is spread across the frame. I think maybe you're on to something," he said, his attention still on the ruby.

Then with an audible exhale, he counted to three, then snatched the ruby with his left hand, placing the rock in its place with his right.

Celeste twined her fingers together, waiting for the ceiling to fall or the floor to open. But nothing happened, the quiet room seeming to mock her fear. Then there was an ominous click, and she watched as the bracket dropped a quarter of an inch, the rock falling with it.

Heart pounding, she waited again, but again there was only silence.

The ruse had worked. The bracket held. Her grandmother had been wrong. She hadn't wasted her time watching too much TV.

Marcus turned to face Celeste, his look triumphant, but as he looked beyond her shoulder, his eyes narrowed, suspicion wiping out all semblance of his elation. "I should have known."

Celeste whirled around, surprised to see her father standing on the other side of the chasm.

"Just making certain you don't get any ideas about my ruby." Her father looked sinister in the flickering torchlight. Almost like a stranger. She turned back to Marcus, her principal thought to let him know that she hadn't known her father was following them, but at the sight of his anger the words died on her lips.

"So all of this was just another of your tricks," he said, his green eyes never leaving her father. "Get your daughter to seduce me into taking her along for the ride, then you swoop in to scoop up the spoils."

"Something like that. Actually there's a lot more to the story than you know. But I'm getting ahead of myself." He moved closer to the chasm, his eyes on Celeste. "Take the stone, Celeste. It belongs to me now."

Her heart twisted, the need to please her father conflicting with the need to protect Marcus. There was something in her father's eyes she couldn't put a name to, but she knew as surely as she knew anything that somehow it meant danger for Marcus.

"I can't," Celeste said, the words coming of their own volition. "I won't."

"God damn it, girl." Her father's voice was condemning. "Don't tell me you've fallen for *him*." The last was said with such derision she almost felt as if he'd physically struck out at Marcus.

"I haven't fallen for anyone. I just don't like you treating me like some kind of trained monkey." It was almost as if her father had morphed into someone else. Or maybe as if she were seeing him for the first time.

"You've fallen under his spell." Her father waved his hand in dismissal. "I should have known better than to send a lamb into the wolf's lair. But you see, my dearest daughter, you've made a horrible mistake. You have no idea who it is you've fallen for. Or did he tell you all his sordid secrets?"

She looked from Marcus to her father, having absolutely no idea where the conversation was headed, but not liking the looks of things. Marcus was holding the ruby so tightly she thought it might cut his hand, his anger giving way to something deeper. Darker.

"He hasn't told me anything at all except that his mother died and that he and his father are estranged. Right?" She looked to Marcus. She might not know his secrets, but she knew him. Knew his heart. At least she thought she did.

He gave her a curt nod, a muscle in his cheek ticking as he stood statue-still, his gaze locked with Cedrik's. "Leave her out of this. She doesn't need to know any more than she already does. This is between you and me."

"Except that I'm standing right here," Celeste said, her own anger rising. "And I have a right to know what's going on. What secrets, Marcus?"

"Yes," her father continued, "Marcus, tell us about your sordid past. All seven centuries of it."

"Seven centuries?" The words hung in the air, taking on a life of their own, Celeste's head spinning, knowing with certainty that this was the shadow that had been standing between them.

"Marcus is immortal, Celeste. He's not human. At least not in the sense that you and I are. Check the cut on his head." Her father's eyes glittered in the light, his gaze flitting from Marcus to the stone and then back again.

"You were there?" she questioned her father, disbelief mixing with her anger. "And you didn't help us?"

"Just check the wound."

Still struggling with her cascading emotions, she walked over to Marcus, knowing her eyes were full of questions. But he said nothing, standing perfectly still, his expression purposefully blank. She reached up with shaking fingers and lifted his hair. The skin was smooth and unblemished.

Her stomach roiled, and she fought to maintain her balance. "I saw it. You were really hurt. There was blood everywhere."

"I regenerated." His tone was flat. As if saying the words had somehow sucked the life right out of him.

She swallowed her fear, her mind trying to make sense of what they were trying to tell her. He couldn't be immortal. No one was. But even as she had the thought, her brain trotted out the image of all his books, his name written in each of them. His ability to read archaic languages. His inability to remember Indiana Jones. His courtly manners. His pirates logs. Faust calling him "Captain." It all rushed at her with the force of a hurricane and she lifted her eyes to meet his. "You can't die?"

He shook his head.

And surprisingly the only thing she felt was anger. "I thought you were dead, you son of a bitch. You scared me half to death. And *I* can die." It was a ridiculous response, she knew it, but the entire world seemed to have gone topsy-turvy.

"There's more." Her father's words cut through her hysteria.

She almost laughed. What else could there be? The man had superpowers and was allergic to kryptonite? She waited, feeling as if the chasm was expanding, threatening to suck her down into its depths.

"My father is the devil." Marcus spoke the words so softly, she almost didn't think she'd heard right. But one look at his face and she recognized the truth. Saw his pain. His vulnerability.

"And your mother?"

"A mortal like you. He pretended to be something he wasn't and seduced her." The irony of his words was not lost on her.

"How long have you known all of this?" Celeste asked, turning back to her father.

"I've suspected for a long time now. But I needed proof."

"And I just provided it." Marcus showed no expression, but she could feel his tension.

"Your admission is icing on the cake. If I'd known you were going to be so forthcoming, maybe I wouldn't have had to take such drastic means."

"What have you done, Father?" Celeste asked.

"Only what was absolutely necessary. I needed access to the ruby. Preferably with Marcus in attendance."

"Why?" Celeste asked.

"Because the Devil's Delight was created from Christ's blood—the power of all that is good. And now the devil's spawn holds it in his hands. The blood of God's son—and the blood of the devil's." He waved at Marcus's still bloodied hand holding the stone. "The prophecy has been fulfilled."

"Prophecy?" Celeste managed.

"In the ancient texts it says that the blood of Heaven and Hell shall combine in rubicund light, creating absolute power. Just look at it." His face contorted in the flickering light. "The power of Heaven and Hell concentrated there in the Devil's Delight."

She could see it actually. The glow spreading out across the cavern. She'd experienced it firsthand, in fact, the memory of the ruby's siren call still resonating inside her. But Marcus had broken the spell, and she'd found the strength to ignore it.

"It's just a stone, Father."

Her father's eyes narrowed. "Come on, Celeste. Surely you can see that it is more than that."

Marcus took a step off the dais, but her father shifted, the torchlight reflecting off the gun in his hand. "Don't move."

"I think we've covered this ground already." Marcus stopped, but his tone held a sneer. "You can't kill me, Cedrik."

Marcus took another step, but her father changed his stance, pointing the gun at Celeste. "You're right. Nothing I can do will harm you. But I can kill her. And I know for a fact that's something you can't stomach. Remember Adelaide?"

Beside her, Marcus flinched.

"That's right, I know all about it. Faust was only too happy to spill his guts."

"Faust would never . . ." Marcus started, but couldn't seem to finish, his eyes glittering with anger.

"He didn't have a choice. You may not be able to kill an immortal, but believe me, there's no problem drugging one."

"Where is he?"

"I assume on the *Apollyon* working off a hell of a hangover. I didn't stick around to see."

Celeste followed the exchange with a numbness that left her feeling almost paralyzed. Her father was threatening to kill her, and the man she loved was immortal. She fought her rising panic and turned to look at Marcus, searching his face for some sign of the demon her father was insisting he was. But all she saw was Marcus—the man that she *loved*.

The realization hit with surprising simplicity, and without thinking she reached out her hand. For a moment she thought he would refuse to take it, but then his fingers closed strong and warm around hers.

"Celeste," her father goaded, "he's a devil."

"No," she said, suddenly sure of her center. "No, he's not."

Her father's face twisted in anger, his desire for the ruby turning him into a stranger, and then the gun fired, the sound echoing off the rock walls. Marcus jerked her arm, pulling her behind him as another sharp report gave testament to the fact that her father had no problem pulling the trigger.

"If you want to save her, Diablo, give me the stone." Her father held out one hand, firing another shot, but Marcus dodged it, careful to keep his body in front of hers.

"That's three bullets, Cedrik. I can wait."

Her father moved the gun, aiming not at them, but at jagged stones that made up the ceiling. "But only one shot will bring down that roof. And while I'm sure you'll live through the experience, I can't promise the same for my daughter."

"Don't listen to him," Celeste whispered. "We'll find a way out. And even if we don't, we can't let him have the stone. Surely you see that we can't let anyone have it."

The ruby glowed red in the palm of his hand, almost as if it were refuting the point.

Or agreeing.

"Can't you feel it?"

Marcus shook his head. "Only a little. But I saw what it did to you."

"Throw it in the chasm," she whispered. "Send it back where it came from."

"Or better still, give it to me." With a hot whoosh of fire, and presumably brimstone, a wiry man with a goatee appeared on the rope bridge, a well-manicured hand extended toward Marcus. "Well done, my son."

A chill followed the heat, and Celeste tore her gaze from the bearded stranger to look up at the man still clasping her hand. "Is that . . ."

"My father," he finished for her.

"Your client." Understanding slid home, even before he nodded. She tightened her fingers on his, telegraphing all the love in her heart. "Whatever you do, Marcus, we're doing it together."

Marcus stared at his father, his mind going a thousand directions at once. Cedrik stood frozen, his attention locked on the bridge. One devil sparring with another. Except that his father was the real deal, which meant that Cedrik didn't have a chance.

Celeste still stood beside him, her hand clasped in his, trust, determination, and something more shining from her eyes. It warmed him in places he'd thought forever cold. She'd seen the truth and still she stood by him.

Whatever he chose to do, she'd be there by his side. His heart sang, as if wakening from a dark sleep, and he felt whole in a way that he'd never dreamed possible.

"Marcus," his father said with a frown, "give me the ruby."

It was starting to be a sad refrain. And suddenly Marcus knew what he had to do. To hell with his life. To hell with his father's. The ruby was dangerous. It had ruined God knew how many lives. Including Celeste's father's.

It stopped here.

He threw the ruby high into the air over the chasm, the stone sparkling as it tumbled downward. Celeste's father dove for the stone, as Marcus's father held up a hand, but just as the ruby's trajectory started to change, Marcus raised both hands, calling upon the powers he had buried for centuries. One second, two, and then blue light emanated from his fingers, the arc connecting with the Devil's Delight—the contact shattering the ruby into glittering particles of dust.

Cedrik teetered at the edge of the precipice, hands reaching for the remnants of the Devil's Delight, as he screamed, "No!" One minute he was standing there, and then he was tumbling downward, his cry still echoing off the rocky sides of chasm as he disappeared from sight.

"*Father!*" Celeste moved toward the edge, but Marcus was faster, his hand closing on her arm.

"He's gone," Marcus said, wrapping her in his arms. "It's over."

But Celeste shook her head, pulling free of his embrace, turning instead to face his father as the last glints of red dust sank into the hole. "You knew this would happen. This was all a test."

"And Marcus failed." His father's eyes sparked with anger. Anger and disappointment.

"Maybe from your point of view," Celeste said, her anger almost matching his father's. "What he did he did for me." She faced the old devil fearlessly, and Marcus's heart filled with pride.

"I'm well aware of the fact," his father said, his dark eyes locking on his son's. "The choice was always yours to make, Marcus. And unless I'm missing something here, I believe you've already made it."

Marcus held his father's gaze, his arm tightening around Celeste.

The old devil nodded once and then disappeared in another burst of flame, the cave seeming abnormally quiet after all that had preceded it.

"O, my God," Celeste whispered, staring at the place where his father had stood.

"That's one way of looking at it, I suppose." Marcus turned back toward the chasm, searching the shadows for signs of life.

"He's dead, isn't he?" Celeste looked down into the darkness, fighting tears. "Maybe it's for the best. He betrayed us both."

"Not intentionally," a cultured voice said, preceding the powerful beam of a flashlight. Faust stepped out of the shadows. "It was the power of the stone. I'm afraid his desire blinded him of what was really important." Marcus's friend blithely crossed the bridge, the ropes not even swaying.

"I just wish it had been different. He wasn't always like . . . like that."

"Power corrupts," Faust said, joining them at the edge of the chasm. "But perhaps in death he has at last found peace."

Celeste nodded, but she didn't seem convinced.

"Are you all right?" Marcus turned to her, wiping away a tear with his thumb.

"I'm fine," she said, reaching up to touch his cheek. "You're the one who's bleeding." She pulled back her hand, the significance of her words hitting home. "You're not regenerating."

Marcus reached up to touch the cut. It hurt like bloody hell. He centered his thoughts, concentrating on rebuilding.

Nothing happened.

"I'm afraid that's not going to help much," Faust said.

Marcus frowned, and Celeste grabbed his hand, as if by touching him she could heal him herself.

"It's only a cut, Celeste. Stop worrying." Faust laughed. "But I'm afraid he'll have to heal the old-fashioned way."

"My choice," Marcus said, astonishment mixing with certainty. "When I chose Celeste, I chose life." He paused, emotion threatening to unman him. "I chose love over immortality."

"That you did, my friend," Faust said, smiling his approval. "That you did."

Marcus closed his eyes for a moment, feeling the blood pump through his body, the air as it filled his lungs and then was released again. It was as if he'd never really felt the sensations before. As if, despite the centuries, he were only just now coming to life.

He felt Celeste's hand on his arm. Felt the question there even though she hadn't put it into words, and in response he swung her into his arms, spinning her around in sheer delight.

"I love you, Celeste Abbot," he said, slowing to a stop, "and if you'll let me, I intend to spend the rest of my days showing you exactly how much."

"Every day." She reached up to cup his face, his blood still staining her fingers, his life held firmly in her hands. "I'll hold you to it."

He bent his head and touched his lips to hers, the kiss a promise of their life to come. He'd lost one quest, but in so doing, he'd won the one that mattered most.

He'd made a bargain with the devil, but in the end his father had been the one to set him free.

Epilogue

"My sons have failed me." Lucifer stared into the mirror, trying to contain his frustration. His own flesh and blood had deserted him.

"Sometimes children need to find their own way." Eustace held the tux jacket as Lucifer slid into it. He would not have accepted the bold assessment from anyone else. But Eustace had been with him from the beginning. They shared a past, and in many ways, the old servant knew him better than anyone living or dead.

Tugging the sleeves into place over the cuffs of his starched shirt, he adjusted his cufflinks and turned from the mirror to face the room. It was dotted with the flotsam and jetsam of centuries of fatherhood. An early painting of Nick's, a cutlass that had belonged to Marcus, and a pair of bronzed gaming dice from one of Jack's many ventures.

In so many ways he was no different than any other father.

His anger sizzled, the resulting sparks of electricity sending Eustace to the safety of the far side of the room.

So much for normalcy.

"I believed in them, Eustace. For once in my life I actually had faith in something."

"Perhaps it was misplaced. It's not as if you spent that much time with any of them." Eustace shrugged, patting out an ember that had lodged in the bedclothes.

"I had other obligations," he thundered. "You of all people should understand that."

"I do understand." Eustace's tone was placating, but Lucifer wasn't fooled. "But sometimes we need to shift our priorities."

Lucifer sighed and resisted the urge to throw something. Love was a complicated waste. Baser instincts were so damn much easier to deal with. "It's just so hard to contemplate. Jack off in Barbados with *Gabriella*. Nick totally wrapped up in that simpering Burnett woman." He sighed, smoothing his moustache, the gesture reflecting his agitation. "And Marcus"—he almost choked on the name—"you should have seen him. Kowtowing to that the girl as if *she'd* gained possession of his soul."

"Perhaps, in a way, she has. Don't you remember how it feels to be in love?"

"Worse than anything I can dish out. That much I'm certain of. God alone knows, I wouldn't wish it on my enemies, let alone my sons. What in Hades name am I supposed to do now?"

"Put it behind you," Eustace said, holding out a stack of contracts for him to sign. "It's always best to move forward."

"Easier said than done," he grumbled, scratching his signature on the proper pages.

"I think maybe you're forgetting something important."

Lucifer looked up, his molten gaze meeting Eustace's. If he hadn't known better, he'd have thought he felt a flare of hope.

Eustace smiled. "You've still got your daughters."